From Dusty With Love

Nina Whyle

First published in Great Britain in 2022 by

Nina Whyle

PB ISBN-13: 9781739219246

EBOOK ISBN-13: 9781739219222

Cover design by: James Bowden

DEDICATION

To our furry companions, Potter, Lolly, Bean and Smudge.

A source of great companionship and amusement - and so easily bribed with treats.

CONTENTS

‘Express yourself, don’t repress yourself.’—Madonna

CHAPTER ONE

Does life follow some sort of GPS? If so, mine has pre-set to an agonisingly slow journey with tolls and a few trolls along the way, ETA undetermined. Surely there is more to life than watching the minutes tick by, and I don't think working as a receptionist at Port-A-Privy, 'For All Your Intimate Occasions', is it!

I wonder if you can actually die of boredom? I bet there's a link between boredom and premature death.

1.35 p.m …

I can almost feel my brain cells shutting down, the life being sucked out of me while my boss, Geoffrey Monks, stomps about like he's the CEO of some multinational corporation, the stock markets hanging in the balance with every decision he makes, a global crash if he doesn't get the next outdoors event tender. My boss takes the world of mobilising poop holes seriously.

Did you know the average person spends approximately two hundred and forty days on the loo in their lifetime? (According to my boss, that's estimating one poop a day until the age of seventy-nine years old.) There's also a World Toilet Day: 19th November. I asked Geoffrey, 'Is that because of the rise of irritable bowel syndrome?' He wasn't amused.

Turns out World Toilet Day is no joking matter. There are around four point two billion people in the world who do not have toilets or access to clean drinking water. Shocking, isn't it?

But we can all feel better knowing that Matt Damon is leading the global crusade for safer water and sanitation. If Jason Bourne can expose the horrors of Operations Treadstone and Blackbriar then he's definitely the man to persuade governments to sort out the world's water crisis. If not, I'd suggest he karate-kick their privileged behinds at the next G8 summit.

But working for a Portaloo-for-hire company is not the destination I had in mind when I came to London. I was heading towards a leading role in the West End or a top TV show. Except real life has a way of crushing dreams. And my only notable acting credit to date is a TV commercial about IBS.

Before I slip further into a black hole of negativity, I get up from my seat and walk over to the vending machine. I don't really want a coffee, but it passes the time and stops me wallowing in self-pity. I select a cappuccino. As I wait for the noxious liquid to fill my cup I casually glance up—and jump backwards with fright. My boss, Geoffrey Monks, is peering down at me from his lofty view on the balcony at the top of the stairs. A shiver goes through me. How long has he been standing there?

I give the vending machine an affectionate pat on its side, just in case my boss is in any doubt why I am not at my station. He turns away and stomps back to the hole whence he came, but not before I imagine whacking him on the head with an invisible wand and watching him tumble down the stairs.

A-LAR-tey WHACK-ih-mah-TOE-sey!

This is another thing I like to do to pass the time. Pretending to have wizard powers helps me get through another mind-numbing day at work. Whenever a member of staff materialises on the stairs, I decide their imaginary fate. Those who have been nice get a bubble and I float them safely down the stairs. Those who have been mediocre, melancholic, or downright rude get an invisible lead bar to the back of the head and come crashing to the ground.

I think it's weird though, how my boss always knows when I'm not sitting at my desk. It did cross my mind that he had the chair alarmed. It isn't. I've checked. I'm not even allowed to go to the first floor to make a proper coffee, and if I want to take a pee, I have to telephone first. What's that all about? My theory is he's keeping tabs on everyone's toilet habits for some weird presentation we'll all be privy to one boring afternoon.

I return to my desk and sit down. I blow into my cup, staring glumly into the cheap plastic vessel. There's really nothing else to look at except the giant clock on the grey building opposite. Not only does my clock-watching drive me insane, it's magnified whenever I look up.

1.49 p.m. …

I slump forward and press my forehead against the desk. My life is heading down the toilet. Literally.

I must have dozed off because an unfamiliar ping wakes me. I jerk up at the sound and look up in surprise as the main front door opens and an actual customer walks in. My gaze shifts to the time on the computer screen.

1.59 p.m. …

Wow, I napped for a whole ten minutes.

I return my gaze to the man walking towards me. At a

guess, I'd say he's early fifties. His gait is rather stiff and mechanical, but what piques my interest is the custom-made navy-blue suit he's wearing. No off-the-peg hangs that well. He is also wearing a dotty blue dicky bow. Very dapper.

No one in this building is particularly fashion-forward. My boss wears the same grey suit and cheap patterned polyester shirt day in day out. But for me, deciding what to wear in the morning is the highlight of my day. 'Good afternoon,' I say with a dazzling smile. 'Welcome to Port-A-Privy. How may I help you?'

He smiles, revealing a perfect set of pearly whites. 'Good afternoon. Could you tell me the time?'

Oh, for goodness' sake!

'It's 1.59 p.m.,' I say, through gritted teeth. But when I look at my computer screen, time has shifted an entire minute. 'Actually, it's two o'clock,' I say excitedly.

The man smiles. 'I have a meeting with Mr Monks at two o'clock.'

'And your name is?'

'Mr Simons.'

'Right, um … One moment, please.' I dial Geoffrey's number, but it goes straight to voicemail. 'I have a Mr Simons here to see you,' I say in my best business-like voice. 'He's here for his two o'clock appointment.' I put the phone down and look at Mr Simons. 'If you would like to take a seat, Mr Monks will be with you in a minute.'

I watch as he walks over to the sofa and sits down, an amused smile playing on his lips. I wonder what has amused him? Is it the cheap polyester sofa or the faint whiff of toilet cleaner? He doesn't strike me as someone who usually seeks temporary sanitary hire. I wonder if he's one of those elite party-arrangers for the über-rich?

Mr Simons looks up, as if he senses me watching him. I give him another smile, then quickly resume my usual façade of being happy at work—fake-smiling against all my inner demons, tapping busily at the computer when, in fact, I'm opening up Instagram. I immediately regret it. My friend Alice has posted a photo of her latest beach shoot.

Alice is a model. I was actually with her when she was scouted. We were fifteen years old and walking to our local fish-and-chip shop when a woman with large tortoiseshell glasses and a crazy hat—totally out of place in our village—jumped out of a taxi and took Alice's photo.

Alice is six foot with shiny blonde hair, glowing skin, and legs up to her armpits. I was the hobbit in tow at a meagre five foot five with dirty-dishwater blonde hair and skin that was prone to the occasional outbreak. But that moment stuck with me. It made me realise that you never know who might be watching, and from that moment on, like a dutiful scout, I have always been prepared. Plus, I'm secretly vain.

Now, my sweet Alice is walking catwalks all over the world and I see her less and less. Although she's ever so thoughtful, always sending me clothes in the post. It's like Christmas morning whenever a package from Alice arrives. Honestly, I don't know what I would do without Alice—or Jodie, for that matter. Jodie is my flatmate, the yin to my yang. We met at university and spent three years getting hammered on cheap spirits and waking up in a variety of situations, which is not conducive to attendance records.

Alice and Jodie couldn't be more different. Alice is posh, her fortune handed down generation after generation. I think her family own some huge brewery in Cheshire—or is it Nottinghamshire? Somewhere ending in -shire. Her parents sit on a few boards from time to time and then hightail it back to their country estate. Alice always said her parents were quite lazy and vowed never to be the same. You might mock and say, 'But she's a model, no IQ necessary,' but Alice is far from dumb—and *you* try working some impractical, oversized headdress while balancing on a pair of six-inch skyscrapers in sub-zero temperatures on a rock in the ocean and still looking sublime!

Between you and me, I love the idea of not having to work for a living. Just imagine it: all the money in the world and not having to lift a finger. I could just do good deeds all day and go to lovely lunches with my friends.

Jodie, on the other hand, hails from Essex, but don't go thinking she doesn't have a brain either. She works as an air hostess. Seriously, I can hear you sniggering at the back. She's actually learning to fly—so there! Her parents are filthy rich too. Her father started his business hiring out inflatable bouncy castles, then progressed into soft plays and now he owns a bunch of trampoline parks. Smart man.

They bought Jodie a two-bedroom flat for her twenty-first birthday. My parents bought me an alarm clock from a second-hand store. My mother said it was to help me initiate my life by starting the day in a timely and more orderly manner—that I might look at it when I'm older with the warm feeling of nostalgia. They've always thought I was a bit of a flake.

My sister got a shopping trip to Harrods for her twenty-first birthday. In their mind, they were backing the winning horse.

Even though my sister and I went to a private school, my parents have always been on the verge of bankruptcy, and our run-down family house looks like it could collapse any second. What with Grandad's care home bills and Mother's horse, Goliath, we never had two pennies to rub together. Interestingly, the paddock always had special Swiss flowers sown in and Goliath never had second-hand anything. New saddles, bridles—

commercial. I sat in a room with a bunch of other women before being wrangled into another room where we were told to pretend to spray deodorant under our armpits, then told, 'Thank you very much, we'll call you.' I didn't get a call. All my energy, time and money amounted to ten seconds of me appreciating my meadow-smelling armpit for a casting director who had already seen scores of other eager young actresses doing the same thing. My parents were right. Acting is a preposterous career choice.

Jodie steps out into the hallway, looking amazing. She has squeezed her legs into a pair of red leather pants and wrapped her torso with a Vivienne Westwood basque. 'I really think things happen for a reason,' she says, looking at herself in the hallway mirror. She blows her reflection a kiss. 'Something good will pop up, babe, you'll see. You've just got to be open to those opportunities.' Jodie was a psychology major. 'Now, how about we Hobnob it out of here?'

Hobnobs is a fashionable bar in the City, frequented by City boys and girls ready to spend their hard-earned cash. Jodie heads straight to the bar and I go and find a table. Jodie loves coming here, although I don't know why. It should be called Hob knobs, as the place is full of them. Personally, I prefer somewhere a little closer to home and a lot less fake. Men with a sensitive, artistic side, men whose art challenges the status quo. I check my phone. Still no message from Cameron.

Jodie returns with two glasses of wine. 'You've just hit a blip, that's all,' she says cheerfully.

'A blip! I think having a boyfriend who can't be bothered to call me, getting fired from another job that I didn't even like, and being unable to get one acting job is a bit more than a blip.'

Jodie takes a swig of wine and pauses thoughtfully.

'Life is a journey, not a destination.'

'Yeah, well, yours are full of those by default.'

Jodie smiles.

'It's okay for you,' I say, hearing the whine in my voice. 'You're doing what you love. You have a lovely flat, a job you actually like, you get to travel, and soon you're going to be a qualified pilot. Me? I'm just flailing around like, like … a turtle on ice.'

'Aww, cute. I love turtles.'

'I've no prospects,' I wail. 'No ocean in sight. I'm just waiting for a … cormorant to gobble me up.'

Jodie gestures at me to drink up. 'It's about working towards your goals,' she says. 'I think your problem is …' Jodie stops. 'Can I say something? And please don't take offence.'

I push my hair back not sure I'm going to like what I'm about to hear. 'Err … okay.'

'I think you've lost your identity.'

'What, my *Bourne Identity*?'

'When we first met at university, you were always the first to do something new. I really admired you for it. You were so'—she searches for the word—'nonconforming. You went off and did that circus gig not giving a jot what society or your parents expected of you. You went to Paris and came back speaking about how you were going to take the world by storm with your one-handed puppet show. Genius, turning puppets into horror theatre, and your show was a triumph in Edinburgh Festival Fringe. *You* were a triumph. You've always bucked against the crowd and the expectations set by others. You've always been my biggest inspiration.'

'Aw, thanks, Jodie.'

'But now it's like you've given up.'

I don't know what to say, or rather I do, but I just can't face admitting that I feel lost.

'It's up to you to steer your life in the direction you want to go.'

'But that's the point, I don't know where that is anymore.'

Jodie's forehead creases into a frown. 'You need to find yourself again. You don't even dress like you.'

'What?' I splutter in outrage. 'That's not true. I happen to dress very well.'

'I don't mean the designer gear. What about all the cool thrift stuff you were always so good at finding?'

'That was only because I couldn't afford designer.' Although I still can't afford designer. 'You always accused me of looking like a bag lady.'

'But you owned that bag lady look,' says Jodie with a grin. 'And it was a compliment, you numbnut. It's like I don't recognise you anymore. I don't even think *you* recognise you.'

Oh, God, this is too intense.

'You're not angry with me?' Jodie asks.

'Well, we can't all have Mummy and Daddy pay for everything,' I retort.

'I knew it! You're angry. I'm sorry, hon.'

'No. I'm sorry, Jodie. I didn't mean to be a bitch.'

'That's okay.' She pauses for a moment. 'And my parents don't pay for everything. I pay for my flying lessons.'

'I know. I'm sorry. But why the big secret?'

'They'd only interfere like they do with everything else. Deciding where I should live, what career I should have, what kind of car I should drive.'

I'd totally forgotten how dominating and interfering they can be. Although some might call it attentive, and caring, and very, very generous.

'Goodness knows what they'd say when I tell them what I really want to do.'

My head jerks up. 'What? Are you keeping secrets

from me?'

'Oh! Um …' Jodie tails off evasively.

'Jodie!' I lean in, my interest piqued. 'Spill.'

Jodie avoids looking at me and takes a swig of wine.

'Oh, my God. You *are* hiding something from me!' I am genuinely shocked. 'But we tell each other everything.'

Her baby-blue eyes travel questioningly over my face.

'You know you can trust me.'

Jodie considers this for a moment, then leans closer. 'Okay,' she says, her voice low. 'I want to join the RAF.'

I give her a blank stare. 'What?'

'I want to join the RAF,' she repeats.

I snort a laugh without meaning to. I was not expecting that. 'Yeah, right.'

Jodie gives me a filthy look. 'I knew I shouldn't have told you.'

I stop laughing. 'Seriously?'

'Yes, why not?'

Why not, indeed? 'It's just not what I expected, that's all.'

'I want to fly a fighter jet.'

My jaw drops to the floor. Jodie is one of my best friends and I thought I knew her inside and out, but this RAF thing has totally thrown me.

'But this isn't about me, this is about you. I care about you. I just want you to be happy.'

'I know, and I'm sorry for snapping.' I'm still trying to picture Jodie as a RAF pilot. 'But it's not like I haven't tried. It's just difficult to stay positive when you're auditioning for commercials that can only be aired during *Embarrassing Bodies*.'

'What about the audition the other week?'

I wince. 'The eczema commercial?'

easyJet.'

'I hope the airline's attitude is as good as its name.'

'You are a naughty boy,' says Jodie, enjoying herself.

'What about advertising? I reckon we could rustle you up a position in virtual sales, virtually anything, gorgeous. Haaaa … umph,' he says, bursting into a snort-like laugh. I wince and lean back from the slime ball.

CHAPTER THREE

I wake up feeling like a rocket has taken off inside my head and prematurely exploded, leaving me in a plume of smoke and debris. I push through the devastation and shuffle into the kitchen, my head spinning from the effort. Coffee and paracetamol, that's what I need. I take the milk out of the fridge, give it a sniff and recoil. No wonder—it's seven days out of date. Also in the fridge is my vape stick. How did that get there?

I find the last stash of paracetamol, swallow two, take a puff on my vape stick and spend the next couple of minutes in a coughing fit, the dry coil scalds my throat.

I'm out of e-liquid. This won't do.

Still in my pyjamas and hair resembling an abandoned bird's nest, I slip into my high-heeled boots from last night, pull on my rain mac and shades, stuff my purse into my pocket and head outside. I am not remotely concerned about my dishevelled dishevelment. I have lost faith in everything, even my precious vanity.

I drag my heels across the pavement, head down, as if simply avoiding eye contact will render me invisible. At least the spinning has stopped.

When I finally reach the corner shop I flinch at the loud, happy music that greets me. I head straight to the back of the shop and shove my head in the freezer compartment. The coldness numbs my brain and blocks out the music. I take a few deep, slow breaths, and for a second it is bliss, but gradually the coldness turns to pain and I pull my head out of the freezer.

Milk, Coke, an apple, and paracetamol. I tick off the items in my head as I pick them up and head to the till. I also grab the local newspaper. The girl at the till is the same girl who's always here. She has that look that suggests she'd rather be anywhere else but here and I feel genuine empathy towards her.

'Good morning,' I say, even though it feels anything but. 'Pack of ten Marlborough Lights, a lighter, and that bottle of e-liquid, please. Tobacco flavour.'

'You know you shouldn't do both.'

'Excuse me?'

'If you're trying to give up, don't buy these,' she says, waving the packet of cigarettes in the air.

'Both, please,' I say through a forced smile, my empathy ebbing.

She shrugs. 'Okay. Your life.'

Yes, it is, and when I last checked it was a free country. Doesn't she know you do not stress a smoker who's trying to give up? You do not enter the world of what's good and what's bad. The smoker already knows, but the more you tell them the more they want to smoke—it's simple reverse psychology. Besides, I will not take advice from someone who looks like a toddler's art project: hair, a mass of ribbons and a face splodged with glitter. 'And a carrier bag, please.'

'That'll be five pence.'

'No, it won't, you're not Sainsburys.'

'Oh, yeah, I keep forgetting. That will be …' She takes ages ringing up the items. I dig into my coat pocket for my purse, unhooking it from a fraying hole in the lining, and find my P45 and something else, which is sticking to it—a business card. On the front is a telephone number and on the back, *Duty Calls. 237 Maurice Embankment* and *Miss Hall. Noon. Ottoman* scribbled by fountain pen.

That's odd.

'Eleven pounds fifty.'

I swipe my card over the card reader.

'Have a nice day,' the health centre wannabe shouts as I shuffle out of the shop.

'You too.' If I'd wanted a lecture, I would have called my mother.

Outside, I wrench open the packet of cigarettes and light up. The heady drag tickles my brain before triggering a wretched coughing fit. I haven't had a real cigarette in six months. Since my last dismissal, come to think of it.

When I get home, I eat the apple and sip the Coke straight from the can. Fizzy pop and apples are my hangover remedy, one of the many useful things I learned at university. I'm just in the middle of making a coffee when the phone rings. I pick it up without thinking.

'Oh, you're home. I thought you'd be at work. I was going to leave you a message.'

I give an inward groan. My mother is the last person I want to talk to right now. 'Day off,' I reply.

'I only wanted to remind you about this Saturday. You are coming, aren't you?'

'Wouldn't miss it for the world!' I trill. I've already excused myself from the last two family gatherings, so there is no getting out of this one.

'Have you spoken to Coco?'

'Not since yesterday when she couldn't decide between tea cupcakes or teacup Yorkie ringbearers.'

'Can you at least feign interest in your sister's wedding?' my mother reprimands. 'And don't forget it's Roger's birthday on Saturday. Have you bought him a card?'

I grab a pen and scribble on the corner of the newspaper. *Roger. Card.* 'Yes, of course.'

A bleary-eyed Jodie wanders in. I motion to the coffee on the counter and she mouths a *Thank you, hon.*

'Are you doing anything nice on your day off?' my mother asks.

'I thought I might visit the British Museum. You know, get in touch with my inner Aztec, possibly join the Aztecs for a spot of lunch. I've never tried cannibalism, but I've always been curious.'

Jodie muffles a laugh.

'That sounds lovely, dear.' Mum hasn't heard a single word I've said.

'Mum, are you grooming Goliath?'

'No, just sorting out his haemorrhoids.'

'Eww, gross!'

'Don't be silly.' My mother continues on with the conversation while sorting out Goliath's haemorrhoids as if this is perfectly acceptable behaviour. 'Roger was saying there is an Arabic ceramic exhibition at the V&A. So, we will see you Saturday?'

'Yes. Yes. I'll be there.'

'Right then. Bye-bye, darling.'

'Bye, Mother.' I hang up the phone and slump down in the chair. 'Well, that's Saturday ruined.'

'I'm sure it won't be that bad,' says Jodie.

'Oh, but it will be. All we ever do is talk about Coco's wedding and how brilliant and perfect her life is and why haven't I met somebody, anybody? Roger will make some crappy joke about my crappy job and I will leave my parents' house feeling worse about my entire existence. Guaranteed to be even worse when I tell them

I've been fired.' I let out a half-groan, half-whimper.

'So don't tell them,' replies Jodie.

'I suppose. Oh, take a look at this.'

Jodie picks up the business card and reads it aloud. '"0207 432 5555 ext. 007."' She turns the card over. Duty Calls. 237 Maurice Embankment. Miss Hall. Noon. Ottoman. 'Who's Ottoman?'

'I have no idea. I found it in my coat pocket. I thought you might know.'

'You were talking to that businessman for ages last night, but I thought his name was Niall, or was it Miles?'

'Neil. He also suggested I could spank my way into his office of love.'

Jodie laughs. 'I think you should go.'

'What? To the office of *lurve*?'

'No. To Duty Calls.'

'You think?'

'What have you got to lose?'

What indeed!

Jodie twiddles the card in her fingers. 'When one door closes, another opens,' she says with a smile.

The kitchen clock chimes and the menacing cuckoo bird bolts out as if it wants to peck a hole in my throbbing forehead.

'I hate that thing,' I say.

'You hate all clocks, Dusty, but if you get your skates on, you can still make it.'

By the time I make myself presentable for a job interview I know nothing about, if indeed it is an interview, Jodie is waiting for me behind the wheel of her white brick of a Volvo. This car has been pranged and scraped more times than I can remember. Its second home is Drew's Garage, conveniently at the end of our street. Jodie's driving is unpredictable, and I can't help wondering how safe she is in the skies. She really hates the car. She wanted a sleek supercar but instead she's stuck with it, thanks to her mother's interference about keeping her safe on the roads, but Jodie loves speed and manoeuvrability—difficult to achieve in London's congested roads with a car that's wider than the Thames Estuary.

'Ready?' she asks, revving the engine.

'Yes,' I say hesitantly, while crossing my fingers over my eyes and hoping not to die, which is the best way to experience Jodie's driving. Jodie has one way of driving: fast and furious.

We arrive at the address in record time and thankfully in one piece. Jodie waits, illegally parked, while I totter over to the high-tech building. It's an improvement on Port-A-Privy. I look at the rows of shiny metal buttons displayed on the intercom and locate the button for Duty Calls. I give Jodie the thumbs-up.

'Break a leg!' she bellows, giving the car horn a honk. Several passers-by turn to witness the loud Essex woman in a white brick with wheels as she does a wheel spin and speeds off down the road, narrowly missing a bus stop and leaving a wake of terrified passengers.

Turning back to the rows of shiny metal buttons, I press the button for Duty Calls. Nerves pinball around in my stomach. At least the pounding in my head has diminished to a light tapping.

'Duty Calls Cleaners,' a voice calls out from the intercom.

A cleaning company? My heart sinks. 'Hi. I am Dusty Hall. Here to see Ottoman?'

'You need to come around the back,' the curt voice instructs. 'Car park entrance.'

A bloody cleaning job. I walk towards the car park, ridiculously overdressed in a pair of three-inch pink pointy heels, chequered dress and co-ordinating jacket. When I get there, there's a huge, bald man sitting in the car park kiosk.

'Excuse me, I'm looking for Duty Calls.'

Two tiny brown eyes blink at me while an oversized hand points to a metal door.

'Thank you,' I say.

As I head to the metal door, I get this really weird feeling in the pit of my stomach, a feeling that something's not as it seems. My palms begin to sweat. I look over my shoulder and the man in the kiosk motions for me to open the door. I shrug the feeling away. It's probably just nerves.

The metal door groans as I push it open. I find myself at the foot of a large stairway. Again, I hesitate. *Come on, Dusty. Don't be such a wet blanket.*

I end up walking up four flights of stairs before I find a door marked 'Duty Calls'. As I step into a corridor there is building work under construction across a large section of this floor. I carefully step around the ladder and bags of plaster, noticing small round holes dotted about in the walls. Next to the round holes is a door labelled 'Cleaning Equipment' and, next to that, a door labelled 'Reception'.

I take a moment to compose myself—deep, succinct breaths. I wipe the sweat off my palms and commence 'make a good entrance' Dusty. There's a keypad, but the code has been written on a sticker and stuck to the wall next to it; clearly security is not high on their agenda. I punch in the code—one, two, three, four—and the door buzzes and clicks out of the lock.

I'm surprised to find a burly bloke sat behind a desk in front of me. He doesn't look like your average receptionist and I can presume he's the receptionist as there's a placard that says 'receptionist'. He looks far more suited to a boxing ring.

'Hi, I'm Dusty Hall.'

He nods curtly and hands me a form. 'Please fill this

out.'

'Of course! Absolutely. Right away.' I take the form and turn to find a seating area, surprised to see two women sitting there, not a smile between them. I notice they are both wearing heavy-duty boots peeking out from combat trousers and sweatshirts, and I immediately wonder if there was a dress code. I take another look at the business card, but there's nothing on the card to suggest there was. I'm about to sit down when the door next to me flies open and a woman and two men step out. I take a hasty step back.

The woman is wearing a brown jacket that is way too big for her, although she has a pretty face. In fact, she looks a lot like my aunt Agnes. She is wiry and tall with a severe haircut. However, my aunt Agnes is fair-skinned, fun and cheery, and likes wearing colourful headscarves. This woman doesn't smile, but then neither does the man next to her. Actually, he looks rather furious. I'm not sure how to respond. I turn to the other man and instantly feel a jolt of recognition.

'Mr Simons!' I exclaim.

So it was Mr Simons who slipped me the business card. Of course he did. Didn't he say I was wasted in that sterile environment? I beam at Mr Simons. 'It's so nice to see you again,' I say as if we are long-lost friends.

'Good to see you again, Miss Hall.'

My gaze flickers to the other man, but he has turned his attention to the Aunt Agnes lookalike and is shaking her hand. 'Lieutenant Khan. It was a pleasure.'

Lieutenant?

'Yes, sir, thank you, sir.' She has a dry Northern accent.

She turns to leave but I am in the way. 'Sorry,' I say, stepping aside to let her pass. She leaves the office without a backward glance.

There's a brief silence when the two men look at me. Mr Simons is friendly and warm, but the other man's gaze is so hostile I flinch. They turn on their heels and return to the office. I'm about to sit down when—

'You can't be serious.' The man's tone is curt.

'Oh, but I am,' replies Mr Simons.

'But she has zero experience, she'll be a liability. Whereas Lieutenant Khan is hungry for it. Perfect performance, academically and physically.'

'She is aggressive, unfeminine and about as alluring as a triffid.'

I stifle a giggle.

'She might need to work on her interpersonal skills, but she's skilled in combat, fluent in Arabic. She wouldn't need a lot of moulding. Totally obedient and respectful of orders.'

'She's too textbook-clean.'

Overqualified, more like. She's way too skilled to be a cleaner.

There's a cough from behind and I turn to see the buff receptionist gesturing to me to sit down. I nod and take a seat. I glance down at the form.

Answer to the best of your ability the following questions. There are no wrong or right answers. We test your ability to be honest and self-aware. If you answer against your first choice, it will be evident to our psychologists.

I've never done a personality test for a job before. How exciting.

1. You see a butterfly with irrevocable damage to its wings. Do you:

a. put it out of its misery quickly or

b. place it to the side, hoping it will recover?

I would put it on a flower with nectar for warmth and shelter. I try to write as neatly as possible. Crikey, that's soppier than a sponge in a monsoon.

2. You are held hostage on an aircraft. Do you:

a. remain calm and keep quiet

b. panic

c. react aggressively

d. start thinking of a plan to overcome your captors?

I circle 'a', then cross it out and put 'd'. If I could talk to the captors, befriend them somehow, listen to their grievances, validate their distress … I mean, we've all got problems, haven't we? Maybe I could talk them out of it. It's worth a shot. I smile at the thought. I would be a hero and all those passengers would be saved. My smile turns upside down, as now it looks like I'm an indecisive Minnie.

3. *What is your favourite word?* 'Forlorn'. I love that word. 'Scribble's' another good one. The French have great words too. 'Bisou' (n: kiss), pronounced 'bee-zoo', and 'pamplemousse' (n: grapefruit), pronounced 'pahmp-lul-moos'. Well, they didn't stipulate in which language. Drat, I've written them all down and they said only one. Now I look as focused as a blurry mirage. Damn it.

4. What is the most dangerous thing you have ever done?

That's easy. I scribble down 'The Wheel of Death'. It was during my circus days and I lay spread-eagled and tied to a wheel and had knives thrown at me. I bet they won't believe me, but it's true.

'Miss Hall. You can go through now.'

My head snaps up. The two women give me evil

stares as if I've somehow jumped the queue.

'I haven't finished the questionnaire,' I reply.

He points to the door. 'I suggest you don't keep them waiting.

I get to my feet and head over to the door, ignoring the glares from the two women. I knock once then enter.

Mr Simons is sitting behind a wooden desk, shuffling through a stack of papers. The other man is sitting in a leather armchair in the corner. He reminds me of a viper ready to strike at any moment. I stifle a nervous giggle.

The office itself is very … beige. Beige carpet, beige-painted walls. The only colour is a wonky scenic painting depicting a grey stormy sea. Not at all fancy like the front of the building, nor does it strike me as the sort of office either of these men spends a great deal of time in. The funny feeling returns to my stomach.

'Sit down, Miss Hall.'

I click the door shut behind me and lower myself into one of the wooden chairs. 'I didn't get to finish the questionnaire.' I slide it across the desk.

'Don't worry about that. A complete waste of time, if you ask me.'

I smile, unsure if he's being serious. 'This is my CV. Although … um, it still shows my previous employer.'

The man in the corner stands up abruptly. 'I'll take that.'

'Yes, that was unfortunate, but I'd say to our advantage,' says Mr Simons with a wink.

I give Mr Simons a grateful smile.

'Miss Hall. I just need you to sign here, then we can proceed.'

'What is it?'

'A non-disclosure agreement. Just formalities. Need to ensure what we discuss here today remains confidential.'

'Sure, you can trust me.' I lean over, puzzled but sign

along the dotted line.

'"My boss is possibly the most boring man to roam the universe, with humour akin to a decaying pool of poo." Isn't that what you said?' says the man in the corner.

'Well, I might have jested.' I give an awkward laugh.

'That is character assassination. Not humour.'

I jolt. I turn to Mr Simons, but his face is unreadable. I turn back to the other man and let out a light laugh. 'There was, um … a description challenge going around on Facebook,' I say with a sudden burst of inspiration. 'You had to write a funny description about your boss.' I look back and forth between the pair of them. 'Real or imaginary. It's a game called, um … Monday to Friday. It was fun, only my boss doesn't have a sense of humour, so the description was a hundred percent accurate and I got—'

'Fired,' retorts the killjoy in the corner.

I stare at him. 'Misunderstood.'

'Sacked,' he counters.

'Taken out of context.'

'Let go.'

'Unfairly dismissed.'

We stare at one another, our gazes locked, mine indignant, his … amused, like an adult waiting to see what silly thing the child will do next.

Mr Simons interrupts with a cough. 'Let's put that unfortunate business to one side and continue with the interview.'

Oh, please do.

Mr Simons leans forwards on his desk. 'What skills do you possess, Miss Hall?'

Skills? Does opening a bottle of wine with my teeth count? Probably not.

'Your achievements?'

'After university I travelled with a circus as part of a

clown acrobatic troupe. We toured the home counties for an entire summer. It was physically gruelling and a real coup for me, as there were a lot of students from my year group who wanted that job. You have to display a variety of skills, it's not all clowning around,' I quip. 'Handstands, flips, cartwheels. I can juggle and ride a unicycle.' Both men are staring at me in astonishment. It's hard to tell if it's in a good way. 'And I'm really skilled at hula-hooping. I can keep it going for hours.' I ignore the guffaw from the corner and focus my attention on Mr Simons. 'My computer skills are above average,' I add.

'You broke into your university tutor's hard drive.'

My head snaps sideways and I glare at the man. 'That was never proven.' *How did he even know about that? That's not on my CV. I mean, you don't put that type of stuff down unless you're interviewing at Cyber-Hackers Limited.* 'And I was never charged.'

'But you did do it.'

I turn to Mr Simons. 'Only to find my personnel file. Nothing sinister. I thought I was about to be kicked off the course, you see. I had to know. My future was at stake. I had a high temperature, I was completely delirious.'

'You broke your leg,' says the man in the corner.

'Yes.'

'How does that constitute a fever-driven act against security?'

Think, Dusty, think. 'I got an infection from the surgery,' I lie. 'Terrible fever, powerful painkillers that made me a bit, you know …'

'Delusional?'

'A little away with the fairies,' I reply.

'Fairies?'

'Figments of the imagination. Hence the word "fairytales". Off to the Never-Never.'

'The Never-Never? Your point?'

How can he be so callous? 'I was woozy from painkillers and a bit spaced out. Not in control of my faculties.'

'Interesting you try to break into a faculty when you lose your own,' he retorts. 'Couldn't you have just phoned or emailed him?'

'How did you know it was a him?'

'A fifty-fifty guess.'

'During my unfortunate and lengthy recovery, I watched a program on how easy it was to hack a firewall. It must have sunk into my subconscious. I didn't know what I was doing.'

'Evidently you did. You brought the entire system down. Not the usual side effect one expects from a high temperature. And how convenient you got a first.'

I don't like his accusations or his tone, and I'm feeling uneasy about how he came by this knowledge. Actually, it is probably not that hard to find out anything anymore. It was a pretty big thing in the local paper, and it was even on the regional TV news. Mr Simon's face is a blank mask, while the killjoy's face is much more revealing. It tells me I am a waste of space.

However, I'm not about to go down without a fight. 'There was no malice intended, just the result of an innocent, enquiring mind,' I respond sweetly. 'I'm certainly not about to bring corporations down with my flimsy IT skills.' I laugh to show how idiotic the suggestion is.

'I thought you said they were above average?'

Does the man never take a break?

'You brought an institution down, not so far away from a corporation, is it?'

'I got lucky. To be honest, a slug with a rubber hammer could have hacked it. Anyway, this was the literature department. Their golden nuggets on poetry disposition were hardly about to be sold to the Russians. Tolstoy wasn't standing on a hill with a homemade satellite transmitter digging out the best prose to plagiarise, although that would have been quite poetic.'

He laughs, and this time it doesn't sound patronising. I glance over at Mr Simons and he gives me a way-to-go smile. At least Mr Simons is rooting for me.

'Not good with IT, a bit sluggish,' says the killjoy.

'I was doing the university a favour,' I say. 'After that little hiccup, the IT department encrypted stuff properly, secured the university network. Anyway, I have other skills besides IT.'

'We're on the edge of our seats,' he replies.

'I am fluent in French,' I say.

'Shall I warn France's internal minister?'

I ignore him. 'I spent some time studying in France and it was a wonderful experience and, um … illuminating.'

'Illuminating. Why, did you get electrocuted?'

I grit my teeth.

'You studied mime,' he scoffs. 'Enlighten me, but how is that relevant to, well, anything?'

'Mime is the mirror into someone's soul,' I reply.

'I thought that was the eyes?'

'"Do not the most moving moments of our lives find us all without words?"' I say, quoting the late great Marcel Marceau. 'When you communicate in silence, you are exploring the very depth of a person's being. Mime makes the unseen seen, just as a magician makes the seen unseen.' Now they're both giving me confused looks. 'Did I mention I speak French?'

'Qu'esperez-vous pour votre avenir?' asks Mr Killjoy.

Of course he is bloody fluent in French! What do I hope for the future? What kind of question is that? Honestly, he might as well have asked how you make a soufflé rise.

'J'espère que avenir est radieux et je peux porter des lunettes de soleil.' Which roughly translates, 'I hope the future is bright and I get to wear shades.' I mean seriously, what do I hope for the future? I've got to get the present sorted first.

Mr Simons lays a pen deliberately down on the desk and I give a little jump. 'Miss Hall, would you say you can turn your hand to anything, a woman of many guises?'

'Absolutely.' I nod. 'Chameleon should be my middle name. I can play the bimbo, the villain, or even the showman … ta-da,' I say with jazz hands. 'Constantly adapting, that's me.'

Mr Simons nods enthusiastically and I realise I might still have a shot.

'I'm a fast learner,' I say. 'You only need to show me something once and then I've got it. I learnt how to make an origami heart with a ten-pound note just by looking at a YouTube video. When I first started hula-hooping, I could barely keep one up, but with some practice a few weeks later I was spinning fifty at a time.'

I ignore the snickering from the corner and concentrate on giving Mr Simons my undivided attention. 'Some things can take a little longer to learn, but I never give up. I can perform CPR.' I really should have started with that first. 'And change a tyre,' I say. 'And my toilets are always sparkling. The trick is baking soda and vinegar. But you probably know that already.'

Mr Killjoy and Mr Simons stare at me. I have lost them, I can see it in their faces. Mr Simons leans forward and spreads his hands on the desk. 'Miss Hall, how would you feel about being involved with a covert company that uncovers illegal business operations?'

I gawp. 'Well, I can cavort as well as the next person,' I respond, completely confused. That's not another way of saying prostitution, is it?

'Covert, not cavort, Ms Hall. My name is Ottoman. I am the chief of a special operations division at MI6. Duty Calls Cleaners is a cover,' says Mr Simons—or not Mr Simons, as it turns out.

'Your name isn't Mr Simons?'

'Not Mr Simons,' he says with a smile. 'And this is Special Agent Adelstein.'

I glance over at Special Agent Adelstein and my stomach does a flip. Now that I am looking at him properly, he looks remarkably tanned and dangerous. I wonder if he's recently been on holiday or on some undercover assignment to some far-flung exotic destination?

'So how about it, Miss Hall, do you think you're cut out to be a spy?'

Without meaning to, a snort of laughter erupts from me. 'Well, I haven't really given it much thought.'

Of course I bloody haven't. Does anyone in the real world think James Bond stuff is real? But now it makes sense. The women outside must be soldiers.

'You know I'm not a soldier,' I say dazedly.

'Yes, that much is obvious,' retorts Adelstein.

I ignore him as James Bond flashes into my head, swiftly nudged out of the way by a bumbling Johnny English. I get back to James Bond and a scene unfolds.

There I am, beautifully made up with perfect skin, clad in a black latex catsuit swinging from a rope just as a building in the background blows up. Bond smiles at me as I make a perfect landing next to him. 'That was amazing.'

'Nothing to it,' I say, flicking back my shiny hair, not a split end in sight. 'Once you've swung on jungle vines, ropes are child's play.'

'Miss Hall?'

I am catapulted back into the room, two pair of eyes staring at me. 'So, I would be working for the government?'

'Yes,' replies Ottoman.

'Like 007?'

Ottoman smiles.

'Can I tell anyone?'

'No, you will be shot,' interrupts Agent Adelstein.

I stare at him. He's joking, right? He's just trying to scare me? I look for a flicker of a smile but it doesn't come. 'Sure, why not, sounds like a hoot!'

'A hoot?' Adelstein eyeballs me.

Ottoman abruptly stands up, calling an end to the interview. 'I think we have heard enough.' He comes around the desk and I get to my feet. 'It's been a pleasure, Miss Hall,' he says, shaking my hand.

'Likewise,' I reply.

Adelstein joins us and takes my hand. His grip is crushing. So too is his gaze. 'Remember you have signed the Official Secrets Act, you cannot tell anyone about this interview, do you understand?'

I nod mutely. I did? It's that what Ottoman got me to sign?

'It would be treason of the highest kind.'

'Yes, yes, I get it.' I nod. He lets go of my hand and I give my fingers a flex, redistributing the bones back into place.

As I step out into the reception area, the bulky receptionist looks up. I'm too stunned to speak. The two women look at me and everybody would have to be deaf not to hear Adelstein's ear-piercing cry. 'Over my dead body!'

I smile when I hear Ottoman's response. 'That can be arranged.'

CHAPTER FOUR

Not that any of it matters now, because obviously I will not get the job. Agent Adelstein will see to that. How dare he underestimate me—that's always been my family's job. I could be a spy. With a little training, anything is possible.

I don't know how long I stand outside the car park in righteous indignation, reliving the interview and cringing at what I said. How dare Agent Adelstein judge me and get me so wrong. Feeling somewhat deflated, I walk towards the Embankment. *Something will come up, I just need to be positive,* I tell myself. Who knows, maybe my dream acting job is just around the corner. It's just about keeping my chin up and looking forwards, not backwards, but I can't resist looking over my shoulder at the Duty Calls building.

I must have walked for about twenty minutes when I feel a peculiar tingling sensation, like someone is following me. I turn to see a sleek black car with tinted windows crawling to a stop next to me. My heart jumps into my mouth as the passenger window slides down. Reacting on pure instinct, I drop to the ground.

'Miss Hall?'

Hang on … That sounded like Ottoman. I look up, confused. Mr Ottoman is hanging out of the window, holding a brown envelope.

I pretend to fiddle with my shoe. 'Dodgy heel,' I say, getting to my feet.

Ottoman smiles. 'I want to give you this.' He hands me the envelope. 'Your training starts tomorrow. 8 a.m. sharp.'

'You're giving me the job?' I say in disbelief.

His mouth twitches into a smile. 'Details are in the envelope.'

I take the envelope, too dazed to say anything else.

'And for the record, Ms Hall, you are precisely what we need.'

'I think your co-worker disagrees.'

'Well, it's a good job I'm the boss.'

A huge smile licks across my face. 'Yes, it is!' I glance over his shoulder at the empty space next to him. 'Where is your co-worker?'

'I left him back at the office. He has the delightful task of informing the remaining interviewees they've been unsuccessful. So, do well in training and prove me right and him wrong.'

'Absolutely,' I say. 'I won't let you down. I promise.'

I watch the car pull away and for a moment I stand there in stunned disbelief, letting his words sink in. I, Dusty Hall, am precisely what this country needs. Okay, not exactly those words but as good as.

I look around me. People are going about their daily lives with no clue what has just taken place. I can't help thinking that my eyes have been opened to a whole new world. Before I was blind, now I can see. Like *The Matrix*. I giggle. I'm about to embark on a new and exciting, quite possibly dangerous journey—and no one knows. Excitement fizzes in my stomach. This is it. This is my chance to make something of myself. To really make a difference. I won't let Ottoman down. I am going to show him and Agent Adelstein—heck, I am going to show King and country!—that Dusty Hall is a force to be reckoned with.

I fish out my mobile from my bag and dial Jodie's number.

'Jumbo jumbo,' she says.

'Jumbo jumbo,' I reply. 'Jumbo jumbo' means 'hello' in Swahili. Jodie and I have this thing where we answer our phones in another language. We can say 'hello' and 'yes' and 'please' in quite a few languages. I don't know why we started doing it. It's a bit naff but it makes us giggle.

'I got the job,' I exclaim. 'And I start tomorrow.'

'Bloody hell, they must have been desperate.'

'Excuse me?'

Jodie coughs. 'What's the job?'

'Oh … err …' Damn it. I should have thought of that before ringing. I feel my face go hot as I prepare to lie. 'Well, it's, um … just the, err … same really—admin, reception, PA thingy.'

'Well, it's a job at least,' replies Jodie, sounding bored already. 'Where are you?'

'Standing on the Embankment, wondering who I could call to celebrate with.'

'Me!' screeches Jodie, bursting my eardrum. 'Where are you thinking?'

'What about that amazing place just off St. Martin's Lane? The place with the Mexican music. Gah! What was it called?'

'Last time we were in Soho we were a tad inebriated,' recalls Jodie.

'Wahaca,' I say in a sudden burst of recollection.

'Okay, hon, see you there in half an hour,' says Jodie.

After a short Tube ride and a little window-shopping, I arrive at the restaurant, famished. The smells coming from Wahaca are divine. The diners are pretty divine themselves, but today I am more interested in what's on the menu, not what tackle the fish have brought in. I chuckle to myself.

'I'm here to eat,' I declare to the approaching waiter.

'Very good,' he says with a welcoming smile. 'We make food to be eaten.'

I give a smile. 'Table for two then, please.'

'There's a brief wait, is that okay?'

'That's fine, my friend isn't here yet.' He's very charming and quite the apéritif to set up a good appetite.

'If you'd like to'—in my mind, I hear myself say, *Yes, your place or mine?*—'follow me,' he continues, handing me a menu and leading me over to a set of cosy seats by the stairs. As soon as I open the menu, my mouth waters and my stomach grumbles in anticipation, reminding me that all I've eaten today is an apple. I gaze around happily, half-daydreaming. This place is full of the Mexican spirit. You could almost believe you were on holiday.

When Jodie arrives, she's in a green sequinned dress and a full face of makeup.

'You know, I can't stay out all night,' I say hesitantly. 'I have an early start tomorrow.' Jodie waves away my concern. 'I'm being serious.'

But Jodie turns her attention to Mr Apéritif, lust licking across her face. 'Hiya.'

'Your table is ready,' he says. We follow Mr Apéritif to our table, slap-bang in the middle of the restaurant. 'Can I get you ladies a drink?' he asks as we settle down in our seats.

'Two margaritas, please,' Jodie says, answering for me. 'We're celebrating. My friend here has a new job.'

He turns to me. 'Congratulations.'

'Thank you,' I say, hoping he doesn't ask me about my new job. Of course he doesn't.

'There's so much to choose from,' says Jodie, her eyes growing big as she scans the menu.

This is the longest I've seen Jodie silent. She studies the menu carefully, then as soon as the waiter returns with our drinks she slaps it shut and places her order in the manner of machine-gun fire without once glancing down. I add a few more dishes to the order and hand the menus back to the waiter.

'Congratulations on the new job!' Jodie says, raising her glass in the air.

I grin back. 'Thank you.' We touch glasses and I take a sip, immediately feeling the tequila buzz course through my veins.

'They must have been very impressed with you to hire you on the spot like that.'

'Or desperate?' I quirk a brow.

'You know I didn't mean it like that.'

'Well, I'm quite an impressive person.'

Jodie smiles. 'I knew that already. So what's the company called again?'

'Duty Calls.'

'And what do they do?'

'They're, um, a cleaning company.'

Jodie screws up her nose. 'I suppose it's a job.'

My nose shifts slightly out of joint. 'Nothing wrong with a cleaning company.'

'No, no. Of course not! And I think a receptionist is an important job. It's the first line of contact and all that. What's your boss like?'

'One of them is nice, the other is a bit of a twat.'

'Don't write that on Facebook.'

'Don't worry, I won't. I've learnt my lesson.'

'Will they give you time off for acting?'

'I didn't ask,' I reply. 'Anyway, I think it's time to

knock acting on the head.'

Jodie breathes in sharply.

'It's okay,' I reassure her as she reaches for my hand. 'I think it's just time to let go, you know, pursue a new passion. Jodie, are you crying?'

'I just don't want you to give up on your dream,' she sniffs. 'You've wanted to be an actress all your life, and you're amazing at it.'

I smile. 'I'm just being realistic, Jodie. There's only so many rejections one can take and now it's time to accept that it isn't meant to be. Aren't you always saying, "As one door closes, another opens"? Well, who knows what this new job might bring.'

'Dusty, it's a cleaning job!' Jodie says in a disbelieving voice.

'Which I'm really excited about. So you needn't worry. I'm not a lost cause.'

Jodie gapes at me, looking totally bewildered, then she seems to snap out of it. 'Well, seeing as this is the new you, and talking of lost causes, what are you going to do about Cameron?'

'Cameron who?'

Jodie beams. 'Marvellous. Maybe Mr Apéritif could fill the void.'

'Don't call it a void. Anyway, I'm not interested. It's you who's in desperate need of a good shag.'

'Chance would be a fine thing.'

'No luck at Treasure Island Hotel then?'

'Barren island, more like,' cackles Jodie.

'Not even a holidaymaker washed up on the beach?'

Jodie shakes her head woefully. 'Nope.'

'Pervy Pete didn't send a message in a bottle?'

'Eurgh!' snorts Jodie. 'I do not want to think about that man in a seafaring way.'

'Oh, Seaman Pete. Is that what you mean?'

Jodie looks like she is going to be seasick. But then

the food arrives and our mouths gape open at the smorgasbord of Mexican delights put in front of us. I can feel myself drooling. 'You go first,' I whisper.

'No, you,' Jodie whispers back.

'Okay, together, on three. One, two—three.'

We delve in like pigs at a trough. The only word to describe the experience is 'heavenly'. The beautiful assortment of tastes that hit my hungry, neglected tastebuds feels like a divine intervention.

'OMG. This is soooo good,' sighs Jodie.

I nod and sigh, my mouth full.

'More drinks, ladies?' Mr Apéritif pops up out of nowhere. I catch Jodie's eyes; our mouths are stuffed with quesadilla. I have an urge to laugh and quickly cover my piggy-ness with my hand. Jodie does the same, but with her other hand holds up two fingers and points to our glasses.

The waiter seems well versed in sign language. 'Two more margaritas coming up,' he says.

'I swear waiters do that on purpose,' I say, still chewing on a mouthful of chicken.

Jodie nods. 'It is delicious though.'

I grin. 'Nom.'

The conversation swiftly moves on to Jodie's gorgeous Manolo heels she wants to wear every day instead of the company-issued bricks they try to blag off as footwear, and the latest gossip from the fuselage sisterhood, which always has a good measure of sauciness. The only irritation to our otherwise heavenly dining experience is my sister.

The thing you need to know about my sister is she thinks everyone should be at her beck and call, regardless of what they might be doing.

Coco: *Is Florists Flor Unikon more in vogue than Scarlet and Violet?*

Me: *Haven't a bloody clue.*

Coco: *Would I look better in truffle or champagne?*

Me: *Definitely, as a box of truffles with the lid closed. I'm busy. Let's discuss tomorrow.*

Coco: *This is my big day.*

Me: *Okay. Go in black. Your funeral anyway.*

Coco: *I don't think that's funny.*

Anyway, I shouldn't be on my phone during dinner. It's rude and I don't like it when other people do it. People should engage more, although possibly not my sister and possibly not to Roger.

'Sorry,' I say, stashing my phone in my bag. 'Bridezilla is driving me insane.'

'You do know she won't stop until the big day,' replies Jodie.

'Unless I drug her until her wedding day. It's the only way anyone's going to get any peace.'

Jodie laughs.

I get up from the table. 'I need a pee.' My stomach feels bigger than the bloated prosthetic one I had in the IBS ad. For no particular reason, but possibly as a result of two margaritas swishing about in my bloodstream, I have an urge to sweep past the tables in the manner of an undercover agent. It's all quite fun until I slam into Mr Apéritif and step on his foot with my heel. He winces.

'Sorry!' I gasp.

'That's okay,' he says and hobbles away. My spy self clearly needs some practice. I head for the toilets and lock myself in a cubicle.

It's actually rather jolly in here. Mexican music fills the colourful space and as I finish up, my feet are toe-tapping on the tiled floor and it's as if the music possesses my body. The music's beat gets louder and I swing my hips. Even when I'm finished, I swish and sway my way over to the sinks like a matador with tap shoes—full dance-off style, arms akimbo. Miss Latina is in the room.

Suddenly, the door bursts open and a woman enters. She giggles when she sees me. I am slightly embarrassed, but then the woman does her own little hip sway and makes her way into a cubicle.

Latino beats are infectious. I turn to face my reflection, tossing my shoulders back. I look positively glowing. I suppose two margaritas will do that to you. As I look more closely, I come to the conclusion I look nothing like a spy. I might have chosen Mr Apéritif for a honey trap, but I am ordinary-looking. I have green eyes, but not the mesmerising type; they're more apparent in summer months or under a dentist's light. My most redeeming features are a well-cut fringe and a plump mouth. I wouldn't break a mirror, but nor would I be the cause to invent one. I'm not beautiful like Alice or striking like Jodie, with her red hair and big baby-blues. I am what people call pretty, in a non-threatening, girl-next-door kind of way. But maybe that's the point. Isn't the whole point of being a spy to blend in and not attract attention? Still, it's all pretty exciting, which is why I better get home to bed.

I return to our table in a normal fashion to find Jodie has ordered two more margaritas. 'One for the road,' she trills.

'I shouldn't. I start my new job tomorrow!'

'Oh, come on. The night is still young and it's not every day you start a new job. Well, maybe it is for you.' Jodie laughs out loud.

She's right. There have been quite a few new jobs over the past two years, but that is definitely behind me now. I accept the glass graciously. 'Okay. One for the road.'

'Super!' Jodie beam. 'You're much better company than Mustard.'

'I should hope so. Mustard is a cat.'

'I think he was a king in his last life.'

'All cats think they're kings.'

'Do you think Mr Apéritif is a queen?' she asks, elbow slipping off the table. She rights herself and takes another sip of her drink. 'So where should we go next?'

'Home,' I reply.

'But it's only eight o'clock.' Jodie pouts.

'Okay, one more place but I need to be home by ten.'

'All right, Cinders. Remind me to buy you pumpkin pie on route.'

CHAPTER FIVE

I wake up with a painful jolt, my phone beeping loudly in my ear. There's a slight rhythmic pounding in my head but on a hangover scale of one to ten, I'm about a six. I have definitely been far worse.

Jodie and I ended up in some random pub cellar-turned-music venue in Islington. We had definitely been homeward-bound but somehow got sidetracked and ended up rocking out to a terrible indie band with a bunch of university students from Panama—so much for getting to bed before midnight. They were a handsome bunch too and Jodie and I were smitten. It would have been rude to have left. Besides, I've never met a Panamanian before. Try saying that after a few margaritas. I secretly switched to lemonade when Jodie wasn't watching, but I don't feel as bright-eyed and bushy-tailed as I wanted to or should be for my first day of training.

Jumping into the shower, I shampoo and condition my hair in record time, dry myself off and double-brush my teeth. I head back to my bedroom and open my wardrobe door. I inhale deeply. My happy place. I pick out a pretty pink floral dress and kitten heels, retrieve my gym bag from the back of the wardrobe and check it still has the yoga gear and trainers inside. It does. I pop in a towel and washbag and hit the road.

I still have plenty of time to get there, and with the cool air surrounding my face (because I can't work out how to get the Volvo's roof up) clarity replaces fuzziness. It seems I *can* burn the candle at both ends.

The training centre is in some godforsaken place in the middle of bloody nowhere. As far as I can tell, it's behind a massive wood, the closest postcode about five miles in the other direction (according to Google Maps). Even when I tried Street View, it is obscured by lorries going past; I wonder if the government did that on purpose? Luckily for me, Jodie's safe brick box of wheels has a built-in swanky sat-nav—and, doubly big bonus, Jodie said I can borrow the car for as long as I need it because she's getting a bike. She thinks I'm attending a lame company-training course in some faceless conference centre.

Jodie is a fitness freak: swimming, running and now cycling. Next she'll be telling me she's entering a triathlon. I probably should take a leaf out of her book and start getting fitter. I have been a bit lapsed on that front.

The roads are empty coming out of London. I turn on the radio, which is playing some eighties throwback tunes. I'm surprised at how many songs I know. Cameron may have been a crap boyfriend, but he was a big eighties nut and I endured hours of rehearsals, cover after cover. The songs must have seared into my subconscious.

After a couple of wrong turns, I find the woodland track and see the training centre in the distance. The butterflies in my stomach turn into excitable hamsters while I belt out the lyrics to Madonna's 'Like a Virgin.'

'Nice pipes!' remarks the security guard as I pull up in front of an enormous wrought-iron gate. My singing peters to a stop because all I can do is stare at the gun hanging off his shoulder.

'Hi, I'm here for some training.'

'Your name?'

'Miss Hall, reporting for duty.' I salute. The guard gives me a smile as he checks his list, takes a photo and compares it to one presumably on his touchscreen.

'Proceed, Miss Hall.' He buzzes the barrier and up it goes.

I'm just done parking up when over the top of the steering wheel I see Adelstein at the door of a greyish building and he is looking straight at me.

I gulp. Is he waiting for me? He isn't smiling. No change there then.

I retrieve my bags from the passenger seat and cross the concrete car park. 'Good morning, Mr … Agent Adelstein,' I say.

His eyes narrow at me. 'I hope that's a change of clothing in your bag?'

'Of course.'

'The other recruits arrived half an hour ago. They're on the field warming up.'

'The letter said 7.45 a.m. It's 7.30 a.m.'

'Then you have fifteen minutes. Follow me.'

I follow Adelstein into the training centre with only the clip, clip, clip of my heels for company. He barks out a couple of instructions—toilet to the left, canteen first floor on the right—while we continue down a long, narrow corridor, down some steps, and finally come to a stop outside a green door.

'The women's changing room,' he says, and for about two of the longest seconds, he stares at me. It's quite unnerving being under the scrutiny of someone who doesn't like you. 'A word of advice, Miss Hall, save your nights out for the weekend.'

I jolt. 'Since when is it a crime to go out for a drink with a friend?'

'We need fresh minds here, Miss Hall. Not fried.'

My cheeks flush. I feel guilty and, well, a bit shaken. How did he know? Was it a lucky guess or am I under surveillance? Do they do that to all new recruits? Or is the entire world under surveillance? I feel a lurch in my stomach. Avoiding further eye contact, I push open the door, then close it and collapse against it for a moment. I've always said you never know who is watching, but now the thought makes me feel decidedly uneasy.

I get changed in double-quick time and put the rest of my belongings into a locker. Adelstein is waiting for me as I exit. He stares at me for a long time.

Oh, for goodness' sake, what now?

Suddenly, his mouth twitches up at the sides and I swear he's trying not to laugh. 'This way,' he says, spinning on his heel. He marches off down the corridor.

I run to catch him up, tripping on every third step. Honestly! Put me in a pair of heels and I am a graceful swan, put me in a pair of flats and I'm like a kid skidding about a freshly washed floor. A quick sideways glance and I can see my ungainliness has not gone unnoticed. He's definitely trying not to laugh.

Well, at least he's not angry.

What the …

A sudden wave of nausea comes over me and I feel slightly faint as I see it for the first time: a gigantic obstacle course.

Adelstein leads me towards the rest of the recruits. Seven in total: four women including me. No one else seems bothered by the immense booby trap in front of them. But I am quite possibly going to die out there. It looks hideous, dangerous and impossible to finish.

look like you're auditioning for a psychedelic fitness video.'

I hear the snickers, but they stop as soon as he looks in their direction.

'You are the only unit here today. It's your assault course. I expect most of you to finish it in less than thirty minutes. I suspect some'—he looks pointedly at me—'Not to finish at all. Ladies first. That includes you two.' He points to the guys.

Everyone moves towards the painted line on the grass and takes up their running stance. I have never done an assault course in my life, and I have a horrible feeling I may never do one again. But they wouldn't make it if you couldn't do it. Would they?

The sergeant blows his whistle and we're off. I focus on Lieutenant Khan's blue baseball cap. If I can keep up with her then I just might make it.

God, she's fast. But I'm totally keeping up.

Oh, God. My chest is hurting and I have a pain running down my side. When will those bloody endorphins kick in?

I arrive at the first obstacle and drop to the ground. The net is heavy and wet. I lie flat on my stomach and start to crawl through the mud. It seems to go on for ages, partially due to me getting tangled up in the damn thing, but eventually I reach the other end. I scramble to my feet and run towards the next obstacle.

I assess the man-made hole. I can't see what's down there. I hazard a bet there'll be spiders. I push the thought out of my mind and climb down the metal ladder, jumping the last rung. I land in water, which seeps into my trainers and up my lycra leggings. Darkness envelops me. The only noise I can hear is the sound of me sloshing through the muddy water. The rest of the recruits are long gone. I feel an anxiety-driven acid reflux creep up my oesophagus. It only goes away when I see the light at the end of the tunnel. I step up the ladder and take off at a steady pace until I hit a brick wall—literally.

I step back and look up at the vertical net. I reach for the rope ladder dangling down and start to climb. By the time I'm at the top, my arms are burning. I swing my legs over the side, grip hold of the rope and climb down the other side. My arms are shaking and when I hit the ground my legs buckle.

I thought I was pretty fit, but every bit of me is aching and my lungs feel at bursting point. I keep going. I focus on putting one foot in front of the other, sheer determination pulling me forward.

What now?

I look at the rope swing and the large , grimy pond and there's just one thing for it. I grab hold of the rope and push off. 'Geronimo!' I holler, bursting into insane laughter.

The tips of my trainers touch the edge of the pond, but I can't get a good enough grip and I am propelled backwards, swinging back and forth several times, momentum petering out, along with the rest of my hope. I'm left dangling a few meters above the pond's surface, Lycra hanging in suspension. I have no choice but to let go.

My heart drops, along with all my internal organs, and I sink into the pond of gunk. I bob back to the surface, covered in algae, and wade through stenchy water over to the edge. I clamber up the side, looking and smelling like the Creature from the Black Lagoon.

I am wet, muddy and smell like sewage, and to top it off I have lost a trainer. I am also making a weird sort of grunting noise, a bit like a walrus. I drag one foot in front of the other until I reach the top of the slope. The mud-laden trainer has all the grip of a custard slice and I end up sliding down the slope on my bottom, which actually speeds me up, landing right in front of some monkey bars.

I attempt two rungs of the monkey bars but I can barely hold on. I clearly have to work on my upper-body strength. I leave the rest and stagger towards a barrier of thick vegetation, then struggle through nature's barbed wire of damp thorny undergrowth. Brambles and twigs poke and prod at my face, snagging at my clothes. I push forward. I am panting so heavily I'm certain that my lungs will pop at any second. An oxygen tent wouldn't go amiss in this dank leaf prison. One more heave and I make it through, with most of the vegetation stuck in my hair and my arms looking like they've wrestled with a wire brush.

I stumble forward onto my hands and knees. I stay there for a second, catching my breath. My mind thinks back to the day before last when I was sitting at a nice clean reception desk, fresh and dry—also bored out of my skull, I remind myself.

A guttural sound interrupts the air like a wounded bear. What was that? I crawl forward on my knees, moving towards the sound, and peer over the edge of a large pit. Lieutenant Khan is at the bottom of the pit. I watch as she takes a run up the side, trying to reach the rope—but someone has cut it and she's way off. She slides back down.

'Can I help?' I ask, my voice coming out in an exhausted rasp.

Khan whips her head around, surprise and disappointment reflected in her eyes. 'Yes!' she says.

'How did you fall in?'

'I was pushed,' she grinds out. 'And they cut the rope.' She points to the rest of the rope coiled at her feet.

'That's awful. What can I do to help?'

She pauses, looks at the rope then at me. 'Do you think you catch this bit of the rope and tie it to that tree?'

Her accent is northern, Lancashire perhaps?

'I think so.'

Lieutenant Khan threads the rope and builds a loop. 'Get ready!' she says. I quickly jump to my feet as she twirls the rope above her head, swinging the freshly made lasso faster and faster.

Oh, crikey, that's really fast.

I brace myself and the rope flies through the air, making a loud whooshing sound. It lands over the top of me. Wow, that was cool.

I pick it up and run over to the tree where the rest of rope is tethered, form a small loop, pass the end of the rope through the loop, and wrap it around the end, muttering the mnemonic, 'The rabbit pops out of the hole, runs around the tree, gets spooked and runs back in the hole.' I pass the end back through the loop and give it a tug. Satisfied, I drop the rope to Lieutenant Khan. 'This should hold,' I shout.

Lieutenant Khan gives it a tug. Her brow quirks, like she's surprised. Then I watch as she expertly scales the steep incline. When she reaches the top she inspects the knot. 'A bowline,' she says, impressed.

'Thanks,' I say. 'My mum taught me how to do the knot as a child. She wanted me to be able to lead horses around safely. It's the best knot to know since there's no danger of it tightening up around the horse's neck when the rope is pulled, yet it's really strong. Never thought I'd ever need to use it again.'

Lieutenant Khan nods brusquely. 'I'm Yaz.'

'Dusty,' I reply.

'Well, thanks.' She hovers for a moment and there's an awkward pause.

'You go.' I wave her on. 'I'll follow in a minute.'

'Okay,' she says, looking relieved. She gives me a half-smile and jogs off. I follow but it's more of a hobble, an uneven, sporadic lunge if you were watching from above. But I can see the finishing line. Well, I hope it's the finishing line and not some weird balancing wire over a burning pit of scorpions. I break into delirious laughter.

No, it is definitely the finishing line. I can see the rest of the group. Sergeant is standing bullishly with a stopwatch in hand, Adelstein is standing with a pair of binoculars in his. The figures grow larger as I get closer. I speed up, and my body cries out in protest, but all I can think is, *I did it. I bloody well did it.* I throw myself across the finishing line, sprawling flat out on my face.

I can hear a chorus of laughter but I don't care, they can laugh all they want. I did it.

'This is not a comedy show, Hall,' Sergeant bellows. 'GET UP.'

But I don't think I can. My body has shut down.

'We haven't got all day!'

Everybody is staring at me, waiting.

I slowly manoeuvre myself onto all fours, lift one knee up and push off with my hands, aware that my bum is sticking up in the air. I stand up but I think my missing trainer has given me vertigo because I feel a little dizzy and I think I'm going to fall. Yaz grabs my arm. I smile at her gratefully.

'Right, you lot of cretins,' Sergeant bellows. 'Next exercise is at eleven hundred hours. Gymnasium hall. That gives you forty minutes to leak and water.'

The group trots off obediently, no aches or pains visible.

Yaz stares at me with concern. 'Will you be okay if I let go?'

'I think so,' I say, aware that I am holding onto her for dear life.

She lets go and I sway. 'I'm fine,' I say, more to convince myself than her.

Yaz jogs away and I stare after her, envious. How

does she have the energy?

'You should get moving. You need to shower and change.'

I lift my head to see Adelstein peering down. 'What, mud and gunk aren't part of Army regulations?'

'This isn't the Army.'

'It's not the *Vogue* offices either.'

'You smell really bad.'

'Oh!' I say, not expecting that. 'Well, I better shower. I wouldn't want to offend your delicate sensibilities.'

A smile flashes across his stern features but evaporates just as quickly.

I turn and limp away, aware that he is watching me. He's what my mother would call an odd duck.

'Did you see her?'

'Clearly out of her comfort zone.'

'Wherever did they find such a castoff?'

'Did you see what she was wearing?'

'I heard she's an experiment.'

'I've seen quicker sloths!'

I know nothing good ever came from eavesdropping but it isn't like they are trying to hide it. I slam my locker door hard and the women jump apart. When they see it's me they burst into hysterical laughter. My cheeks burn with humiliation.

Lieutenant Khan, who is sitting away from the others, looks up at me. 'Just ignore them.'

'What ya saying over there, Khan?' says Brickhouse. 'I'd hate to see you fall into another pit.'

'Pratton, there won't be a next time,' snaps Yaz.

So her name's Pratton, and she's a major prat at that. I smile gratefully at Yaz, grab my towel and head for the shower cubicles.

CHAPTER SIX

I can still hear the women cackling as I shower and I start to cry, tears rolling down my cheeks as the water pummels down the back of my neck. I bet they would love to see me fail—the Barbie doll who couldn't hack it! Why do people have to be so judgemental? Why can't they let me be? I'm obviously no threat to them.

Well, I will not fail. Not this time. Ottoman singled me out for a reason. He sees something special in me and he's the boss around here. Since when do I care what other people think? I may not fly around the obstacle course at the rate of a triathlete but it's my first day—give me a break!

As the water washes away the gunk and foliage it also washes away the self-pity and self-doubt. Those women better not write me off just yet—and neither should my parents. I am a force to be reckoned with. Just you wait and see.

The place is empty by the time I've finished up, but my jaw sets with a renewed determination, further boosted when I get to my locker and find my lost trainer and a note inside: *Leave no man—or woman—behind.*

Well done, Miss Hall. And it's signed *Ottoman.* I didn't even know Ottoman was here. I break into a huge grin. Also next to my mud-encased Lycra is a freshly cleaned tracksuit and a note from Lieutenant Khan: *You can borrow these. Yaz Khan.*

Suddenly, the world doesn't seem like it's out to get me. Or is it? I hold up the jogging bottoms for inspection and my nose wrinkles.

The tracksuit is not my style, but anything is better than trying to squeeze back into soggy, muddy Lycra and I don't think the dress will be appropriate. The tracksuit is … roomy. I look like a convict due for the exercise yard. I roll up the sleeves and the bottom of the jogging bottoms, which is a slight improvement. I give my muddy trainers a quick wipe and stick them under the hand dryer. They're still damp when I pull them on, but bearable. To finish the convict look, I scrape my hair back into a ponytail but can't resist dabbing on a little glittery eyeshadow because … well, why not. I leave the changing room much taller than I walked in.

There are a few sniggers from Pratton's table when I enter the canteen, which I ignore. Yaz is sitting alone and, judging by her body language, she wants to keep it that way. I get myself a coffee and find an empty table in the corner. I pull out my mobile. It rings as soon as I switch it on.

'Where have you been? I've been trying to get hold of you all morning.'

I let out a loud groan. 'Coco, I'm at work,' I hiss down the phone.

'Why haven't you got your phone on alert when I call?' And without pausing for a breath she continues her tirade. 'Is it too much to ask for curly willow branches with white and pink rose pomanders, wrapped in crystal butterflies and hanging votive candles? No, I think not. But you'd think I was asking for the moon. I'm going elsewhere if Jorge doesn't grasp my vision soon. Oh, and Grandad is refusing to wear a suit. He's threatening to turn up in his Navy uniform … You've got to talk to him. Dusty? Dusty? Are you listening?'

'I'm sure he's only joking.' I say, picking up my coffee.

'I don't think he is. He turned up at Gemma's christening in his full medals and battle dress.'

'He is very proud of his naval career.'

'But it's *my* day,' she whines. 'And it is your duty as chief bridesmaid to make sure *my* wedding day goes absolutely perfectly. Besides, he's always had a soft spot for you. You both have frequent bladder needs.' She giggles at her own lame joke.

'I'll see what I can do,' I huff, taking a sip of coffee. As I look up I see Yaz and the other candidates get up. 'Look, Coco, I've got to go. Speak later.'

'But I haven't told you about—'

I cut her off mid-sentence and switch off my phone. I finish my coffee and hurry after the group.

CHAPTER SEVEN

When I arrive at the brightly lit gymnasium Pratton and her satellites have lined up in the centre of the room. Sports equipment and punching bags are towards the back of the room and out of place by the side is a long table full of … non-gym stuff. I walk over to the table to take a closer look. Basically it's a table full of different objects, mostly kitchen stuff, some vases. Yaz is standing at the table. I want to say thank you for the tracksuit but she is so focused on the contents I don't want to interrupt. I look at the various objects. I particularly like the pretty blue-and-white vase.

The door to the gymnasium bangs open and in walks Sergeant followed by Adelstein. 'LINE UP,' hollers Sergeant.

Yaz and I share a look.

'NOW!' shouts Sergeant.

We jump to it and join the others in the middle of the room, but not before catching Pratton's smug look.

'You need to be aware of everything always,' remarks Adelstein. It's the first time he's addressed the group. 'This includes carefully assessing the people and objects around you. Who is your target? What is your target? You must be aware at all times. Remember, it's all in the detail.'

I have no clue what he's talking about.

'We assume you have all looked at the items on the table?' said Sergeant, covering up the table with a big blackout sheet. 'Who can tell me what is on this table?'

There's silence. No one speaks. Then Twitch pipes up. 'Some kitchen stuff.'

'SOME? SOME WHAT? A KITCHEN CUPBOARD? A WASHING MACHINE? A MIDGET ON A BAKING TRAY? TWO CLOWNS IN A MICROWAVE? A FROG MAKING ASHTRAYS?'

'Err … small stuff, used in kitchens.'

'Oh, well, that narrows it down. Your observation skills are sublime, just out on their own. What did I just say?'

'It's in the detail, sir,' squawks Twitch, turning red, a vast improvement on her normal pallor.

'What is the bloody detail? You idiot.'

Twitch's cheeks are now at boiling point.

'Anyone else?'

I raise my hand tentatively.

'Well, go on then, we haven't got until infinity.'

'A set of chef knives; a deflated red balloon in a cup; two pots, one round, low and cerise, the other tall, funnelled and blue with black handles; a crossover handbag; three cloths, each depicting a Biblical event from the Old Testament; a thimble in a glass; four wooden spoons varying in size; a stainless-steel kettle; a cafetière half full of coffee; six espresso cups, one without a handle; an orange saucepan; and a pretty Ming vase from the Ming dynasty—obviously a fake.'

The group's scorn quickly turns to gawps of disbelief. Even Adelstein looks surprised.

'Didn't she do well,' says Sergeant, stomping down

the line; no one can look him in the eyes.

'That is exactly the detail you need to process. Take heed, airheads, when you're reporting we need the flipping details,' says Sergeant, thudding his stick on the floor. It's all very dramatic. I suppose that's Army psychology for you—theatre with thunder.

Adelstein stealthily appears from behind him and removes the sheet from the table. 'But it's no good remembering the details if you can't get yourself out of danger,' says Adelstein. 'You need to be able to defend yourself in the quickest, most effective way, and you won't always have a gun to hand. You will need to improvise.' Adelstein pauses and takes a moment to look at each person. 'The purpose of this exercise is to prepare you to counteract-counterattack. To be ready to respond to threats and challenges at the beat of a butterfly's wing. Which you will need if you intend to survive life as a covert operative.' Adelstein's voice is serious. I still don't have a clue what he's talking about. 'Hall!'

I jolt. 'Yes, sir?'

'Select something from the table.'

'Er, okay.' I wander over to the table and pick up the fake Ming vase. Adelstein picks up a kettle and before I know what's happening, he wraps the cord around my throat. It's not tight, but it's disconcerting all the same. I clutch the vase to my chest.

'What are you doing?' Adelstein lets the cord go slack.

'Shouldn't I be asking you that?' I wheeze. 'You're the one with a cord around my neck!'

'Why didn't you hit me with the vase?'

I stare at him. 'It's not mine.'

'Do you think an assassin is going to do an inventory before they get the upper hand?'

My cheeks flush. 'No, of course not!'

'There is no time to think, only act.'

'You lot with me,' Sergeant's voice suddenly booms. 'Except Robocop and Roboflop. You two stay put.'

He means Yaz and I, and I know which one I am.

The group amble off, sniggering to themselves. Yaz seems a bit miffed about being lumped with me.

'Thanks for the loan of the tracksuit,' I say.

Yaz shrugs. 'I always keep a spare.' There is a pause as she stares at me intently. 'Do you have a photographic memory or something?'

I snort a laugh. 'No, I don't think so. I guess I'm just good at remembering things.'

Yaz frowns. Even Adelstein is displaying the same frowny expression. 'We're going to do things a little differently with you two,' he says. 'Khan, I want you to show Hall some rudimentary techniques.'

'Yes, sir.'

'Hall has a lot of ground to cover. Think supercontinent and you'll get the picture.' He turns on his heel and walks away.

Yaz turns to me, her lips pursed. 'Have you done any combat training?'

I shake my head.

'But you did the initial sixteen weeks, phase one?'

'Er … no.'

Yaz frowns, squinting her eyes. 'So it's true? You *are* an experiment?'

'I guess I am,' I say flatly.

She nods, curls her hands into fists and gestures for me to do the same. 'Let's get you started with the basics. Just copy what I do.' Yaz names a few different punches, demonstrating each one by punching the air. I do the same, bouncing lightly on my feet. This isn't so bad. 'What exercises do you do?'

'Does hula-hooping count?'

Yaz smiles. 'You're funny.'

She thinks I'm joking.

'The base of the throat is one of the most sensitive spots on the body. A light punch to the throat can cause someone to choke. The groin area is another suitable spot. Nose, eye, chin, a good stomp to someone's ankle can break the joint or ligament. Side of the neck, jaw.'

'I get the general picture. Basically, every part of the human body is vulnerable,' I deadpan.

'As you have little upper-body strength, you'll want to use your elbows and knees. You can put more power behind them. But first you need to know how to block.' She punches me in the arm.

'Ow! That hurt.'

'You need to block or move out of the way.' Yaz hits me again.

'Can't you give me a bit of warning?'

'You've got to be ready at all times.'

'Oof!'

This time she kicks out my knee from behind, and I fall backwards onto the floor.

'A kick is always good. You can put a lot of power behind a kick.'

'Can I get up or are you going to attack me again?'

She smiles.

I get to my feet and steel myself for what comes next. My primary tactic is avoidance. Each time Yaz goes to kick me, I run.

'HALL! This is not the 1920s. A little less Chaplin and a hell of a lot more Chan, if you please,' barks Sergeant.

'Dusty, you need to get over the fear of being hit,' says Yaz.

'But it hurts.'

'So what are you going to do about it?' She swings out a punch and it lands on my shoulder.

'Ow!'

I throw a punch. It misses Yaz by a mile and, judging by the grin on her face, she's loving this.

'I'll never be able to do this,' I groan.

Yaz stops and takes pity on me. She places a reassuring arm around my shoulder. 'You will. It just takes time.' Then she grabs me by the arm and sends me spinning to the floor. I land heavily on my bottom.

Good job the floor is padded because otherwise I would have broken a bone or two by now. I ignore Yaz's offered hand and hoist myself up.

We go again, and again, and again, and gradually I start to catch on. I learn how to hold myself and how to move my body. I let my muscles relax to absorb the hit but keep the strength when throwing a punch and soon I am ducking and blocking like a ninja. Well, I like to think that's the look I am pulling off but probably 'electrocuted bunny' would be a fairer description. I am sweating profusely but feeling strangely elated. When we stop, I turn around to see Adelstein and Sergeant watching. I'm tempted to give a little curtsey but think better of it.

'Ow.' I say. Yaz punches me in the back of the legs again, paralysing me to my knees. 'What was that for?'

'Concentrate,' she barks.

She comes at me again but this time I'm ready. I grab Yaz by the knees and pull them from under her. 'Gotcha!' I yell triumphantly, as she topples to the ground.

I see Adelstein looking over and I can't help pointing to Yaz on the floor. He acknowledges my success with a brief nod of his head.

From the floor, Yaz raises her hand in the air and we high-five.

'There's hope for you yet.' She beams.

My arms feel like they're detached from my body, so

much so that I have to use both hands to turn the shower on. Twisting the thing off feels like I'm going to rupture a tendon. Even drying and dressing takes a huge effort. Not to mention my legs feel like mounds of jelly.

When I eventually dress it's time for the next lesson. Yaz waits for me and we walk to class together. I can't believe I've actually found an ally and I think we might become friends—in time, perhaps.

As we take our seats I notice the classroom is surprisingly light and airy, with old leaded windows lining the right side and some steel filing cupboards at the back, a few white tables with rigidly laid out pencils at forty-five-degree angles and a large projector screen at the front. I am feeling hopeful that this next exercise won't be physically demanding. Seriously, if they ask me to do more hand-to-hand combat, a three-day-old banana sandwich would offer more resistance.

Sergeant storms into the room, his jaw so hard a vessel on the side of his neck is visibly throbbing. I don't think he knows how to walk into a room any other way.

'PAY ATTENTION TO DETAILS. IT WILL COUNT.' He pulls out a remote control, zaps the windows and the blinds close automatically. He marches to the back of the room.

Result! We're going to watch a film, and I'll be able to enjoy it without Adelstein breathing down my neck.

Actually, it's quite interesting. It's about a femme fatale who tracks down different contacts. Really hammy acting and I guessed the ending, but still preferable to being pulverised in the boxing ring.

Suddenly the blinds are up and lights streams through the window. Sergeant drops a test paper on our desk. 'You have thirty minutes to complete this test. Your thirty minutes start NOW.' Sergeant turns about, walking up and down the middle aisle with his whipping stick, knocking the desk legs.

I don't let it distract me.

Question: *Was the third man in the pub on the left or right of the bar?*

Answer: *There was no third man.*

Question: *Was the woman at the hotel reception wearing earrings?*

Answer: *Only one in her left ear.*

Question: *How many steps down to the cellar?*

Answer: *Thirteen.*

Question: *Was the door open or closed when they got to the cellar?*

Answer: *Ajar.*

I'm rather good at the small details. Actually, I've always been good at remembering names and faces and what people are wearing or any interesting quirks.

'TIME'S UP, MOLLUSCS. Hand your papers in and get lost until tomorrow. 0800 sharp. If you're late, you're out. Dismissed.'

Returning to the flat, I feel physically and mentally exhausted. I dump my stuff in my room and drift into the living room. Jodie glances up as I collapse onto the sofa next to her. 'Hard day at the office, hon?'

'You have no idea.' I sigh.

'Shall I get you a glass of wine?'

'That would be lovely.' I lean back against the sofa. I close my eyes for barely a second when I suddenly come to my senses. 'No!' I sit bolt upright. Jodie jumps, staring at me from the doorway. 'I can't drink tonight. I need to be firing on all cylinders tomorrow.'

Jodie continues to stare, trying to work out what the word 'no' means in correlation to wine. 'Are you sure?' she asks hesitantly.

I nod. 'Yes.' Jodie turns ashen—even her fake tan can't hide her shock. She stares at me with mouth gaping open. 'But don't let me stop you.'

'It's not that. It's your nails,' she says, aghast.

'Oh, yeah.' I give a sad sigh. The obstacle course seems like a lifetime ago. 'Filing.'

'Are the files made of breeze blocks?'

I laugh.

'I can't leave you looking like that. I'll go get my nail kit.'

I can't help but smile to myself as I close my eyes.

I hear Jodie trot off into the kitchen and return moments later with a glass of wine and her nail kit in hand. 'Your mum rang earlier. She said to remind you not to forget this weekend.'

I groan.

'Oh, and your sister rang. She said you must call her later.'

I let out another groan as Jodie takes my limp hand. 'Hounded by that woman day and night. I'll call her tomorrow. I don't want to talk to anyone tonight.'

'Not even Mustard?'

'Except Mustard. One must always greet royalty with polite conversation and the utmost civility.'

Mustard stretches languidly on the armrest as if he senses we're talking about him. I lay my head back against the sofa, wanting to zonk out.

'It's like fixing a rag doll.'

'Hmm-hum,' I murmur.

'I'm off tomorrow. A long-haul trip, remember. I'm going to be away for a few weeks, and may get stuck southern hemisphere. Don't forget to feed Mustard.'

I lose whatever Jodie says next, something to do with engines refits, as I drift off to sleep ...

... clinging on to the sides of a deep well. It's dark and the walls are slimy and I don't have the right shoes on. I'm slipping further down, into blackness ...

My heart pounds and I wake with a start.

'Dusty, you're dribbling.'

'Urgh!' I wipe my mouth with the back of my hand. I look at my nails. She's painted them a vivid red colour. 'They're gorgeous. Thank you.'

Jodie beams. 'You're welcome, Officer Dribbles!'

'How long was I out?'

'About half an hour.'

Wow. It barely felt like five minutes.

CHAPTER EIGHT

I've stopped counting time. Now I count bruises. Sixteen so far including the mothership of all bruises that has dwarfed all the others and covers my entire right buttock.

Morning drill involves a race around the assault course. Then there's field sprinting, crab crawls, burpees, lunge jumps, plank holds, sit-ups, push-ups, not to mention hand-to-hand combat.

It's day three and there have been many moments when I have wanted to swap places with the nearest bin—you know, let people throw things at me, because that is how it feels on a daily basis. But at the same time I have never felt more alive or more exhilarated. The experience is … changing me. It's as if I am being pulled apart and rebuilt. Into what, exactly? I've yet to find out.

And I have made a friend. Well, friend might be stretching it a bit. Yaz doesn't mind sitting with me or being teamed up with me. She is unlike anyone I have ever met. She's a total badass and yet so straightforward.

'What's happened to the projector screen?' I ask,

joining her at the desk.

Yaz looks up. 'I hadn't noticed.'

Sergeant bangs his swagger stick loudly on the floor and everyone jumps. 'Now listen up, you pathetic cretins. We will test co-operation, trust, and reliance. We're looking for teamwork. As an agent, you rely on your teammates. There is no room for one-trick ponies here. Do I make myself clear?'

'YES, SIR.'

'Right then, you miserable molluscs. Find a sucking wall.'

Yaz and I exchange blank glances. No film then.

'You dopey bits of plankton. Find a partner!'

The sergeant marches to the back of the classroom, where there's a door. He signals for us to follow him.

We get up from our seats and follow him into a dimly lit corridor, which leads to another room. This room has nothing in it but a strange grey wall, which seems to be suspended by industrial metal cables.

'One of you will be blindfolded. It will be the other's job to direct their team member around the obstacle course in the fastest time. This calls for precise, short, lucid communication. Now move closer.'

The grey wall is a large material screen with a dark room on the other side. Yaz stands at the front, and I hang back. Sergeant switches the lights on and the room illuminates. It's not just me who draws an inward breath. The room is a giant maze of deadly booby traps.

'Khan. Hall. You two up first.' He thrusts the blindfold at Yaz, and she thrusts it at me.

'This should be interesting,' mutters Pratton behind me.

'Just do as I say,' says Yaz firmly. 'You'll be fine as long as you follow my instructions. You can follow instructions?'

'Of course I can follow instructions.' I pull on the

blindfold. 'I can't see anything.'

Yaz chuckles.

The blindfold has an earpiece attached to it. I clutch for Yaz and she grabs my hand, squeezing it really hard.

'Come on. We haven't got all day,' bellows Sergeant. And with that bark in my ear, he pushes me through a flap in the wall.

'Don't worry, I'll take into account your heels,' says Yaz.

I feel cheated. I thought we were going to watch a film, so I changed into my civvies: a short, floaty dress and a pair of three-inch stiletto-heeled black pixie boots. I can't see a damn thing and my head spins in the darkness.

'*Schisss*,' the radio hisses in my ear. I reach out in front of me, but all I can feel is empty air. What was that? I twist my head as I hear a clank of metal and the murmur of voices disappears. Was that the door locking?

'Dusty? Nod if you can hear me.' Yaz's voice comes through the earpiece, calm and concise. I nod. 'Good. Now I want you to follow my instructions,' she says.

Hearing Yaz's voice focuses me. I can hear my breaths quicken and take a couple of deep ones to calm myself down. An overpowering instinct takes over. I will not let Yaz down.

'You can do this,' I hear over my earpiece. 'Trust me.'

Yaz is the one person I do trust.

'I want you to take a step forward.'

I do as she says, taking a small step forward.

'That's good. Now do that again. Six times.'

I count slowly. One, two, three, four, five, six.

'Good. In front of you is a row of boxes. Reach out and swing one leg over as far as it will stretch. Step carefully. The boxes have dirt on them to show disturbance. The gaps between them are narrow and uneven, so let the other leg follow carefully.'

The mere mention of dirt makes my legs obedient. They have gained strength with all the morning not-so-fun runs and I do not want to ruin this dress.

'Last box, Dusty, it's slightly higher than the last.'

I feel like a praying mantis warning off a spider. With perfect balance, I straddle the last box, clipping one heel on the top.

'Well done. Now get on your knees and shuffle forwards. I'll tell you when to stop.'

Oh, dear, there goes my modesty.

'Stop!' she says and I immediately halt. 'Stand up and turn right, bend down thirty degrees for five steps, then stop, move left, and reach up ninety degrees. It's a tunnel with a funnel at the end.'

I clear the tunnel without touching the sides, mainly because of the pygmy steps and shuffles dictated by my high heels. I get my hand through the above funnel without touching it. 'Now reach a little higher and grab the rungs of a rope ladder. Climb for three steps. Have your feet tilt backwards towards your heels.'

I pull myself up and complete this quickly.

'Now kick your right leg out at a forty-five-degree angle to catch a net. Once you've got one heel in, throw the other leg over whilst still holding onto the ladder. The net is spinning slowly, so anchor your heels in until there is no give.'

My shoes stop the net spinning off. High heels have their advantages!

'Now swing the rest of your body over to where your feet are.' For a second, I worry about falling backwards, but then I remind myself to trust Yaz. I twist my body and make a successful transfer, as if dismounting a horse from the championships of high-heeled gymnastics.

'Now let go. You will land on a soft podium where there is a slide on the other side. Push your bottom forward until you feel your feet lower. Then push yourself right over and slide down, keeping your heels up and your arms folded.'

I twirl and twist down what I think is a tube slide, then land on a big inflatable cushion.

No sooner do I land than I hear Sergeant's booming voice in my ear. 'Quick, quick, prattle off, Prêt-à-porter.' I am so relieved to be on solid ground I don't notice my dress has ridden up to waist height. I scuttle away as fast as I can, whipping off the blindfold and pulling my dress firmly back in place. Just before I reach the door, I hear a voice over the tannoy.

'May I suggest trousers next time, Miss Hall? This isn't an audition for *Moulin Rouge*.'

My head whips around. It's Adelstein smirking from the observation window above, and next to him is Ottoman. Ottoman nods approvingly. At what, I'm not sure—was it my amazing agility at passing through the booby-trapped maze or my *revealing* performance? At least the lacy French knickers saved some of my dignity. It could have been worse. I could have been wearing a transparent red thong with a go-to glitter spot.

I stumble out of the door and into Yaz's arms. 'You did it,' she says.

'*We* did it,' I say.

Yaz grins at me, and it's the first proper grin I've seen from her. It shows off her perfectly straight teeth. I also notice the rest of the group. Their faces are twisted in shock and disbelief, their jaws slack and not one snide comment amongst them. Even Sergeant has a fresh look of respect in his eyes. I suppose they *are* nice knickers. He checks his stopwatch and nods.

We return to the classroom (after a quick dash to change my outfit). I feel on cloud nine. That was my chance to shine and I nailed it, if we ignore the knicker faux pas. Yaz sits down and looks at me in awe. 'I'm really glad we are partners,' she says.

Oh, wow. I think I may cry.

'I … I feel the same way,' I say, choking up.

There's a tiny silence, during which we both look at each other, grinning wildly, until my mobile pings with a text. I look at the screen and sigh. 'It's my sister. I'll have to text her, or she'll keep pestering.'

Coco: *Why are you not answering my calls?*

Me: *Is it urgent?*

Coco: *Of course it's bloody urgent.*

Me: *I'm busy at work. We can talk later.*

I stuff my mobile into my jeans. 'Honestly, she expects the world to stop spinning at her every whim,' I say to Yaz.

Yaz frowns. 'Why?'

'So she can marry a buffoon.'

Yaz stares at me blankly.

'You'd have to meet her and him to understand,' I say. 'Do you have any sisters?'

Yaz shakes her head. 'When is she getting married?'

'Not soon enough. So there's still weeks of misery to go. She's been planning it for a year but she wants to change everything.'

'Are you a bridesmaid?'

I grimace. 'Maid of honour.'

'That's nice.'

'Not really, it's like a prison sentence but without the perks.'

'Don't you like your sister?'

I frown, confused. 'Not at the current time! But she is my sister.'

Yaz looks perplexed for a second then nods in understanding. 'Family always comes first.'

'C'mon. Up you get,' booms Sergeant as he struts into the room. 'Change of plan. We're going to shoot ourselves some targets. Chop, Chop!'

'You better not let anyone see you have a mobile on you.'

'Roger that.'

'Keep your finger straight and off the trigger until you are ready to shoot,' says Yaz helpfully. 'And get one of your legs behind, it will help balance you out.'

'Okay.'

I stare at the weapon on the stand. I have never held a gun before. Actually, that's not true. I did hold a gun fifteen years ago when Alice and I thought it would be a lark to shoot her father's clay pigeons down in the copse on their estate. We knew squat about recoil or loading the thing. First, it was bigger than us, an antique musket rather than a rifle. The concept of clay pigeon shooting was totally lost on a couple of ten-year-olds. I went first, fell backwards with the recoil and thought I'd shot Alice, who had fallen over in shock as the gunpowder blasted out of the barrel. That gun's safety needed some maintenance. We found it in the boot of an old Aston Martin in her father's barn. He likes to collect vintage cars.

'Attention!' Sergeant bellows. 'You need to shoot at a hundred percent precision, not ninety-nine percent. A hundred percent on target. You may not get a second chance.'

He waits for absolute silence and begins in a new voice devoid of the usual bombastic, fear-inducing bark. 'Even when the target's moving, keep your breathing even, your hand will be steadier. If you keep your eyes on the ball, the target is less likely to start a ping-pong match.'

I take a deep breath to stop my hands shaking.

'Listen up! This could be the difference between maiming and death. There won't always be backup in these situations. Drones can't fly over and see how you're doing. It is not an afternoon tea party.' He continues to rant on about modern warfare. I don't understand a word he's saying.

I concentrate on breathing to quell my nerves.

'Ear defenders on,' shouts Sergeant.

I carefully pick up the gun, handling it the way an auctioneer might handle a Fabergé egg. So, this is what a gun feels like. I stare at the weapon in my hand. My stomach gives a lurch.

'Remember. Precision. Breathe. Shoot or death,' Sarge repeats in a low resounding voice. Now I'm scared.

My heart is pounding as I look at my target. Okay, this shouldn't be too difficult. It's not moving for a start.

'Weapons ready.'

I hear sounds of clicks and locks and loads echo around the room. Sergeant does a line walk, checking everyone is correct. He stops when he gets to me. 'Hall, what is this?'

'Er … a gun, sir.'

'Take the safety off like so.' He unclips the catch.

'Thank you, sir.'

'Hold the gun with both hands.'

I do as instructed.

'Now aim and fire.'

I face the target, my hands trembling.

'Hall, either you're the best shot ever, or you might want to open your eyes.'

'Yes, Sarge.' I take aim, keeping my eyes open, and—

Bang! Bang! Bang!

The recoil sends me stumbling backwards and I don't see where the bullets go, but when I steady myself I see they're not anywhere near the target. Sergeant says nothing. I raise the gun and aim. This time I am ready for the recoil. It makes my hands jump back, but my feet stay planted. A bullet hole appears at the edge of the target. Sergeant awards me the faintest of smiles. 'We may make a marksman out of you yet, Hall!'

A further twenty rounds or more and I manage to hit the middle of the target. At first I put it down to a fluke, but then I do it again. I look to see if anyone has noticed. Yaz is looking at me. She gives me the thumbs-up.

It's a strange sense of power, holding something so small, yet the damage possible is so large. I guess that is the attraction for the gun-obsessed.

It does not come as a surprise to see that Yaz is an ace shot and hits the bullseye every time. She could totally give Lara Croft a run for her money.

My mobile vibrates in my pocket. I try to ignore it, but then it vibrates again. I put the gun's safety on and place it down on the table and pull out my mobile.

'Coco, I can't talk, I'm at work,' I whisper, crouching down low so Sergeant doesn't see me.

'You're not answering my text messages.'

'That's because I'm at work. Now is really not a good time. I'm … in a meeting,' I say. 'Err … taking minutes.'

'I don't care if you're in the middle of elective surgery, nothing's as important as my big day.'

'I'm sure it can wait until tomorrow.'

'Don't you dare hang up on me! Don't you—'

I cut her off. The mobile immediately starts vibrating again. 'Do your ears have cement in or is your brain too tiny to understand?' I hiss down the phone. 'I'm working.'

'Oh, that's nice. Really understanding from the chief bridesmaid.' Then, without taking a beat, Coco says, 'Are those gunshots I can hear?'

'No. Now go away. We can talk about this tomor—'

'UNBELIEVABLE!'

I jump with fright and my mobile flies out of my hand and slides across the floor.

'Who do you think you are, Mellennial Dirty Harry?' says Sergeant.

'Who's that?'

'Now get down and sniff dirt.'

I stare blankly at Sergeant.

'Fifty. NOW, Miss Vodafone.'

I drop to my hands and knees and begin push-ups. When I get to thirty, my arms are shaking like a wet Chihuahua. I collapse onto the floor.

I hear the group sniggering like a bunch of hungry hyenas out for the kill.

'Quiet!' roars Sergeant.

The room goes silent and all you can hear is Coco's tinny voice. 'I can't decide on the blush pink for the napkins or powder pink. What do you think? Dusty? Dusty?'

I look up and give Sergeant an apologetic grimace, but he's already walked away. 'Did I tell any of you to stop?'

I crawl over to my mobile and hit the power-off button. I lie on my back, trying to catch my breath and my dignity. I look up to see Adelstein looking down at me, holding my gaze for a few seconds longer than is strictly necessary.

He offers me his hand. I look at it suspiciously. He tilts his head to one side, a bemused smile on his face. 'Do you want a hand or do you intend to lie there on the dirty floor?'

I grudgingly take his hand. 'Thank you.'

'You're welcome.' He is still looking at me. Not in a bad way, but not in a good way either, possibly how someone might look at the village nut. He gives me the faintest smile, then walks away, no doubt mentally jotting down all the ammunition (so to speak) ready to tell Ottoman that I should rejoin the circus. The class clown everyone laughs at.

So that's pretty much how I begin and end my first week, flat on my back, in dirt, and way out of my depth.

CHAPTER NINE

I have always lived for my weekends but this is the first time I've wanted to sleep my way through one. Not that I'll get a chance.

I'm on a train, rattling towards the Kent countryside. I open up an Army training manual, determined to make good use of my time: *Countering Insurgency*, Chapter 1 …

Suddenly, I jolt awake, disorientated, the training manual lying wide open on my lap. It's a good job I'm not holding any state secrets. Then an even worse thought hits me and I have that all-too-familiar feeling that I've missed my stop. I look out of the window and read the station sign.

Dammit. I'm in Etchingham.

I leap from my seat and literally throw myself onto the platform, the training manual and my bag skidding across the ground. That was close.

I pick up the training manual and bag as I dial my parents' number. I am not looking forward to this conversation.

'Hello, Mother, it's me.' There's no immediate recognition from the other end. 'I've missed my stop.'

'Coco,' my mother shouts in the background. 'Can you go and retrieve your sister?'

I hear my sister's response. 'Where is she?'

'Where are you, dear?'

'Etchingham station.'

I wait patiently outside for my sister to arrive. It doesn't take her long to get here. She pulls up in a red Porsche convertible. 'How on earth you get from A to B is a mystery. Have you lost weight? Did you see that Britney Spears documentary? You have your final fitting next week. They'll probably have to take it in. It will cost you.' She says all this without pausing for a breath. I hop in and we hug awkwardly.

'Is this a new car?'

My sister nods enthusiastically. 'Roger bought her for me. He's so kind, and thoughtful, and heartbreakingly handsome—'

I snort a laugh, which stops the gushing.

My sister glares at me. Let's be clear, Roger is not heartbreakingly handsome, but they do say beauty is in the eye of the beholder.

'So, did you go for blush pink or powder pink?' I ask.

Coco is only too happy to have the conversation turn to her. 'I want everything to be perfect. I'm pleased to say that Jorge is finally taking my vision seriously and has truly outdone himself. There's a mock-up of my centrepiece on Mother's dining table.'

'Is it edible? Because I bet lunch isn't!'

Coco scowls. 'Stop it, Dusty. Mother and I have made a real effort for Roger's birthday.'

'I don't know why you want me here.'

'Roger loves seeing you.'

'Only so he can take the micky out of me.'

'That's not true.'

'Mother doesn't really want me there. If she had known what a disappointment I would be, she would have put me in a wicker basket at birth and cast me downstream.'

Coco laughs. 'Mother is very fond of you.'

'Fond" is like saying you're fond of the opera. It's not quite love, slightly more than a casual liking.'

'Mother is fond of Father,' says Coco.

'My point exactly. Father is the firewood-fetcher. Bale mover. Heeder of instructions and little else.'

'Mother's very fond of me.'

'You've always been her favourite. You get the haute couture name and I end up with a dreaded household chore.'

Coco laughs again, then moves the conversation back to her favourite subject, herself, prattling on about the wedding as we speed along country lanes. 'Roger and I have been taking dancing lessons. Lionel, the dance instructor, thinks I've got great poise. Roger's no Fred Astaire, but he's come on leaps and bounds. We've got a fantastic first dance routine worked out.'

I zone out and put my head out of the window like a dappy Labrador and, for that, I get a dead leg.

Our family house is an old, detached cottage with a small paddock to the side. The paddock's only resident is Goliath, the ageing horse that always had better shoes than me. Coco has her own stables at Ascot, far more convenient for her when she's at work. And no, the snobbery aspect didn't go amiss.

Coco pulls the car into the driveway and barely puts the handbrake on before leaping out and striding into the house. I bend down to pick up some fallen apples and throw them over the fence for 'beloved Goliath'.

'I've got her,' Coco trills.

'Hello, Mother,' I say, pecking her on the cheek.

There's nothing mumsy about my mother. She wears riding clothes all the time: riding boots, jodhpurs, a coarse brown jumper, and a green gilet. She also treats humans as horses.

Neither is she a whizz in the kitchen. Her repertoire comprises something in a big pot and that's it. So seeing my mother grab the pestle and mortar with the vigour only seen in an exorcism is disconcerting. Coco strips the artichokes with ample aggression.

My mother adores Coco and acknowledges I might be vaguely related.

'You look tired. Let me see your gums.' A large part of my childhood memories is my mother pushing my lips back and checking the colour of my gums without invitation. 'You are desperately pale. How can you have bags under your eyes at your age?'

'Dodgy genes,' I mumble. I immediately revert to a sulky thirteen-year-old whenever I return home.

'Over-partying, more like,' says Coco.

'Coco, do you turn to dust in actual sunlight?' I retort.

'What is the price for crack these days?' she replies instantly.

Mother looks over with disapproval.

'Need any help with lunch?' I ask.

'I think we have it under control,' says Mother. 'Why don't you go in and say hello to your father and Roger? Lunch won't be long.'

I find my father and Roger in the lounge, watching a re-run of *Antiques Roadshow*. The room has recently been redecorated and on the wall are Coco's horse-riding cups, academic prizes, homemade prizes awarded to herself, etc., and Mother's copious horse-riding trophies. Polishing those trophies was the only bit of housework I ever saw my mother do willingly and without complaint. If you didn't pick up after yourself, it would just get left where it was, usually on the stairs until you tripped over it on the way up, which then became a quick way down. I had figured out by age four to put cushions at the bottom.

I still remember taking all my clothes to the stream, as they were too dirty to wear even to a six-year-old, and it was so hot that summer I thought it would be a good idea to wash my clothes in a nearby stream. Mother was on some hunt season, training the horses, no time for household chores. It was quite funny to see her in front of all the gentry witnessing her younger spawn wading down the stream trying to catch her entire wardrobe shouting, 'I have no clean knickers and the brown marks won't come out!'

Even the hounds stopped for the wailing waif in the stream—an epic embarrassment for my mother. So, at six, I was instructed in the finer workings of a washing machine. But those trophies and cups were and are on the housework rota. Mother polishes them regularly, keeping them always shining. My couple of riding rosettes (just for taking part) are somewhere on the back wall. I think she flicks those with a duster, hoping they'll fall off in bits, banished into molecules forevermore.

Things to know about my father: he's a big cricket fan, enjoys drinking port from a silver goblet and is not quite with today's reality.

'This is obviously sixteenth-century Delftware,' the ceramic expert stutters out with ridiculously posh vowel sounds, while handling what looks like something you'd pick up in a jumble sale.

'It's obviously a poor reproduction, my good man,' Roger tells the TV.

As for Roger, he's an antiquarian. I didn't have a clue what that was when he first mentioned it, or should I say the many times he dropped it in conversation, as though the job defines his very stature. In a nutshell, he sources ceramic antiques, which have been looted around the world, and finds rare pieces to sell for the top auction houses. Apparently he is highly respected in his field, or so he tells me. He wears far too much aftershave. You can't help but choke in proximity. Eau de dead muskrat rather than cologne.

I give Father a peck on the cheek. 'Hello, Pops.'

He looks up fondly. 'Etchingham station, eh, pumpkin?'

'I fell asleep.'

'Night-time is for sleep and beds are for sleeping in.'

'At least it wasn't Hastings this time,' says Roger.

'Happy birthday,' I say, handing Roger his birthday card, which is a little crumpled. The picture is of cheap junk food. The text says: *Mc-Smythe-Donaldsen's Posh Meal deal.* A basket of paupers being forced fed and minced into foie gras. The punchline: *What to do with commoners.*

'You shouldn't have,' he says. He studies it for a moment. 'No, really, you shouldn't have,' he says, but chuckles.

'So, how's the world of dusty potties and unkempt pointy beards?' I ask. I'm not as impressed with Roger as my family is, but on the whole, he's all right. A harmless, posh twat.

'Well, Dusty, at least *my* potties aren't in use. How is the usable potty business these days?'

'Steaming.' I say, to deter further questioning. Roger's face screws up in disgust.

I haven't told my family I got sacked. I've decided this is on a need-to-know basis.

'I have an acquisition coming in next week, from Egypt. Very exciting. I adore the Naqada period. Imagine that—made 4000-3500 years BC.'

'You must get your Marigolds out then, Roger, imagine the stains.'

'Your wit must elevate your spirits in times of overflowing Portaloos.'

Coco rushes in. 'Chop, chop. Sit. Sit. We don't want the rucola to wilt under the weight of the truffle oil.'

'It's called rocket. Or are we Italian now? Last I heard it was called *rocket*, mia cara.' Father raises a hand to muffle a snigger.

Coco has a unique ability to ignore what is going on around her. She's utterly and totally oblivious.

I turn to Father. 'Oh, God, please no. She's not trying to be gourmet again?'

'Smile and eat something,' says Father, beaming inanely.

We all follow Coco into the dining room.

'Well, as long as it's not guinea fowl. Remember the toilet visits?' I whisper in my father's ear. 'I think I'll stick to the veg. She can only give a small dose of *E. coli* through those vessels.'

Father chuckles.

'Today's menu is a choice from bouts of diarrhoea to vomiting or, quite possibly, death,' I add.

Roger grimaces. 'I'm still rather full from breakfast,' he says, patting his stomach.

'Nonsense,' says Coco.

The dining room is my favourite room, especially in the winter when the huge fire is lit. The beams are old, the leaded window crooked on its long sill. All the glass panels are original, as in warped—some of them shoot rainbows from their prisms. I remember watching them as a child, thinking it was magical rays from another world.

For a room with so many dark and heavy features it's incredibly light. The unusually large window bounces the light even on dull days. It smells of burnt wood, soot, and old lives. I always used to sneak into this room to read when I was little. Sitting inside the fireplace somehow felt secretive. No one else came into this room, so it became my place to get away from the ramblings of a sister at full volume and a mother on Operation Horse from dawn to dusk.

It hosts a heavy, wooden sideboard, a ten-seat table made from three planks of thick oak, and a sword mounted on a coat of arms hanging over Granny's and Gramps' Hall urns. The feel is medieval and it still is the most atmospheric room in the house; the rest is a mishmash of bad modernisation throughout the decades. Nothing ever gets completed. By the time my parents decorated the bathroom, it had a white toilet, a pink sink and an avocado bath, the shower cabinet akin to a serial killer's makeshift sauna. You could call it shabby chic but you'd be wrong, it is just plain shabby. But the unspoilt dining room makes my heart lift. I'm forever a princess looking out of the window for her prince, which one day was an escaped goat chewing up the daffodils.

After a muffled exchange of exasperation, Coco and Mother come in with the last dish. Jorge's elaborate centrepiece sits in the middle of the dining table, dwarfing the spread.

'So, Dusty, I heard some poor unfortunate soul got their arm stuck in a portable loo trying to retrieve their handbag,' says Roger. 'That wasn't you, was it?'

'For your information, I have left the world of porta-potties. I have a new job.' I announce to the table, immediately noticing the shared looks of panic between parents, Coco and Roger.

'Have you moved up to whole bathroom suites?' jokes Roger.

'Oh, Dusty, you can't keep chopping and changing your career willy-nilly. Take Coco, she's been at her job for …'

'Five years. But Mummy, Dusty and I are *very* different people. Dedication and hard work isn't for everyone.' Coco gives me an evil grin. 'Ambition just isn't natural to some.'

I poke out my tongue.

'Perhaps you should listen to your sister. If you paid more attention, you might do better.'

'Can't work miracles,' Roger says, guffawing.

'Roger!' says Coco, only half-admonishing.

'Dusty knows I'm teasing,' he says, swigging back red wine.

'So, what is this new job?' asks Coco.

'I'm a PA,' I say.

'What's the company called?' asks Coco.

'Duty Calls. They're a cleaning company,' I mumble.

'What a bummer,' Roger guffaws.

The table erupts into giggles.

'Funny, Roger. I wonder how all around you don't collapse from the constant hilarity you spread.'

'Enough of Dusty's problems, let's *please* look at Jorge's masterpiece!'

And for once, I'm relieved Coco wants to talk about her wedding. Everyone dutifully looks at the centrepiece. If only I could tell them what I was actually doing. Can you imagine the looks on their faces?

Coco witters on about the centrepiece and I look out of the window, across to the field, willing myself away. A scene forms in my mind.

I'm sat at a bar in the obligatory scarf and sunglasses of a femme fatale, nursing a martini, and looking hot but ever so cool. A Russian man approaches. I speak a Russian code word to him, and he hands over a black velvet bag. I hand him a shot of vodka, which he downs in one. I stub a long, slim continental cigarette out in the shot glass with purpose. I dismount from perching on the stool and trot away in incredibly high heels. I am oh so sophisticated ...

'Earth to Dusty.' Coco clicks her fingers annoyingly

in my face.

'I hope you don't space out like that at work,' says Mother.

'Isn't a girl allowed to think about something else other than a stupid wedding?' The words come out before I have a chance to rein them in, and the table gasps as if I have just said something sacrilegious.

'I thought this was Roger's birthday, not Kent's annual wedding fair,' I mumble. But the damage is done.

'That's just great. Just great. The most important day of my life …' Coco tears up and dramatically blows her nose. 'She,' she says, pointing at me, 'can't be bothered.'

'Do get a grip, Coco. Is it your hormones?' I retort. 'You're not pregnant with a mini-Rodgepot, are you?' I laugh, but the joke doesn't go down well with the rest of the table and Roger chokes on his wine.

Coco suddenly leaps from her chair and flees the room in a torrent of tears.

'Dusty! Your sister is very fraught at the moment,' says father.

'Oh, come on, she's tearing up if she sees a new shade of pink or a crooked vol-au-vent these days.'

The meal, suffice to say, is cut short, which I'm happy about. I grab a bit of chunky bread and a lump of cheese and decide I may as well head home. Father offers to drop me off at the station but Coco says she'll do it, like she's doing something exemplary. Coco loves a bit of martyrdom.

'That's nice, isn't it, Dusty,' says Father, willing the peace talks to start. I attempt a smile, but don't quite pull it off. 'I don't like seeing you two quarrel.'

I climb into Coco's car and wait for the engine to start. It doesn't and we sit there in silence. Coco thrusts a printout in my face.

'A list of your chief bridesmaid duties,' she says.

'Oh, how lovely,' I say, failing to keep the sarcasm from my voice.

'Of course, I've done most of this myself,' she says scornfully. 'You haven't been particularly helpful.'

I scan the printout.

1. Help the bride shop for her dress.

2. Go to vendor meetings. This includes florist, ceremony and reception sites, photographer, band, DJ, caterer, etc. Surely this is a groom's duty, not mine.

3. Help pick out the bridesmaid dresses.

4. Assist the bride with assembling 'save the dates', invitations, and favours.

5. Host hen night. MUST BE SPECTACULAR!

6. Keep track of all the gifts that the bride receives at hen night and wedding and help write ALL the thank-you notes. Keep receipts in case of bad taste.

7. Attend the rehearsal ceremony.

The list continues on for a further two pages.

'I suppose I must sort out my own hen weekend too,' Coco says.

'No. No. It's all planned,' I say. I even add a dramatic eye roll.

'Really?' Coco breathes a sigh of relief.

'Of course,' I say, swallowing hard.

Satisfied, Coco turns the engine on and off we go.

How the hell do you make a hen party spectacular? I was thinking a cheesy nightclub at a seaside town, some embarrassing outfits and lewd paraphernalia, lots of alcohol and recovering on the train back. My impossible-to-please sister is expecting St Tropez, private catering with bells on top. I'm doomed.

On Sunday, Coco rudely awakes me from my slumber with an urgent text. Is there any other kind with her? She has texted me a list of what she doesn't want for her hen party. I suspect she has used up all her data allowance sending me this mammoth SMS.

Nothing distasteful. That includes: tawdry seaside resorts mixing with binge drinkers; bars that aren't members only; or cop-out picnics by the river. Anything that advertises itself as a 'perfect hen weekend'—boats, barges, hen party accommodated—anything like that is a DEFINITE NO. No action outdoorsy team-building rubbish adventure. No tents. No caravans if you want to see Christmas again. No horse-riding either—too everyday, wouldn't you say? Nothing around where we grew up, otherwise Mother will gatecrash with her friends and probably her horse. And please, no common stereotypical additions—no garish pranks, ridiculous activities, or tatty clothes, and absolutely no rude entertainment. I will walk out and never speak to you again. Spa weekend is a good option, peace and tranquility at a very reputable mansion house or the like. But nowhere that's open to the public, only the residents.

My sister is such a control freak and a killjoy. Hmm … I should introduce her to Adelstein. I flip up my laptop. I really thought a seaside jaunt would be a passable idea. Make a weekend of it, some silly stuff in the day followed by a fun night out at a hilarious club. Who wants to sit in a spa, silent and sober? Now I really don't have a clue what to do. Maybe Coco's friends will have a better idea.

Hi, everyone, this is Dusty, Coco's sister. As you know, the hen party is nearly upon us and Coco wants a tasteful, non-eventful time. Any suggestions to the opposite? Thanks, Dusty x

I decide to get out of bed. Besides, Mustard is walking across my laptop demanding I feed him. I mosey into the kitchen, feed Mustard, make a cup of coffee, pull out the packet of cornflakes and plonk myself in front of the TV, declaring I will not be moving unless it's absolutely necessary. With Jodie away on some remote island in the middle of the Pacific somewhere and my phone switched off, I can't be reached by anyone. I will spend the entire day in pyjamas, watching spy films. I'll start with *The Spy Next Door*, followed by Daniel Craig in *Casino Royale* and then move onto the Bourne trilogy. With my day planned out, I settle comfortably onto the sofa, pulling a fluffy blanket over me, munching on cornflakes straight from the packet. I realise I haven't even thought about Cameron at all and I'm actually glad I don't have a boyfriend. Well, at least not one who is ever present.

It's only when I'm going to bed and check my email that I see most of Coco's friends have already replied.

The suggestions so far:

How about going to the Champagne region and staying in a château with all the rich aristocrats? Land a husband, or just land them. Hugs, Andrea x

How big are these girls' budgets? Yeah, why not book two châteauxs?

A farm weekend. We can do cow-milking, bog-jumping, and bread-making. Love, Michelle xoxo

Can't imagine Coco jumping any bogs or wearing wellies, let alone touching udders.

How about an arts and crafts weekend? Seriously, what age is she, twelve? I read on. *We can choose from making fascinators or lace, pottery classes or maybe a nude life-drawing class. Sarah x*

Hmm, that's not as bad as going bankrupt. It's still pretty bad though.

There's a reproduction of Sense and Sensibility *in the Cotswolds where Emma falls foul of a horrendous crime. It's a murder mystery evening and the hen party have to work out who the killer is. You get to dress up too. Yours sincerely, Bernie*

Definitely need to look at that one—as if the

excitement of a bonnet and a murder would constitute a wild hen party.

Las Vegas—and stay at the oasis in the desert. Get her drunk, hire in a band of hunky masseurs for the entire weekend, and make one of them strip. Philippa xxx

God help me! Not a common thread between them, apart from Andrea and Philippa, although different continents.

CHAPTER TEN

I spend the next few weeks in intensive training, which, by the way, is true to its description, and suffice to say I lose track of the outside world. I have hardly seen Jodie but I have my suspicions she is up to something, as I caught her slumped on the sofa with a pot of tea on the table and a RAF textbook, not the mandatory wine and magazine. She was also drooling and muttering something about crosswinds in her sleep.

Training has intensified to include jumping off mock buildings and manic memory tests. I'm rather good at picking out the same person from a myriad of expert disguises. The class and the overseers always seem so surprised by this. I've also learned how to shoot with various guns, ranging from pistols up to full-whack automatics. Turns out I'm rather good at this too. A couple of months ago, I wouldn't have even been able to pick one of those mean machines up. Now, I could give the Terminator a little friendly competition.

Yaz has proved to be a loyal, steadfast comrade. She is without fear. I haven't seen her flinch at anything, even when I charged at her with a machete.

I believe I have had some positive influence on Yaz. She has plucked her eyebrows and looks so much softer in the face. The other day she asked me to teach her to walk in heels. I think this is purely for training, so she doesn't scream out 'elite Army squadron' when she walks through a door. I've managed to make the grey sweater and sweatpants more flattering. I nipped them in at the waist, sewed turn-ups and added a few studs for decoration.

'Remember, one steady breath before squeezing, Dusty,' Yaz hisses as I hold the automatic and fire, hitting the first target, then the second target. B-B-BLAM! Another burst and I kill all targets, dropping the magazine on the floor like some American action hero, locking and loading. All I need is a cigar to chew on and the image would be complete.

Yaz looks up from behind cover and sees all targets obliterated. She throws me a double thumbs-up. But before we have time to start the girls-on-fire-who-can-fire congratulatory club, a booming voice cuts in.

'KHAN. HALL.'

I pull the earplugs from my ears and look across at Yaz. She shrugs.

'Report to room seven on floor sub-sub-zero,' says Sergeant handing her a plastic card.

I don't have the foggiest idea what he's talking about, but by the Cheshire Cat grin that's suddenly splitting Yaz's face, I have an inkling she does.

'Sir, we don't have the security clearance,' Yaz says.

'You do now.' Sergeant turns to me. 'Hall. You have been … surprisingly special. Word of advice, keep your wits about you and your hemline intact.'

'Is this a goodbye, sir?'

'For now.'

I've become quite fond of Sergeant, in a masochistic, dependable way. I open my arms for a hug. He looks appalled and folds his arms.

'Bye then.'

Yaz and I leave our guns and return to the changing rooms, where I immediately start emptying my locker. 'What the hell is floor sub-sub-zero?' I ask.

'Sub-sub-zero is underground. Only top personnel and the SSS know its whereabouts.' She seems very excited by this.

'The SSS?' I gulp.

'You know, secret squirrel stuff,' she says, totally deadpan.

Yaz attempting humour. Are my ears deceiving me? I love it. 'So, do we take everything with us?'

'Everything? What don't you have in there?' asks Yaz, amused.

'Just the essentials.'

'I think we need to have a talk about what you determine an 'essential',' says Yaz.

I stuff the tampons, antibacterial hand-gel, vape stick and juice into my already overloaded tote, followed by an Alvin and the Chipmunks toy from a McDonald's Happy Meal, ibuprofen, a smashed granola bar, four miniature wine bottles (no idea how they got in there!), three pairs of sunglasses, and two plastic neon orange monkey cocktail stirrers.

'Your emergency survival kit, eh, Dusty?'

'Precisely.' I loop the cocktail monkeys around my ears and waggle them. Yaz laughs.

As we walk across the car park I turn back, wanting to give a parting glance to the place that changed me for the better, when I notice an outline of a figure watching us from the upstairs window. I nudge Yaz and she follows my gaze.

'Pratton,' I whisper.

We both stare at her. 'If looks could kill!' says Yaz. A

shiver runs through me.

Yaz gives her a farewell wave. Pratton returns the gesture by giving us the finger.

'Come on, let's get out of here,' I say.

CHAPTER ELEVEN

I'm back where it all started and boy, does it seem like a lifetime ago. Who even was that person back then?

I stroll into the car park, feeling a genuine warmth for the place, clocking the security guard with the oversized hands. He waves at me from inside his kiosk.

'I have an appointment with Duty Calls,' I say, striding towards the metal door.

It really is true what they say, as one door closes another opens. Getting sacked was the best thing to happen to me.

Yaz is waiting for me, but instead of the stairs she walks over to the wall underneath the staircase and pulls the pass from her pocket.

'Don't we go upstairs?' I say.

'Nope, that's just the front office. It's down, down, down.'

She brushes the security pass over a small hole in the wall and the wall slides open. Proper Hogwarts stuff. I peer ahead. Is this an old disused Tube tunnel? One of the Second World War secret ones? Yaz grabs my arm and pulls me through. The door clunks shut behind me.

'Timer-controlled,' she says. 'You need to move quickly. No dilly-dallying.' She hands me a similar-looking security pass. 'This is yours.'

'Thanks.'

'Keep it safe.'

I pop the security pass around my neck and follow Yaz to a large industrial double door the size of a bank vault. Yaz strokes the security pass down one side and there's a dull click as it opens.

It opens up to another tunnel, which appears to be some sort of service corridor, with huge pipes and noisy vents. The doors shut heavily and we're left in orange light.

'I thought room sub-sub-zero was a myth,' Yaz whispers in a hushed tone, her face as excited as a puppy that's found a treat. 'Apparently built during the Cold War.'

'I thought being overground would be warmer than underground,' I reply.

'No, Cold War as in …' She pauses and looks at me. 'Ah, a joke?'

I smile.

'By the way, I don't think you're stupid,' she says.

'Most people do.'

'But you're not. You have a razor-sharp brain.'

I snort a laugh. 'You are possibly the only person who has said, or will ever say, that to me.'

Yaz walks underneath a pipe and over to another door.

'I don't think hula-hooping and mime are high on the list of skills for His Majesty's Secret Service,' I say.

Yaz smiles, waving the magnetic card down the side of the door, but it doesn't open.

I give the door a push. There's a square mirror on the door and I glimpse my reflection. I tuck my sweaty hair strands back behind my ears and give my ponytail a tight tug. Looking closer, I have smudged my mascara so start wiping.

CRUNCH!

I jump back in surprise as the door opens.

'Retina recognition. Why didn't I think of that? Good work, Dusty.'

The creaky door opens up to a spiralling stairwell. I peer over the side. It's so dark I can't actually see the bottom.

'Come on.' Yaz darts down the steps, the sound of her pounding feet echoing in the cylinder.

I follow, getting dizzier and dizzier by the second. When I finally reach the bottom, my head is still spinning.

'You okay?' asks Yaz.

'Perfectly freaked out, thanks,' I reply.

Yaz grins. 'I know, it's so cool, right?'

Not the word I was going for, but I don't want to spoil Yaz's fun. 'Any deeper and we'll wind up in Australia.'

'The security is state-of-the-art stuff,' replies Yaz.

'If there's ever a nuclear war, I know where to go.'

A secondary door automatically opens. Yaz squeals in delight. 'We're in!'

A door flies open and a man in a business suit whizzes past. The normality surprises me. Yaz strides purposefully down the corridor and I hurry to catch her up. It's funny to think that all this secret stuff is going on underground while the people of London are walking above, oblivious to what's beneath their feet.

'We need to find room seven, but none of the doors have numbers on them,' says Yaz with a frown. Another man in a suit zips past, this one clutching a file marked 'Top Secret', a worried frown etched on his face, followed by two women in lab suits. The place is a hive of activity.

'Here,' I say.

'How do you know? There's no numbers.'

I point to the doors behind us. 'Just counted from left to right, that's assuming we start at one. If it isn't this one, then it could be the one opposite.'

Yaz accepts my logic and knocks on the door, then without waiting for an answer pushes it open. Two heads turn from the window. One person is male and looks a lot like the actor, Daniel Craig. I mean, his total doppelgänger. 'Sorry, wrong room.' Yaz ducks out and closes the door.

'The one opposite then.'

Yaz knocks once and pushes open the door. Ottoman and Adelstein look up from the large conference table.

'Good, you're here,' says Ottoman, gesturing to us to sit down. 'Khan. Hall. We have something we'd like to discuss with you.'

Yaz and I take a seat. Yaz sits in hers as straight as a metal arrow.

'But first we have a couple of questions,' says Adelstein.

Ottoman rolls his eyes, but he lets Adelstein continue.

Adelstein directs his question to Yaz. 'What makes you think you'll make a good spy?'

Yaz isn't the least bit intimidated by him and gets straight to the point. 'I have been in Iraq on security detail for eighteen months as a linguistic officer. I completed the APFT last week, so my fitness is up to the required level. I specialise in point shooting and kickboxing. I speak fluent Hindi, Urdu, Marathi, French and Arabic, and I have a degree in Islamic Studies.'

I give Yaz a discreet thumbs-up, which she returns with a grin.

'What about you, Ms Hall?'

My head snaps up. 'Me?' I squeak. But in all honesty, how the heck do I follow that? The only certificate that springs to mind is twenty-five metres swimming and a couple of rosettes for taking part in a horse event. I swallow and lift my chin. 'I can't compete with Yaz's impressive skillset and you'd be fools not to hire her.' Yaz's eyes meet mine, and I know I've made a friend for life. 'But … I think you'll agree I am a quick learner. These past few months I have shown I can put my mind to anything and adapt to my environment.'

'Quite,' says Ottoman.

Or did he say quiet?

'You didn't tell us you had a criminal record,' Adelstein interrupts.

'I don't have a criminal record!'

'You were arrested,' says Adelstein. 'For assault.'

At first, I'm confused and then realise what he's talking about. 'I was seventeen years old. My friend and I were at a concert and this bloke was on his phone, kept chatting, chatting louder and louder … Well, my friend asked him to stop and then he slapped her. So I punched him.'

'You broke his nose.'

'I got a standing ovation,' I reply.

'This is all water under the bridge,' says Ottoman, looking at Adelstein with a tired and wholly annoyed frown on his face.

'If I may be permitted to speak, sir,' says Yaz.

'Go ahead, Khan,' says Ottoman.

'Dusty is fearless and courageous. She has a photographic memory; no one outdid her on the memory tests. She's an ace shot and she's incredibly quick to adapt to situations and learns on the spot.'

My jaw drops open. I am completely taken aback. I think that has to be the nicest thing anyone has ever said about me.

'I agree with you,' says Ottoman. 'Which brings me to the reason you are both here. We think you make an excellent team. We have noticed how well you work together and we have an assignment that needs you both.' I risk a look at Adelstein and my heart plummets. The look in return is stony-eyed with added icicles.

Ottoman pushes a couple of files across the table. I take one and hide behind it. Yaz picks up the other.

'Ahmed Al Sahid,' says Adelstein. I peek over the file and Adelstein is referencing the screen on the far wall. He directs us through a series of headshots of a good-looking Middle Eastern man in various poses: on a yacht, playing polo, motor-racing. 'Owner of the Carlitz Hotel,' says Adelstein, 'which he took over from his father and which now makes a suspicious two billion a year. We know in the past it has housed al-Qaeda operatives from Liberia and Sierra Leone, and his head of security is this man.' He clicks through to another headshot. 'Mohamed El Hakim Fakhouri. Hardcore fundamentalist and suspected member of the Salafia Jihadia group. Arrested in connection with the 2003 Casablanca bombings but later released without charge, as he was a child.'

'We believe Ahmed's hotel is just a front for his more lucrative business—diamond smuggling to fund weapons,' says Ottoman.

Click—a photo of some diamonds.

'Ooh, a natural blue, that's called an emerald cut,' I say. 'Must be ten carats, at least. The proportions are perfect. Look at that canary yellow, what a lovely princess cut.' They all gawp at me. 'I once worked for Garibaldy Giraffay, you know, the Bond Street jewellers. The owner was a colonial slavedriver and would flip if you didn't identify every diamond quality by loop. You've got a human rights tribunal waiting to happen right there. You should open a file on him. Racist tyrant. I'm surprised it's not in my file, everything else is.'

'We can't keep track of *all* your career choices, Ms

Hall,' retorts Adelstein.

'Moving on … three thousand carats of clean white diamonds went missing; they were on the way to the Bourse in Antwerp. An unidentified dealer had already paid thirty percent. Dusty, your mission is to get close to Ahmed Sahid.'

'Close? Define close.'

'We're not asking you to sleep with him,' says Adelstein.

'But if you do, you won't be judged,' replies Ottoman.

Adelstein scowls, as does Yaz. Oh, c'mon, those two need to lighten up, Ottoman is just joking.

'We have managed to secure an opening with their head housekeeper, Alif Bassam. They're looking for a new cleaning company for all their hotels and you both will be pitching for the contract. You will need to be good but not too good. We don't want you to actually win the contract.' Ottoman slides over two glossy brochures. 'You fly to Marrakesh next Thursday.'

Ottoman speaks into the table. *Eh?* 'Jacob and Morley, can you come in?'

Two geeky guys enter. 'Morley, brief our agents about the technicalities of this mission,' says Ottoman.

'You will be wired at all times and we'll also have visual biometrics, in addition to remote tracking devices on your person, should anything go astray,' says Morley, peering at us over the top of his half-moon spectacles.

'You are talking about people? If people go astray?' I ask.

'Yes, it will be placed on your person and if that should go astray we will be able to find the body,' Morley monotones, all matter-of-fact.

'Body? BODY?' My stomach churns nervously.

'Yes. We will have a direct feed from SBAS. It triangulates your position.'

Jacob, a tall, blond, skinny Dane with thick-rimmed glasses and a ginger goatee, spins what appears to be a lollipop as he speaks. 'Yes, a code vord would be appropriate for de ladies. Maybe even just a sound. Ve vill discuss now. The sound of the wind?'

'Well, if one of you feels like the situation is getting dangerous you should say'—says Morley—'"the sky is luminous".'

'Oh, come on, you'd never drop that into a casual conversation. What about …' I pause to think. '"My heels are killing me." You know, something that a normal woman would say.'

Ottoman nods enthusiastically. Adelstein glares at me. 'Okay, "my heels are killing me",' he apathetically concurs.

'You should have worn flats to work,' I quip. Adelstein's mouth twitches into a reluctant smile.

CHAPTER TWELVE

Yaz and I are standing at the bottom of the stairwell; it was bad enough coming down, now we've got to walk up it.

'Drat! I've left my jacket in the conference room,' I say.

'You can pick it up tomorrow.'

'I can't, it's got my car keys in it.'

Jacob, the tall, skinny blond Dane with the glasses and goatee, comes out and walks over to a wall. He waves his pass across the wall and the wall slides apart.

There's a lift! Yaz and I exchange glances.

'Go on, you go ahead,' I say. 'I'll see you tomorrow.'

I dash back to room seven and get my coat. I am just leaving when the door swings towards me and connects with my face. My head whips back, and the pain is immediate. 'Ow! Ow! Ow!' I press my hand to my face, trying to stem the insane throbbing.

'Hall! I didn't realise you were there. Are you okay?' Adelstein actually looks concerned.

'Do you always try to take a door off its hinges?'

'You're bleeding.' He seems aghast.

'Am I?' I say as some blood drips into my eye.

'You've got a cut on your forehead.'

I stare at him dumbly. I can't see anything. I stumble forward and he reaches for me. I can't see anything beyond his chest, which feels solid under my touch. The subtle scent of his aftershave fills my nostrils.

'Hall, are you going to faint?'

I inhale. He smells good. I shake my head. 'I don't think so.'

Adelstein gently guides me into another room and sits me down. He fetches a wet cloth and presses it to my forehead. I don't know where we are, but there's a chair and a first-aid kit. 'You have a cut across your eyebrow.' He pulls out a plastic sticky stitch thing and starts attending to the cut.

'It really hurts,' I say.

'You'll probably have a black eye tomorrow.'

'I know you don't like me very much, but I'd rather you didn't try to kill me.' I give him a tiny half-smile.

'Keep still, otherwise this won't stick.' His lips press together in a tight line. 'I don't want to kill you,' he says, handing me an ice pack.

'But you don't like me very much.'

His brows pinch into a frown.

'You frown a lot, did you know that?' I think concussion is getting the better of me.

He sighs and, after a long silence, says, 'I just don't think you should be here.'

My heart sinks. I knew that was what he thought, but hearing him say it out loud makes it a hundred times worse. It takes every ounce of willpower to meet his eyes. 'I have as much right as anyone else in training.'

'This is not some silly school outing. This is actual life. The dark side.'

'I know.'

'No, you don't. You are too inexperienced. There is

no second chance, this isn't training anymore. One wrong decision means life or death.'

I feel a surge of anger. 'Look, I may not have had six years in the Army. I may not have given it a second thought until the job presented itself to me, but I've worked hard and more than proven myself.' I can hear my voice rising with emotion. 'You're wrong to underestimate me.' I throw the ice pack at him, and it hits him in the chest. I get to my feet, wobbling slightly. He reaches to steady me and I shrug him off. 'I think I can manage on my own.'

On the drive home, I feel pretty deflated and my bad eye is beginning to close up. Why do I care so much about what Adelstein thinks? He made it clear from the start. I guess I was hoping he might change his mind.

My eye-hand co-ordination is further tested when I try to open the gate. With my good eye, I can see there's a large bag of rags on the doorstep. What the hell? As I get closer, the bag of rags moves.

You've got to be kidding me! Cameron? The ex-boyfriend who I haven't heard from in months? 'What are you doing here?'

'Is that the way to greet your boyfriend?'

'Boyfriend?' What a joke.

Cameron reaches in for a kiss and I take a step back. 'What happened to your face?' he asks.

'I haven't seen or heard from you in months,' I say, ignoring his question.

'Lost my phone, didn't I?'

I find myself appraising him properly (with my good eye). He looks like he just rolled out of bed. His greasy brown hair has gotten so long that it now falls past his shoulder blades. His tall, skinny frame, which I always admired, is swamped in a trench coat that seems five sizes too big. This is interesting. I don't find him attractive at all.

'Doorsteps are the new phones,' he says, as if he's being terribly clever.

'And these doorsteps take months to find, do they?'

'You know how I get when inspiration strikes. I've been writing and writing until time ceased to exist. It doesn't mean I haven't been thinking of you, sweet flower of mine. What happened to your face?' He runs his eyes over me.

'What are you doing here?'

'I thought maybe I could come in? I'm starving.'

'You're unbelievable.'

He gives me a cocky smile.

'It wasn't a compliment. You think you can just show up and, what, pick up where we left off?'

'Are you angry?' He sounds surprised.

'What do you think?'

'Ahh, cuppy-cakes, don't be like that.'

'I have no idea why you're here.'

Cameron steps closer and reaches for me. 'Let me show you.' He leans in for a kiss.

'Urgh!' I say, pushing him away. 'Cameron. I'd like you to go.'

'You don't mean that.'

'Yes, I do.'

'You sent me like a gazillion texts. The band was calling you my personal stalker.' He laughs. 'Then you suddenly stopped texting.'

'You said you lost your phone?'

'I did, and then I found it. Like a phoenix out of the ashes, all mystical and that.' He grabs me by the arm and tries to kiss me again.

I pull away. 'It's over. Go away.'

'Nothing's ever over. Time is a continuum, baby.' He goes to grab me again.

'Cameron, I said go away.'

'Don't be like that.'

'I said it's over. Now go.'

His mood changes and his face scrunches into a scowl. 'I've been waiting here for over an hour.'

'What a hardship for you.' I shrug. 'Do you need a pound for some food?'

He reaches for my waist.

'I said don't touch me.' With lightning speed, I knee Cameron in the groin and shove him away. He lands in the peonies. Before he can pick himself up, I let myself into the house and slam the door shut. I leave Cameron swearing and banging on the door. I let myself into the flat and wander into the kitchen. Mustard is asleep under the kitchen table.

I'm starving; all this exercise makes a girl want proper food. Carbs. I look in the fridge and it's as empty as usual, although the gooey thing neither of us will handle looks like it's in another stage of metamorphosis—it's blue, white and green today.

Mustard saunters from beneath the table and purrs at me. As I open the drawer and give him a treat, I hear the door click open and my head jerks up.

'What happened to the peonies?' asks Jodie, walking into the kitchen, carrying a motorcycle helmet under her arm. Jodie's jaw drops when she sees my face. 'OMG! What happened, babe?'

'Well, the peonies were unfortunate collateral damage. I had a problem with an idiot wanting to come in for food.'

'What, Mustard was too lazy to use the cat flap again?'

'Not Mustard, Cameron.'

'Blimey, I thought he sailed away on the hopeless boat yonks ago?'

'So did I but he thought he could just pick up from where we left off.'

'You didn't really have anything to pick up from. He only bothered you when broke or hungry.'

'Like dating a tramp.'

'Least a tramp would be grateful.'

'I kicked him in the balls. He's always been such a …'

'Cockwomble!' she offers.

'Yes, a cockwomble.'

'Did he do that?' she asks, pointing to my face.

'No. I got clipped by a heavy door at work. It's throbbing now. Have we got any frozen peas?'

'I haven't been in the freezer for a year; goodness knows what's in there. Be my guest, but take a crowbar, think it needs de-icing. How about a takeaway?' Jodie looks at me hopefully.

'Why not?'

Jodie grabs all the menus out of the overstuffed kitchen drawer, which is really the true purpose of kitchen drawers.

'What's that?' I ask, pointing to the snazzy helmet.

Jodie looks at me like I've just asked a really dumb question. 'Babe, it's a helmet.'

'Yes, I know that. But when you said bike, I thought you meant a push bike.' Now I come to think about it, there's been a flashy red motorbike parked outside our house for weeks, I just thought it belonged to someone else on the street.

Jodie chuckles. 'I'd hardly be able to get much speed on a push bike, now would I?'

'That's what I'm afraid of. You are careful on that thing?'

'Aren't I always!'

CHAPTER THIRTEEN

'Oh, Dusty! You are positively more groomed than Goliath at his first dressage win,' coos my mother.

'As long as we overlook the big fat shiner on her face,' retorts Coco.

'It's not that noticeable,' I say. 'The concealer covers the worst of it. Besides, it'll be long gone before your wedding day.'

'It had better be,' she replies.

'Dusty, I'll give you one of Goliath's ointments. That'll help the swelling go down.' Mother's quite serious too. I catch the seamstress's eyes as she raises her brows above her thick glasses. I think I may have found an ally.

I refocus on the mirror, not my family, and watch the seamstress check for length and fit.

'The dress is really pretty,' says Michelle.

'Thank you,' I say.

As dresses go, it's exquisite. Coco relinquished her tight grip on her 'big day' and let the bridesmaids choose their own dresses. But first she insisted on trying at least seven different wedding shops, dithering whether to change the colour to peach or lilac or peppermint or lavender. I reminded her she already agreed on blush rose because it reminded her of the Tuscany sunset the evening she met Roger, where they shared a bottle of local rosé, and the first piece of jewellery Roger ever bought her, a small but natural pink diamond pendant. Coco was touched that I remembered. On top of this, everything from the placemats and the flowers in the venue are all based around this colour. She went with blush rose, she chose this colour out of five million others, she's going to have to stick with it.

I found a beautiful spaghetti-strap long dress with a sassy slit down the side for me. The other bridesmaids had different ideas on what they wanted, from middling puritan to downright trashy, but as long as the colour was identical they got their way. I gaze at my reflection, smoothing down the silky fabric.

'If you made a bit of an effort occasionally, you might even find someone to take you out,' says Coco, standing next to me.

'Why, thanks, Coco. Really touching. I see you've been practising those pep talks again.'

'You have to admit your clothes can be … a bit avant-garde. You're not still dating that loser Cameron, are you? You won't get taken to fine restaurants by someone like that. I like your shoes.' She ricochets this all out in one breath.

All fashion is avant-garde to my Sloaney sister. If it's not Ralph Lauren, Barbour or tweed it's just plain wrong to wear. They all look like costumes to her, that's what you get growing up with *Horse & Hounds* and *Country Life* as your fashion bibles. And there's no point wasting your time explaining haute couture, 'because that's just silly.'

'Cameron is out of the picture,' I say.

'Thank goodness for that.'

Another bridesmaid rushes in, totally out of breath. We all look up here and for a few seconds there is dead silence. All eyes swivel to Coco and then back to the bridesmaid.

'Sarah. What. The. Fuck. *Hap-PENED. TO. YOUR. HAIR?'* Coco's voice pauses between each word, increasing in volume. I can see why Coco is alarmed. It is rather fire-engine red and looking patchy. I think Sarah may have done it herself.

Sarah looks crestfallen. 'You don't like it?'

'No, I don't fucking like it! Tell me it washes out.'

'Language, Coco, really,' says Mother, looking apologetically at the seamstress.

'I'm not sure, I'll have to read the packet.' Sarah bites down on her lip.

I begin, 'I think it looks …' Coco narrows her eyes at me, daring me to say another word.

'I think it suits you,' remarks Michelle.

Coco turns on Michelle, her look thunderous. 'What are you wearing that for?'

Michelle touches the tiara that is balancing on her head. 'I was just trying it on.'

'Take it off,' says Coco, whipping it off the top of Michelle's head. 'I'm the only one wearing a tiara.'

Sarah pulls out a pair of black stiletto open-toed sandals from her bag and I can see steam coming out of Coco's ears.

'And what are those? I hope those are not your bridesmaid shoes? Did you not get my email? I specifically said closed-toe shoes with a two-inch heel—'

'What size are you?' I interject quickly.

'Err—six,' Sarah says.

'I'm a six too. I have another pair similar to these.'

'Are they closed-toe?' demands Coco.

'Yes.'

'Fine,' says Coco, then turns to the seamstress. 'Have you finished with Dusty?' The seamstress has gone pale and is staring at Coco, her mouth gaping. 'Well, have you?'

The seamstress nods, seeming too afraid to speak.

'Okay then, tomato head, you're up next,' Coco barks at Sarah.

I slip off my shoes and give them to Sarah. 'If we kill her, we could stuff her body in that silk dress protector and all our problems would be solved,' I whisper.

Sarah giggles. 'This is so unlike your sister. She's usually such a sweetie pie.'

My sister a sweetie pie? 'I have never ever thought of my sister as a sweetie pie. A sour drop, but definitely not a sweetie pie.'

Sarah giggles again.

'So, how is the new job going?' asks my mother.

I peer at my mother. She never takes an interest in my jobs. 'It's really challenging,' I say, 'but rewarding.'

'I'm sure popping appointments on a calendar is a real brain-ache,' interjects Coco.

I shoot my sister a withering look. 'As a matter of fact, I have a business trip next weekend.'

'Next weekend?' Coco pulls the tiara off her head.

'That's wonderful, darling,' says my mother. 'Be polite. People always like manners. And don't be greedy at the table. Never take the last of anything. People notice everything, you know, and you need to stay a while at a place to be noticed at all. Don't loiter though, I don't mean loitering. You should never loiter …'

'Shut up, Mother,' snaps Coco. 'Did you say next weekend as in my hen weekend? The weekend planned for my hen night? That weekend?'

Oh, Good God, is that next weekend? The other bridesmaids look at me, and the smile on my face starts to slip.

'Because it absolutely has to be next weekend, it's on the spreadsheet. Everyone has booked the weekend off. Roger is in Paris on business.'

'You're sure we can't do another weekend?'

Coco goes deathly quiet. There's an eerie sort of calm in the air, the type of calm before a storm, and I brace myself for what comes next.

'No!' Coco thunders. 'I knew it. I knew you'd screw this up like you screw everything else up. You never do anything right, you're a ...' Big, fat tears roll down her face. 'You ruin everything.'

Coco flings herself onto the pile of veils lying on the floor and has a tantrum like a two-year-old. Shop assistants and passers-by look on with horror.

Embarrassed, Mother grabs the nearest long thing she can find, which is a diamante-covered cane, and prods Coco with it as if she's a naughty horse. 'Coco, darling, get up! Stop making a scene. Calm yourself down. I'm sure Dusty has an explanation.'

'Coco!' I say, clapping my hands on my thighs and making the other bridesmaids jump as I try to keep the quaking terror out of my voice. 'I'm just messing with you. Of course your hen weekend is next weekend.' I give a short, fake laugh. 'I have it sorted. Trust me.'

The other bridesmaids look at me with surprise. I smile at them reassuringly.

'I'll email you with the details,' I say.

My sister gets up off the floor, her tears drying instantly. I don't know whether to be impressed with her recovery or have her sectioned. Then she laughs like a madwoman. Her nerves are at breaking point. 'You better not let me down.'

Sitting on the Tube on the way home, I feel like I'm going to throw up. What the hell am I going to do? Because two things are certain:

1.) The hen weekend has to be next weekend. Otherwise, Coco will kill me.

2.) The mission has to be next weekend. Otherwise, Adelstein will kill me.

It's good to have choices!

CHAPTER FOURTEEN

I get very little sleep and at 5 a.m. I'm still wide awake, but now I have a plan! I go for a jog (yes, out of choice) because I need to think through my plan. By 5.45 a.m. I'm in the shower and by 6.15 a.m. I'm out of the door, knowing exactly what I need to do. Time is no longer my enemy. In fact, there's often not enough hours in the day. Jodie is still in her dressing gown, hair awry from over-styling, coffee in hand and a corner of toast hanging from her mouth in astonishment as I wave cheerio.

When I arrive at work, Adelstein is already there. So much for thinking I'd be the first in. It wouldn't surprise me if he were a synthetic AI life form, an experiment they built at the lowest level of sub-zero, floor negative fifty-nine. His eyebrows quirk up when he sees me. I give him a half-hearted wave, saunter into the office and get to work on my brilliant plan.

In no time, I've booked flights and rooms at the Carlitz Hotel, I even blag a twenty-percent discount with complimentary champagne for the rooms. My credit card is maxed out but it's going to be totally worth it, and there is no way Coco can sniff at this. I've emailed all the hens and given them prices, which should be more or less than their daily pocket money. When it's all done, I sit back triumphantly, rejoicing at how devilishly clever I am.

'Am I late?' Yaz asks, striding into the room. Once a soldier, always a soldier.

My heart thuds. 'No,' I say. 'I'm early. I wanted to go through the profiles.' Wow, how easy the lie trips off my lips. I casually tuck the reservations into the file I've labelled 'H' for 'hen folder' and slip it into my bag.

Shuffling in behind Yaz enter Morley and Jacob. Morley is carrying a large briefcase and Jacob is sucking on a lollipop.

'What you got there?' I ask nosily.

Morley smiles with geeky glee and snaps open the briefcase. Yaz and I wander over to take a look. Inside the briefcase is the oddest assortment of things. I pick up the lipstick and unscrew the top. The colour appeals to me. Peach Pop. Nice. Morley and Jacob cower. 'It's a pistol,' stutters Morley.

'Relax,' I say as I carefully screw the lid back on. 'I know what I am doing. After all, I am a trained spy now.'

'Agent,' says Morley. 'No one says "spy".' Beads of sweat have formed on Morley's forehead and he pushes his glasses up his nose. He places the briefcase on the table and takes out a necklace. 'You both get a visual receptor. We've disguised it as an amulet,' he says. 'While you are wearing it, the camera will be able to hear and see everything.'

'Ve shall cover your frontal outlook,' says Jacob.

Morley chuckles, then coughs. 'We will have you, your surroundings under surveillance. You will be safe.'

'I don't wear jewellery,' remarks Yaz, her hand

shaking a little as she lifts it up and fastens it around her neck.

'It is made from microscopic layers of graphene and gold flex,' says Morley.

'A good material to vithstand bullets,' interjects Jacob.

'Really?' Yaz clasps her hand around the amulet, now on side with the Army-issued jewellery. 'It's beautiful.'

'We've disguised the tear gas as face powder. And this key ring is a mini-explosive, creates a smokescreen. This pen is equipped with a small laser beam for cutting through anything.'

Yaz is transfixed, whereas my heart starts to hammer in my chest. This mission has suddenly got very real.

'We also have these fertiliser nodes so you can place the bugs all round the foyer and restaurant in the plants.'

Jacob hands Yaz a passport. 'Penny Palmer.' Not a bad photo, as passport photos go. She is wearing make-up, her brows have been plucked, her posture looks nice and confident.

'Where's mine?' I ask.

There's a shifty sort of silence. Morley looks at his feet uncomfortably and Jacob sucks hard on his lollipop. 'We don't have one for you.'

Yaz frowns. 'That can't be right.'

My throat tightens. *Maybe they've had second thoughts about me? Maybe I'm not going to Marrakesh?* This is a disaster. I have to be on this trip. I've just booked the hen weekend.

'Not yet, but we have something that'll cheer you up,' interjects Morley. 'We've taken the liberty at Liberty's, as you instructed, and brought the wardrobe you specified.'

'All of it?' I ask, stunned.

'Yes.'

Yaz turns to me. 'His Majesty's Government

wouldn't be buying you work clothes if you weren't coming.'

She's right. They wouldn't spend so much money if they didn't see it as an investment. I feel a flutter of excitement when Morley and Jacob disappear and return moments later, wheeling two rails of clothing. My rail is bulging with colourful garments, and I immediately start pulling outfits together. 'This for sure, oh, and this, and this.'

It doesn't escape my notice that Yaz's rail is rather sparse and my trusted partner has gone quiet. I immediately assess the situation and take charge.

'This won't do at all. No, no, no. We're cavorting with the wealthy, seducing rich criminals. Yaz, you'll need Balmain, Valentino, Manolos.' Luckily, we're a similar size. Yaz is just a few inches taller than me. I pull a few items from my rail, and Yaz soaks up everything I say. 'You need Westwood, Prada, Pucci, Chanel, darling.'

'You heard her,' says Yaz, turning round to face Morley and Jacob. 'What are you waiting for? Go, go, go!' she bellows unnaturally. Yaz turns to me as if Christmas has come early.

'Right, my job here is done,' I say with a grin. 'I'm just popping out for a sec. Will you cover for me?'

'Sure,' replies Yaz.

I grab my bag and head for the stairs, finding a spot that is far enough to be out of earshot but still close enough to see if anyone is coming up or down. I can't wait to hear the utter surprise in Coco's voice when I tell her the plans for her hen weekend. Disappointingly, it goes straight to voicemail: *Hi, you've come through to Coco. I'm unable to take your call. Pease leave a message after the bells.*

A ridiculous wedding bells sound effect pounds into my eardrum.

'Hi, Coco, it's me. I hope your passport is up to date because your hen weekend is on foreign shores,' I whisper down the phone. Coco is not going to know what hit her!

I sit for a while, half-expecting Coco to ring me back, when I hear voices coming from the stairwell.

'You can't let her go.'

'I thought we cleared this up.'

I lean forward, my heart pounding. I can't see Adelstein or Ottoman but I recognise their voices.

'She's a liability.'

'That's where we disagree. Agent Hall is the only one who can get close to him, you know that.'

My stomach gives an anxious lurch as I realise they are talking about me.

'It's the perfect plan,' retorts Ottoman.

'She's going to screw it up.'

'Enough!' Ottoman growls. 'Now let me make this clear, crystal clear, clearer than the Priory on St. Patrick's Day. I don't care what that damn file says about her, she is the right person for the job. We need her.'

'Don't say I didn't warn you.'

When I know they've gone, I let out a shaky breath. I feel a flash of irritation that Adelstein still doubts me, but not as much as I doubt myself. Maybe he's right, maybe I will screw it up. Fear and doubt gnaw at me from the inside, taking chunks out of my newfound confidence and sense of purpose.

CHAPTER FIFTEEN

I'm in the middle of packing when I realise I haven't figured out my spy character. I'm travelling under my name, which I think is a massive oversight. Just because it's the Secret Service doesn't mean they're infallible.

I was really looking forward to having a new identity and a new name. Doesn't mean I can't get creative. The question is, who is Dusty Hall if she isn't me?

Top businesswoman, travelling to Marrakesh to win a lucrative cleaning contract. So, how does a top businesswoman dress? Not in jogging pants, T-shirt and a pair of bunny slippers. I tut at my reflection and change into a black wrap DVF dress and a pair of shiny black Manolos. I finish off the look with a pair of black sunglasses and strike a sexy pose. Now I look like a nineteen-sixties Italian widow.

'Why, Signore, it is not I you need to speak with, it is the clandestine order of my late husband's church. I cannot see you anymore. It is too dangerous. There are eyes everywhere, from the mountain to the lake. Go now. I will meet you at the boathouse. Midnight. If I am still alive.'

'What are you doing?' asks Jodie, standing in the doorway.

'Oh, just messing about.' I drop the glasses on the bed.

'I thought acting was behind you,' she says, coming into my room and picking up a sexy cocktail dress. 'Is this new?'

'Yes.'

She looks at the label. 'Prada.'

'Just some new clothes for work.'

'Alice hasn't sent another parcel you're not telling me about?'

'No,' I say, affronted that she would even think such a thing. 'I would never do that.'

'Have you won the lottery then?'

'Chance should be a fine thing.'

Jodie picks up another dress and inspects the label. 'Miu Miu? Oh, God, Dusty. You're not a call girl, are you?'

I snort with laughter. 'Don't be daft.'

'You're definitely hiding something.' She picks up a sexy slip and narrows her eyes. 'Have you met someone?'

'Stop being so nosy.' I snatch the undies from her.

'A rich sugar daddy?'

'Nope.'

Jodie squints at me. 'Okay, Miss Secretive,' she says. 'Don't tell me then. You're not the only one with secrets.'

My heads snaps up. I knew it. Jodie is hiding something, I can see it in her baby blues. I desperately want to ask her what it is, but then I would have to tell her mine. 'If you'll excuse me, I have to finish packing.'

'Are those Manolos?'

'They are.'

Jodie frowns. 'If you're in trouble, you know you can

tell me.'

I give Jodie an exasperated eye roll. 'I'm fine.' I whirl away and start walking up and down my room. 'I just need to wear them in a bit so they don't rub.'

Jodie does a tiny gasp, and I look up. 'You don't need to wear them in. Manolos do not rub.'

With that, she turns on her heels and leaves me be.

Twenty minutes later, I've just zipped up my suitcase when I hear a scream. I run into the kitchen, grabbing an umbrella, just in case, to find Jodie standing in front of the fridge. She gives the umbrella a quizzical look.

'Jesus, Jodie, I thought we had an intruder.'

Slowly, Jodie turns and opens the door to the fridge.

I peer inside and give her a wide grin. 'I'm away for a few days, so I thought I would stock up on some proper food. There's homemade stew—well, homemade by Waitrose—and I know how much you like hard cheeses. Oh, and there's some pickles, and the jalapeños were on special offer, and olives …' I stop. 'Jodie, are you crying?'

Jodie dabs at her eyes. 'You did this for me?'

I nod, smiling at her. Jodie is definitely sentimental when it comes to hard cheeses.

CHAPTER SIXTEEN

I step out of the taxi with a spring in my step. I am ready to do my bit for King and country and I'm not the least bit nervous. I'm already in character. I've decided that I am an astute businesswoman with top business credentials. I'm totally dressed for the part too: Valentino tweed skirt and matching jacket, hair in a neat French plait, smart Manolo pumps. I've developed a really cool voice too. Imagine a female version of Morgan Freeman.

BrrrrrrrING! I blink at the phone. Does she ever relent? Phone wedged between my ear and shoulder, I gather my luggage and walk briskly towards the terminal. 'Coco, do you know what time it is?'

'Dusty, is that you? You sound odd. Have you got a cold?'

'No, I haven't got a cold,' I say, returning to my own voice. 'What do you want?'

'Can't you at least tell me where we're going?'

'No.'

'Not even a hint?'

'Nope,' I say, rather enjoying her desperation. This is

absolutely killing Coco.

'It's not Ibiza, is it? You know I do not do clubs.'

'All will be revealed tomorrow. Michelle has the tickets. Now I've got to go …'

'Wait! I've had an idea for the wedding. I'm going to have a gazelle as ringbearer and put a bow tie on it. Grace passing to grace, i.e. moi …'

I look up and realise I'm in the wrong part of the terminal.

'… people include all types of animals at their wedding: horses, ferrets, iguanas, leopards, gerbils, turtles, pigs, rabbits … a goldfish even …'

'Bugger!'

'Excuse me?'

'Not you. I'm in the wrong terminal.'

'Oh, dear, I hope you aren't lost. Where is it we're going? Which terminal are you in?'

'Nice try. See you tomorrow.'

I end the call and break into a speedy half-walk, half-jog, wheeling my extra-large suitcase behind me. I don't have time to be an astute businesswoman. But once I've checked in and passed through airport security, I remind myself to get back into character and feel a familiar swarm of excitable butterflies in the pit of my belly, the kind I always get when I go on stage.

I find my group sitting in a café.

'Good morning,' I say.

Yaz frowns. 'What's wrong with your voice?'

Oh, I'll just forget the voice.

'You are late,' Adelstein remarks.

'Security was a nightmare and I couldn't get my sister off the phone. She wants to hire a bloody gazelle for the wedding. A bloody gazelle!'

Yaz giggles.

'Would anyone like a coffee?'

No one takes me up on the offer, so I head to the

counter on my own.

'Hello, what can I get you?' says a peppy girl.

'Flat white, please.' Oh, and what the hell. 'And an almond croissant.'

A few minutes later, caffeine and sugar passes over the high counter and I return to the table. To my dismay, it's just Adelstein sitting there. 'Was it something I said?'

Adelstein looks up from his mobile phone with a tiny flicker of a smile. 'Now we're all accounted for, Yaz has gone to get some duty-free and Morley and Jacob have gone to the electronics shop.'

I sit down and Adelstein goes back to his mobile. The silence feels punitive, like the dreaded sound of a school assembly. I drink my coffee and focus on eating the croissant as quietly as possible. Actually, it's quite nice, this silence. I take the time to savour every mouthful and come over all Zen. Who needs talking, anyway?

As if on cue, my mobile rings. 'Urgh!'

'Let me guess, your sister?'

I nod, letting it ring out. 'She has turned into a nightmare. Not that she wasn't a nightmare before.'

As soon as it rings out, the ringing starts up again. I hit the off button.

'She is persistent, I'll give you that.'

'I'm never getting married.'

'You surprise me. I thought you'd love the pomp and ceremony.'

'Well, you'd be wrong. I guess not everything about me can be found in a file.'

Adelstein frowns.

'Do you have any siblings?' I ask.

'Two.'

'Are they married?'

'Yes.'

'Are you?' I ask.

'No.' He quirks an eyebrow. 'Any more questions?'

I have quite a few, but he's already turning away to look at his screen. I don't mind. It's probably better we don't speak. A man not interested in engaging with the world. Or is it just me he doesn't want to engage with?

I absent-mindedly fix my lipstick and look around. It occurs to me how normal Adelstein and I must look. Nothing spy-like about us. For all anyone knows, I am a businesswoman on a business trip with my business colleagues. In fact, if anyone asks, I'll say I go to Marrakesh all the time … for business. Absolutely not on a top-secret mission. I always thought undercover stuff would happen at night or on a private jet, not in broad daylight in full view of the public. I turn back and catch Adelstein watching me, making me feel oddly nervous, and I wonder if I've smudged my lipstick.

'Gate 18 for Flight AZ451 to Marrakesh is now open.' My ears prick up at the announcement coming over the loudspeaker.

Adelstein jumps up from the table. 'That's us.'

Morley and Jacob suddenly appear, followed by Yaz, who's slightly breathless and holding a duty-free carrier bag as if it were a bomb.

I've never travelled business class before. Everything is so lovely and luxurious: big wide seats, no fighting for overhead lockers, so much nicer than monkey class. My knees don't come close to the chair in front and I can kick my legs out at will.

Yaz catches me and does the same, but her legs are longer than mine. She's not travelled business class before either. Across the aisle, Morley is tapping away on his notebook, Jacob is rummaging in his electronic bag and sitting in front of them is Adelstein.

'Would you like some champagne?' asks the air hostess.

Champagne? How decadent. 'Ooh, yes.' I turn to Yaz. 'Yaz, you going to join me?'

'It's the morning!' She stares at me, aghast.

'It doesn't count when you're flying,' I inform Yaz. 'And anyway, you never turn down champagne when it's offered.'

'Make that two then,' she says to the air hostess.

There are a few minor bumps as we climb above the rain clouds and then pure sunshine beams through the cabin, making me blink. I pull the window shutter down slightly. 'What did you get from duty-free?'

'Some perfume.' She whispers it, like she's done something naughty.

'Oh, yes, which one?'

'Hem-ez. I think I'm pronouncing it right.'

She means Hermes. 'Air-mez?'

'Could be.' She shrugs. 'It cost a lot.' She takes it out of the bag.

'Elixir Des Merveilles. My friend is the face of Elixir Des Merveilles,' I say proudly.

'What, the woman on the posters?'

'Yep, that's Alice Tambling-Goggin, she's a model. We grew up together.'

'She's beautiful.'

'She is. I'm wearing Coco Mademoiselle, but I've always had this romantic notion of someday discovering my signature scent, something unmistakably me.' I shrug. 'I haven't found it yet; the perfume is as elusive as a good man. Probably doesn't even exist. Do you have a boyfriend?' I ask without taking a breath, in true Coco style.

'No,' Yaz says, picking up an inflight magazine. 'Waste of time.'

The flight is a little turbulent until we reach the Mediterranean, where the air becomes smoother and the plane heats up nicely. Yaz and I chatter a bit, but she's a closed book with anything personal. Then before I know it the seatbelt sign flashes on and the captain is announcing we are about to land, and then we're gathering our things and making our way off the plane. Adelstein sets the pace—no time to waste, quick march.

Marrakesh airport is a white honeycombed structure, with the travellers moving like tropical bees, buzzing around in a giant queen's nest. It's bright, but cool.

Talking of cool, Jacob and Morley are relatively cool for geeks, and I don't know why I didn't spot it before but they could be twins except for the fact that Jacob is white and Morley is black. Tweedledum and Tweedledee. Even more so now that Morley has swapped his half-moon spectacles for a pair of dark-rimmed glasses matching Jacob's. They look like a couple of exchange students rather than operative technicians. I presumed they would be awkward, but I keep forgetting these people are trained and they've done this many times before. Most of their equipment has been sent on ahead, disguised as innovative cleaning products. Genius, really.

Adelstein continues with his air of formidability: *I can kill you with one finger if I so choose*.

We pass through security without hiccup. It's not exactly quick but neither is London. Then we're in a people carrier heading to the hotel and I'm starting to get nervous. I don't know quite how it happened, but I end up sitting next to Adelstein, and his close proximity makes me fidget. I clasp my hands together and look out of the window as we speed along, the desert landscape barren with the occasional blobs of green sprouting off random rocks. The air conditioning in the car has been switched to freezing, so much so that my skin turns goosepimply. Adelstein notices and hands me his jacket.

I take it and pull the jacket up to my chin, grateful for the warmth and surprised at his gallantry.

When we arrive at Carlitz Hotel, Yaz and I gasp in wonderment. It is so luxurious that it's on another stratosphere: a bright blue river moat surrounds the hotel, and we cross a drawbridge to reach a majestic gilded gate, which is flanked by two columns, each with its own bird of paradise perched on top. The gate automatically opens and a porter in a blue and white uniform greets us. Yaz and I exchange glances and step inside. Our jaws drop as we take in the large, colourful courtyard, surrounded by tall marble arches, glistening pearly white in the sun, each with its own golden railing.

Blue-and-white stripes echo throughout the hotel, but it's the gold that truly glitters, from the planters holding the tall palms, to the grouting between the mosaic tiles—even the pool in the centre of the courtyard is glistening gold. But that's nothing compared to the bordering-on-gaudy staircase. We enter the lobby under a large marble archway and my mind blows. The staircase is like something out of the Renaissance period, with intricately decorated balustrades and a stair runner of deep blue flecked with gold. It really is a feast for the eyes.

While Adelstein checks us in, we sit down on one of the many chairs scattered around the lobby. The air inside is pleasant, cool. I find myself sitting a little straighter, as though in a posture class.

Yaz gives me a strange look. 'Do you need the loo?'

'What? No.'

In no time, we're checked in and in our rooms. Yaz and I have room two-sixty, Jacob and Morley room two-sixty-two and Adelstein room two-sixty-four.

Our room is large, opulent and elegant, with two double beds floating on a mini-mezzanine central platform. It's a room fit for a princess. Not that I expected anything else. I slip out of my tweed jacket and skirt, my blouse just about covering my bum. Yaz turns away, embarrassed. I head over to the balcony, whisk the sheer white curtains back and step out onto the balcony. My eyes widen in awe. 'Oh, Yaz, come look at the views.'

'I will in a sec. I want to unpack first.'

The ghostly mountains stick out like minarets in the far distance. I pull out my phone and snap away; I also take a couple of selfies, making sure I get the view in the background. I won't post them—I know that'll be a breach of national security—but I really don't want to forget this moment.

'Yaz, you really need to come and see this.' I've just stepped back into the room when the adjoining door bursts open and in walks Jacob and Morley. What the … I pull the curtain around my semi-nakedness.

'Haven't you heard of knocking?' Yaz demands, outraged on my behalf.

I watch as Morley and Jacob pull out electronic detectors and sweep the room for bugs. Adelstein enters.

'Hall and Khan, your objective is to …' Adelstein's head swivels as he looks to locate my whereabouts, finally seeing me hiding behind the flimsy curtain. His eyes travel down to my legs. My face colours. He quirks a brow. '… to get dressed and head to the bar. You need to make contact with the suspect. We know he takes a drink this time of day.'

Dying of embarrassment, I nod. 'Okay. Got it.'

'Yes, sir,' says Yaz, pulling out a sexy minidress and holding it in front of her, a frown trailing across her face.

'Oh, Yaz, you should totally wear that. It will go super with the Givenchy sandals.'

Adelstein glances back at me. 'You have fifteen minutes.' He turns on his heels and strides back through the adjoining door. Jacob and Morley, however, don't move.

'Are you expecting us to get dressed in front of you?' barks Yaz.

Jacob's eyes light up in hope.

'Bugger off and fiddle with your gadgets,' she snarls.

I giggle as they scamper away, tails between their legs.

CHAPTER SEVENTEEN

The magnitude of where I am and what is expected hits me suddenly. I'm both nervous and excited. Yaz and I grin at each other as we sit down on the stools at the bar. This is so cool. A smart-looking bartender with great teeth comes over.

'Hello!' I say with a friendly smile. 'Two cosmopolitans, please.'

The bartender responds with a beaming white smile and immediately gets to work in front of us.

I pretend to casually look around while taking in as much detail as I can. Low lighting, lots of plush sofas and chairs, a couple of honeymooners, two bearded guys. One of them looks at me and winks. I smile back, twiddling the locket around my neck, then realise what I'm doing and stop. I don't want to interfere with the sound. Morley and Jacob explained that it has a hidden microphone and tiny camera in it.

'We probably should have ordered soft drinks.' Yaz gives me a worried look.

'It would look suspicious if we did,' I respond confidently.

'I suppose,' she says, eyeing the drinks sceptically as the bartender slides them over. She takes a tentative sip, then goes in for a bigger sip.

I giggle. 'Whoa, not too quickly.'

'This is good.'

I take a sip and sigh with pleasure. 'Perfect. Not too sweet, not too tart.'

We're onto our second cosmopolitans when a familiar smell catches my attention. I sniff the air in astonishment. Yaz looks at me strangely. 'What is it?'

Surely not. It couldn't be. I swivel around on my stool. 'Roger?'

Roger does a double-take. 'Dusty?' We both stare at each other, completely thrown. 'W-wh-wha … What are you doing here?' he asks.

'I could ask you the same question,' I say, aware of Yaz's eyes digging into me.

'I'm here seeing a friend. What's your reason?'

'I'm here for an interview.'

'Don't tell me you've been given the big heave-ho already?'

I pull a face. 'As a matter of fact, I'm representing Duty Calls and we're here to bid on the cleaning contract.'

Roger guffaws. 'Oh, dear, and they sent you?'

I ignore him and turn to Yaz. 'This is my colleague … Penny.'

'Hello, Penny,' says Roger.

'You know, I could have sworn Coco said you were in Paris.'

'Change of plans.' He gives a dismissive shrug. 'Actually, Dusty, I'd prefer it if you didn't mention seeing me to Coco.'

I narrow my eyes at Roger. 'And why is that?'

'Err, well … the thing is—'

'Roger, are you going to introduce us?'

I jolt as if I've been tasered. Ahmed Al Sahid gives Roger a friendly slap on the shoulder. How the hell does Roger know Ahmed Al Sahid? Ahmed then turns to me and gives me a charming smile. I throw him my very best beatific smile. God. He is much better-looking in real life.

'Ahmed, this is Coco's sister, Dusty,' says Roger. 'Dusty, as in if the back door of a pyramid was left open and a sandstorm blew in, it would be dusty.' Roger chortles to himself.

Ahmed gives Roger a blank look.

I smirk at Roger. 'You're the only one who finds your jokes funny.'

'Roger, you never told me Coco had a sister, and one so beautiful.'

Roger looks appalled, and I giggle.

'Enchanted,' says Ahmed, taking my hand and planting a soft kiss on the back. His gaze turns briefly to Yaz, who lets out a girly giggle.

'Hi, I'm Penny,' she says in unrecognisable girlishness.

Ahmed kisses her hand too, and then his eyes return to mine. 'What brings you to Marrakesh?'

'Work,' I reply, and lean forward. 'But what I want to know is how do you know this buffoon?'

'Boarding school,' replies Ahmed.

Oh, that explains it. 'So, was Roger studious?'

'Studious?' Ahmed laughs, and the crinkles in the corners of his eyes lengthen into tiny crow's feet. My stomach flutters. 'Only if it turned a profit. Roger was more of a negotiator of stolen tuck.' Ahmed's English is superb, unsurprising if he boarded at Roger's ludicrously posh public school.

'Next time you are in London we should meet for a drink,' I say flirtatiously.

'Not that ghastly Hobnobs,' says Roger. 'It's

Dusty's local debauched AA hotspot.'

'Don't listen to Roger. His idea of fun is polishing old pots.'

Ahmed laughs, and the look he gives me is definitely flirtatious. Roger looks like he's going to throw up. 'Right, well, it was good seeing you, Dusty, but Ahmed and I have business to discuss.'

'Work, work, work, that is all Roger thinks about. My good friend, when enchanting creatures wander through your land, do you not stop and enjoy the spectacular view?' Ahmed takes my hand. 'You must join us.'

It isn't a question, and something tells me he's used to getting what he wants. 'We would love to.'

'If you would just excuse us for a second, my heels are killing me,' says Yaz.

We all look at Yaz's four-inch shoes.

'We wouldn't want that,' says Roger, ogling her legs. *Urgh! Better not let Coco catch you doing that.*

'Dusty, can you come with me?' says Yaz, looping her arm in mine and pulling me with the formidable power of a rhinoceros.

'Can't keep you away from those rooms, can we, Dusty?' says Roger. 'Now you can take a Penny in them too.' He snorts like a donkey.

I look pointedly at Ahmed. 'How do you keep your sides intact with this joker around?'

Ahmed chuckles. 'I like her,' he says to Roger.

Roger grunts a noncommittal reply.

Yaz doesn't speak until we're in the restrooms, and only then once she's checked the cubicles are empty and bug-free.

Satisfied, she turns to me. 'I'm bursting for the toilet,' she says, while indicating for me to switch off my amulet. 'We don't have long. Did you know Roger and Ahmed were friends?'

'What? No. Bit of a crazy coincidence, eh?'

'I don't believe in coincidences,' replies Yaz.

'Err … but just because Roger knows Ahmed doesn't mean he's involved in anything dodgy. You heard him, they met at boarding school.'

'Hmm.' She doesn't sound convinced.

'And Roger deals with antiques, not weapons. Unless you count a samurai sword from the ninth century.'

Yaz remains silent.

'Do you think I should warn Roger?'

'And jeopardise the operation? No!'

'Oh, yes, I hadn't thought of that.' I bite my lip anxiously. 'I'm sure there's a simple explanation.'

'Dusty, this mission is very important,' says Yaz, as if I needed reminding.

'I know that.'

'The dangers are very real. We must stick to protocol.'

'Yes, yes, I get it.' I shift nervously. 'The thing is …'

Yaz stares at me for a moment, an indecipherable expression on her face. 'What is it?'

I swallow nervously. 'Well, I sort of arranged my sister's hen party here in Marrakesh. Kill two birds with one stone.'

Yaz explodes. 'You did what!'

'And they arrive tomorrow.'

Yaz starts pacing up and down, muttering something that I suspect results in my murder. Eventually she stops, her voice clipped with fury. 'Well, good luck with that.'

'You won't say anything?'

She folds her arms and glares at me. 'I haven't decided.'

Yaz switches on her pendant and flushes the loo. I do the same.

Back at the bar, there's a bottle of expensive champagne waiting for us. I look at Roger and he gives me his usual condescending smile.

'Erm … Roger, there's something I need to tell you,' I say in a low voice, covering my amulet with my hand. I notice Yaz does the same.

'What is it?' asks Roger.

'Coco!' I say.

Roger sits bolt upright. 'What? Where?' His head swivels round.

'She's not here. Err … not yet, that is. She arrives tomorrow.'

'Good God!' He stares at me, appalled. 'She thinks I'm in Paris.'

Folding my arms, I can feel my anger rise. 'Yes, and why is that?'

Roger stalls. 'Well, you know how much she loves shiny stones?'

True enough. 'Yes.'

'You can save a small mortgage outside Europe. It's a morning present after D-Day.'

'D-Day?'

'Dragged Into Matrimony Day.'

I give a snort of laughter without meaning to. 'Don't let Coco hear you saying that.'

I look at Yaz with an I-told-you-so face. Of course Roger would have a perfectly good reason for being here.

'Dusty, Coco mustn't know I'm here.'

'Careful, Roger, the mapping of a marriage is where the roads will lead one day,' says Ahmed. 'One wrong turn and you get lost in the wilderness of lies.'

'That is so true, Ahmed.' I take my hand away from the amulet and flash him a smile. 'And now, Roger owes me big time and I will make him pay for … eternity. So, is your business jewellery?' I ask Ahmed.

'No, I am many things, but a jeweller is not one of them. I am an avid collector of ancient Arabic ceramics and pottery. Over the years I have acquired one of the most important collections in the world,' he says proudly. 'I sometimes have advantages over the museums.'

'I advise Ahmed,' Roger adds. 'Often if a museum doesn't have the funds Ahmed buys it and lets the museum borrow it for exhibitions and study. Of course, he rewards me handsomely for my consultancy capabilities.'

I fake a yawn.

Ahmed looks wounded. 'My dear, ceramics is not boring. No, indeed not, as long as someone reveals the life force, the magnificence of the story behind the shape, the structure, the decoration, what it depicts about the people at that time, their stories. Let me show you my collection of golden urns and I promise you will see the true untarnished beauty.'

'I'd love to have a look at your golden pots,' I say, flirting outrageously. Roger looks like he's going to throw up.

Another man joins us and I instantly recognise him as Hakim Fakhouri, head of security.

'Hakim, this is the delightful Miss Dusty Hall,' says Ahmed, 'And her friend …' He's already forgotten Yaz's name.

'Penny,' she reminds him with a smile.

He smiles broadly. 'Penny for your thoughts. I won't forget again. Dusty … Penny, this is Hakim Fakhouri, he's my head of security.'

'Why do you need security for your pots?'

'Not for my pots, but for my hotel.'

'You own this?' I say, like I didn't already know.

He smiles, showing off his white teeth. 'It is my pride and joy.'

Hakim lowers his mouth to Ahmed's ear. I look over at Yaz and can see she is listening intently.

Ahmed dismisses Hakim with a flick of his hand, turning to me with a smile. It's a real shame Ahmed's a criminal, he's rather handsome to look at. 'Of course, old pots, as you put it, are not my only love. My passion is collecting beauty … and you are beautiful, Dusty. Perhaps you will dine with me tomorrow night?'

Who doesn't like being called beautiful? 'I would love to.' I beam.

'Until then, my sweet bird of paradise.' He kisses my hand and I feel all tingly inside. I give Roger a sisterly peck on the cheek and watch them disappear.

'Hard to believe he's done all those bad things,' I whisper to Yaz on our way to the lift. 'He's so charming, don't you think?'

Yaz looks appalled. 'Don't be fooled by his charm. And Hakim doesn't trust us. I make him nervous. Ahmed told him to relax, called him an impatient cougar. He also called you a harmless dizzy English butterfly.'

'Ahmed said that?' I'm a little disappointed. But isn't that the role I'm here to play? Although I wasn't actually playing.

When we return to our room, the adjoining door flings open.

'In here,' says Adelstein, holding the door open.

Yaz and I follow Adelstein to where Morley and Jacob are sitting. They are huddled over a couple of monitors. Hakim's face is being run through the database and it's a match to MI6's most wanted list. On another monitor is a photo of—

'Can you identify this man?'

What the hell is this? I don't understand.

Roger Montgomery Clinch. Residence: Chelsea. Fiancée: Ms Coco Hall.

Roger Clinch has many diplomatic connections. He is very active on the Middle Eastern circuit. Member of the polo, golf, and private men's clubs of Chelsea.

Mr Clinch has a variety of international relationships away from various museum's databases. He went to Eton and graduated from Oxford. He was always in the company of rich Arabs in Oxford. Shared rooms in Eton with an Ahmed Al Sahid, also shared a house in their last year at Oxford.

I stare at them, feeling ambushed. 'Yes, that's Roger … but … he advises Ahmed in ceramics and borrows antiquities from his collection.'

'We raided his financial files,' says Morley. Roger's bank account pops up on screen and the figure displayed is huge. I'm shell-shocked. Good God, I didn't know he was that rich.

'He said that Ahmed paid him well,' I reply feebly. 'Roger's family are wealthy …' I tail off. No one is listening to me.

'Can you confirm what they're saying in this recording?' asks Adelstein.

Yaz nods and starts translating. 'Hakim asks, "Who are these persons? We are here for business, there is no need for an audience, it's delicate."'

The recording starts up again and Yaz translates. 'Ahmed says, "Relax, my impatient cougar. Business is part of life. Life interrupts business. Drown your demons in your own time, Hakim. This is the sister-in-law of my friend. She is a harmless, dizzy English butterfly." Hakim then says, "I do not like her or her friend. Stop wasting time on whores."'

Whores! I catch Yaz's eyes but she doesn't seem the least bit offended.

'Ahmed then goes on to say, "I am a man of many worlds, Hakim. Don't forget you are just a small part of mine." Sounds like he's getting a bit angry at this point.'

Adelstein asks Jacob to run the skeleton program, whatever that is.

Yaz and I return to our room and I drop the amulet onto the bedside table and head out onto the balcony. The evening air is warm. I'm really not sure what to make of this latest development. Roger might be a pain in the butt but he's not a terrorist. But how does that explain the money? No wonder he can afford that amazing flat in Chelsea and the most lavish wedding this side of Versailles. I just thought he was a silver-spooned twat.

'Have you really arranged your sister's hen weekend alongside a covert mission?' Yas asks, joining me out on the balcony.

I nod.

Yaz shakes her head in disbelief. 'It's so reckless, not to mention stupid. A hundred percent moronic.'

'I know that but honestly, if you met my sister, you'd understand. I had no choice.'

'The things we do for family,' she says, staring out into the night sky. 'The stars are so bright. You don't get this back home.'

I nod in agreement. 'Too many rainclouds. You won't say anything, will you?'

'No, your secret is safe with me.'

'Thank you.'

'But you do know if Adelstein finds out you're dead.'

I laugh nervously. 'You're not really serious?'

Yaz raises her finger and moves it across her neck. I gulp. 'Worse than dead.'

'Is that even possible?'

'Oh, yes,' says Yaz, and I really can't tell if she's being serious or not. 'But if anyone can pull it off, it is you,' she adds cheerfully.

CHAPTER EIGHTEEN

The lights are dim and the words 'Cleaning and Maintenance' appear on the big screen in front of us. Who the bloody hell starts a conference at 8:30 a.m. in the morning? I didn't even have time for breakfast and I would have overslept if Yaz hadn't woken me, or more specifically dragged me up by Darth Vader's choke grip. I just turned over, insisting on one more minute. And then there was her hand, and that was moi up whether I liked it or not.

I didn't sleep particularly well. No surprise, considering Roger is connected to all this. I'm still hoping there's a simple explanation though—association rather than participation.

A series of toilets appear on the giant screen—when you've seen one toilet, you've seen them all. I'm really not listening but judging by those around me you'd think that Steve Jobs was talking. The speaker's name is Ikram Hassi and the audience appear to be hanging off his every word. My old boss Geoffrey Monks would lap this up. 'Toilets are the first and last thing a customer sees and we pride ourselves on having clean, spotless toilets

…'

'What are you doing?' I whisper.

'Taking notes,' Yaz whispers back.

'In case we get asked some questions?'

Yaz raises her eyebrows. I'm not sure she heard me.

'Like undercover stuff,' I whisper.

She looks at me with amusement. 'We are undercover.'

'Shall I take notes too?'

'It's not necessary.'

I pull out my pen anyway. 'Who are all these people?'

'They're our competition.'

I look around, confused.

'For the contracts. These are the other companies competing for a cleaning contract.'

I sit up a little straighter, giving the speaker my undivided attention, pen at the ready.

'… the freshness of our toilets is imperative … but our toilets go further than cleanliness and freshness … We adapted our facilities to accommodate Western sensibilities … toilet paper rather than water …'

After the first page of note-taking I give up.

'… hygiene builds confidence … heated toilets seats … soft rolls are crucial …'

I nod, pretending that I am listening, when my phone bleeps, making me jump. I look down at my phone and show it to Yaz. It's a text from Adelstein: *My heels are killing me.* I can't resist tapping out a response: *Heels aren't for everyone.*

Yaz and I stand up and slip out of the room. A few faces gawp at us, but not suspiciously, it's more of a smirk. I also notice the speaker pause and write something down. Doesn't look like we're going in his good books.

As Yaz and I emerge from the conference room and head towards the lift, Hakim passes us. 'Good morning,'

I say politely. He attempts a smile but it comes out as a dark scowl.

The lift pings open. 'Happy fella,' I say, pressing our floor.

'He distrusts everyone,' says Yaz. 'But particularly women. We need to be cautious around him.'

'So, it's a swipe left if he pops up on Tinder, then?'

Yaz gives me a blank stare.

'Don't tell me you've never used Tinder?'

'No.'

'Actually, you're not missing much. So does your father have the same views of the female kind?' I ask before I realise how clumsy the question is. 'Sorry, I didn't mean—'

'I wouldn't know and couldn't care less what he thinks. He left us when we were small.'

'Oh, sorry, I didn't mean to pry.'

'Don't be. I'm not. My mum brought my brother and me up. She's amazing. Taught us to be independent, freethinking, and fearless of religious prejudices. She escaped a life of misery, emptiness and oppression.'

'Crikey, that's pretty heavy. I didn't know.'

'Why would you? You didn't grow up in a country of fanatics and religious constraints.'

'What about your brother?'

'My brother's dead.'

My head whips round in shock. My small talk leaves something to be desired today.

Yaz chews her lip. 'It happened two years ago.'

I reach over and give her arm a squeeze. 'I'm sorry.'

'You're not the one who has to be sorry.'

I can't help but notice the threat behind her words. I want to delve deeper but think better of it.

I tense as soon as we step into Jacob and Morley's room and there on the monitor, appearing larger than life, is an image of Roger. I swallow. I can feel Adelstein watching me. My eyes meet his briefly. I really don't know what to say. I feel like Roger is somehow my fault.

'Hall, I want you to get into Roger's room and bug it,' instructs Adelstein.

'Okay,' I say. Yaz's eyes meet mine, and she nods reassuringly.

'Yaz, you return to the conference with Jacob.'

'Yes, sir.'

Jacob jumps up and quickly steps next to Yaz. Yaz frowns at him and he takes a step away.

I pull out my mobile and walk away from the group. Roger answers on first ring. 'Hey, Rodgepodge, it's me. Are you in your room?'

'Yes, but I'm just about to leave.'

'Oh? Where are you going?'

'None of your beeswax.'

I cup my hand over my mouth. 'I just thought you might like to have Coco's itinerary for the weekend, so you know where she's going to be, but if you're going to be like that …'

'You did an itinerary?'

'Yes.'

'Bloody hell, Dusty, rather grown up and organised for you.'

'Spreadsheets are not just for the boring,' I reply.

'Okay, but you have to be quick. I need to leave in five minutes. Room 437.'

It takes me just five minutes to get to Roger's room. He answers on my first knock,

'My, my, you really are full of surprises,' says Roger as he ushers me inside. 'I thought you were bound to get confused between riads and rooms.'

'Here's the itinerary,' I say, shoving it in his hand.

'Wow. Your room is so much bigger than mine.'

'Naturally.'

I wander over to the large box on his bed. The lid is opened and I peep inside.

Roger literally dives over and slaps my hand away. 'Don't touch!'

'All right, keep your hair on,' I say.

'It's a fritware spouted jug.'

'And I'm supposed to know what that is?'

'Of course not,' he says rather condescendingly. 'But trust me, it is very rare, so no touching.'

'It isn't even very pretty.'

'Well, that may be, to the untrained eye.' Roger smirks. 'Right, come on, chop, chop. I've got to get going.'

'Where are you going?'

'Nowhere you need to know. Now hurry up.' He closes the lid and picks up the box.

'Ahmed is an interesting character. Is he very rich?'

Roger pauses and gives me a stern look. 'Now listen, Dusty. Ahmed is not a man for you.'

'Shouldn't I be the judge of that?'

'Ahmed is … a man of the world.'

'Better and better.'

'No. I mean, he's a player. He has a new girl on his arm every week. Better not to get involved with him.'

'Oh, come on, Rodge, I'm a big girl. I know the type.'

'Err, no, you don't,' he replies. 'I'm only looking out for you, like a big brother-in-law should.'

'Don't worry about me. I know all about men.'

There is a knock at the door and Roger's head jerks up in alarm. He rushes to the door.

'What is keeping you …' Hakim stops when he sees me standing there.

'Hello.' I wave and give him a smile.

'Dusty was just giving me my fiancée's itinerary.'

'May … I?' He doesn't wait for a reply and whips the itinerary from Roger's hands. His eyes scan over it, and then, satisfied, he hands it back to Roger. 'I didn't realise your visit was going to be a shared family experience.'

'It wasn't meant to be,' Roger replies.

Hakim holds the door open. 'You need to keep to the agreed schedule.'

'I was just leaving,' says Roger. I have no choice but to leave with them. I didn't have time to place the bugs.

'Oh!' I shriek. Roger and Hakim turn round in surprise.

'What?' asks Roger, looking concerned.

I peer down at my legs. 'Time of the month.'

Roger looks mortified. Hakim looks confused.

'Menstruating,' I explain to Hakim. Hakim's confusion turns to disgust. 'Can I use your bathroom, Roger?'

'Yeah … sure,' he says, recovering from his embarrassment. 'Just make sure you, err … flush and, err … shut the door when you leave.'

'Will do.'

I wait in the bathroom until I hear the front door click shut, then whisper into my locket. 'Roger is on the move.'

'Roger that.' Morley snorts. 'I mean copy that.'

I get to work planting the bugs: one in the potted plant in the bathroom, another on the bedside table, and another on the top of the balcony doorframe. 'The greenflies have landed,' I say into my locket mike.

'Copy that.' It's Adelstein. 'I want you to head to the corner of Bab Fteuh and Souk Semmarine. Jacob and Morley will be in a yellow camper van. Use your GPS.'

'Okey-dokey. Bab for two? And suit seminar? Err—got it.' I grin, feeling a moment of pride, a job well done. I'm just letting myself out of Roger's room when Hakim appears behind me. I jump in fright; I did not expect to see Hakim so soon. 'Sorry. You startled me,' I say, trying to pretend I'm not fazed. 'I was just admiring the view. It's really something.'

Hakim looks past my shoulder but doesn't go inside. I close the door and make sure I hear a click. We're halfway down the corridor when Hakim suddenly grabs my arm; his grip is unnecessarily tight.

'You must work out with a grip like that. Is wrestling big here?' I try to keep my tone neutral.

'What are you talking about?' he says, letting go. He follows me into the lift and we travel down to the ground floor in silence.

I can feel him glaring at me. I smile, pretending to be unperturbed by his presence. 'With that body, you really should be pay-and-display,' I gush.

'What?' He gives me a baffled stare.

'So, what do you do besides pumping?' I mime lifting weights.

'Yes, yes, I lift weights. I can lift five times my own body weight.'

'Wow! Impressive.' The lift pings, and I step out, my body flooding with relief.

'Are you not going to the conference?'

I bring a finger to my lips. 'Ssshhh, don't tell on me. I thought I might have a look around the market.' I wink, bending down to adjust my shoe, making sure his eyes only have my derrière to feast on, rather than where I'm going. He scowls, but it does the trick.

The city's souk district near Djemma El-Fna Square is open all day, but I am told that the best time to experience the place is at night, so the plan is to come back tonight with the hens.

When I arrive at the square, I find the place crammed with stalls. I weave my way through the busy market, captivated by the sounds and scents all around me. I take my time walking from one stall to the next, pausing to buy some Turkish Delight. Mother loves Turkish Delight, and it's not like Adelstein stipulated a time.

Just off the square I notice some other souks, a labyrinth of stalls selling everything from wickerwork, to rugs and spices, to leather goods and love potions … wait. I halt at the stall and reread the label. Might be worth a shot, if not for me, then Jodie. Imagine having the power to make anyone you desire to fall in love with you. Would you even want that? It's mythical nonsense, but I reckon Jodie would find it amusing, and no harm in a few drops. I hand over twenty dirhams.

The stall owner smiles as he hands over the potion. He looks a bit like Gandalf. I laugh to myself. 'Utilisez-le avec precaution,' he says.

'Oui, je serai prudent,' I say.

I cross over to the next stall and pick up a gorgeous, silky kaftan. The beautiful rich colours of this print take in the full beauty of Africa—the bright yellows of the Sahara and the deep crimson of a bold sunset. Perfect for a hot summer's evening. I brush the fabric on my cheek, so soft, when suddenly my nostrils twitch at a familiar scent. A scent so strong it can dampen the most exotic spices even out in the open air.

I turn to see Roger, carrying that box with extreme care. He stops for a moment and looks around. I dive behind the kaftans. Then I watch as he enters a shop.

'You buy. I give you good price. Cheaper than Primark.' A weathered face is at my shoulder, his eyes hopeful and devilish.

'Sorry, I'm just looking—'

'I give you two for two hundred dirhams. I can't take a dirham less, not one euro, not even a dollar,' says the stall owner.

'Two hundred?' That's not bad.

'What are you doing?' The question comes through my earpiece. It's Adelstein. I forgot the earpiece and microphone were still live. Fumbling for the locket mike, I turn away from the stall owner and whisper into my chest. 'On my way, sir.'

'I can see that. But as a matter of national importance, can you hurry up and choose between the multi-coloured kaftan and the other multi-coloured kaftan?'

How on earth? I whip my head around. Adelstein is standing just a few feet away.

'Okay. Two for a hundred and fifty dirhams.' The stall owner raises his palms in defeat. 'You drive a hard bargain, lady.'

Adelstein continues to stand there, watching me. At least he's smiling.

'I cannot feed my goat for that, it's very best, the very rocky bottom,' says the stall owner.

'Oh, hello,' I say, swallowing hard. 'Fancy bumping into you.'

Adelstein raises his eyebrows. 'You had a run-in with Hakim.'

'Nothing I couldn't handle.'

'I heard.' He seems impressed.

'And you've been hot on Roger's tail ever since.'

'Yes, I have.' No need for Adelstein to know any different. 'Roger went in there,' I say, pointing to the door.

We both turn and watch the door.

'Okay, okay, you make my goat size zero. One hundred my final offer,' says the stall owner.

I whirl around and whip out my purse. 'Deal,' I say, slapping the money in his hands.

The stall owner beams and hands me two kaftans.

Adelstein nudges me, and we watch as Roger exits the shop, disappearing into the crowd. There's something odd about it, though. He's still carrying the box, but …

then it hits me. This time he's holding it with a little less care, a lot less care.

Adelstein lifts his arm to his mouth while he takes my arm. 'Khan. Subject is mobile. Get on it.' His hand slides down around my waist and we walk towards the shop. 'Hall, you're with me.'

The shop is carved out of stone, literally, the sides chiselled out for irregular shelves. On the floor, Persian rugs are scattered underneath overloaded tables. Not one thing matches. It's very exotic.

From the doorway, I notice a man with a salt-and-pepper moustache wearing a typical Moroccan djellaba. He's holding up a vase in the back of the room where an antique till sits on a stone table in the centre. The top of the till is brass with three wooden drawers underneath, its only companion an elaborate blue shisha pipe. Carefully, he places the vase into a box and then a crate. An assistant sees us looking and nudges the man. The man turns and walks towards us, pulling a curtain across the back section. 'Can I help you?'

'Well, that all depends now. Do you have a seventeenth-century Safi vase for sale?'

I whip round in surprise. Adelstein is talking in a Georgian, Deep South 'Old Atlanta' money accent.

'We only sell replicas, err … reproductions here.'

'They are beautiful,' I drawl in a matching Deep South American accent. I love the slow Southern drawl, no hurry to finish a sentence.

'Our work is honoured all over the world,' the owner says. 'My name is Waffif.' He hands Adelstein his business card.

'Oh, honey, look at this.' I pick up a ceramic vase with golden etchings on it. 'Isn't this adorable? It would be perfect for the orangery. You know, by the bonsai garden.'

Let him think we are just a couple of dumb American

tourists.

'Our craftsmen are highly skilled. This is one of our rare pieces of work. Many hours, eight thousand dirhams apiece.'

'That's like two of them big notes. Not much at all, honey.'

Stupid and rich and American!

The door opens and a tall Moroccan steps in. He's wearing a colourful djellaba and he turns his back so neither of us gets a good look, but from the way Waffif reacts he must be important.

'Excuse me,' Waffif says, leaving us quickly.

The Arab man hands the shopkeeper a small brown paper package, which he stuffs behind his djellaba, and they disappear behind the curtain. Waffif returns moments later with the open crate.

'That vase is identical to the vase I saw Roger with,' I say in a low voice. 'It's a fritwarey something-or-other jug. Why would they make a replica of the vase? It's not even pretty.'

'Let's go.' Adelstein grabs my hand and we head for the door.

'But honey, I only spent twenty thousand of that funny money today, just the loose change in the bottom of my bag.' Looking back over my shoulder, I see the men's ears prick up. Mine would too, because that's about fifteen hundred quid.

Once outside, we make our way over to the kaftan stall, Adelstein's eyes firmly fixed on the shop door while I caress the beautiful kaftans and silk scarfs. They would make splendid gifts. I could get one for Jodie and Alice and maybe Mother's birthday? She never likes any of my presents but at least she could wrap Goliath's dodgy knee in it.

'You come back for more, yes? You like that one?'

'It is gorgeous,' I say, wrapping it around my head.

One of us has to behave like a tourist. I move over to the mirror, admiring the swirls of colours and vibrant flowers, which is when I spy the Arab slip out a side door. I shove the scarf into the stall owner's hands and grab hold of Adelstein's hand. 'Side door.'

Adrenaline pumps around my body as we follow the Arab through the market. I realise I'm clutching Adelstein's hand a little too tight, but it's all very thrilling.

'Where did he go?'

Adelstein suddenly pulls me in front of him and I bump against his chest. I look up, but his eyes focus on a point past my shoulder. 'He's getting into a car.' Adelstein's voice is low and I can feel his breath against my cheek. He reads out the number plate and I realise he's not talking to me, but to Morley and Jacob.

'Right, Hall,' says Adelstein.

'Yes?' I say, somewhat breathlessly.

'We can head back to the hotel.'

My brain refocuses. 'Err … sir, if you don't need me, can I hang around here?'

Adelstein looks at me. 'I know what you're up to.'

His eyes travel over my face and I gulp nervously. 'You do?'

'It's okay, Hall, we can afford to spare you. I'm sure the stall owner will be pleased to see his favourite customer return. Just keep your mobile switched on.'

I nod vigorously. 'Kaftans. Yes, I want to pick up some for my friends. Might even treat my mother.'

Adelstein watches me and smiles. He doesn't suspect a thing. 'Well, have fun.'

I give an airy wave. 'Bye.'

Wow, that was easy. I did wonder how I was going to get away to pick up the hen party, and it all conveniently lands in my lap.

I return to the stall when a thought hits me. Roger!

If I hadn't seen it with my own eyes, I wouldn't have believed it. But Roger is wrapped up in all of this. To what extent I don't know, but he's not here just to buy Coco a stonking big ice rock. Then another thought crashes through that thought. Coco! How am I going to break the news to her? This is going to totally push her over the edge. Unless Coco is in on it? She's materialistic enough, and people do many things for love. OMG! Half my family is operating in the criminal underground, and I knew nothing about it!

No. No. Stop. I'm overreacting. Coco is far too holier-than-thou; besides, you have to have nerves of steel and her nerves are barely anchored in a paddling pool. As for Roger, I just can't believe it. He's just a buffoon—unless it's all an act? Then he's a better actor than I am.

That doesn't sit well with me.

Keep calm, I tell myself.

I head over to the kaftan stall, purchase three more kaftans, run to the outer line of stalls and hail a taxi. Coco and the hens will be descending soon. I glance up at the sky. Hens falling out of the sky around about—I look at my watch—now.

It isn't quite the taxi I had in mind, but beggars can't be choosers and I don't want to be late. Five haggles later and I am on my way to the airport with one bearded driver and a bunch of clucking chickens on the roof rack.

CHAPTER NINETEEN

'Dusty!'

I glance up to see Coco waving frantically at me. Surprisingly, she is wearing the hen T-shirt I insisted they all wear—I didn't dream she'd unwrap it, let alone wear it. I thought she would have banished it to the sick bag on the flight over, for being 'too trashy'. On the front of the T-shirt it says 'Climb on or cluck off, I'm on a hen weekend,' and on the back 'Mares at large in Marrakesh. Do not attempt to feed by hand.'

I unbutton my blouse to reveal my own T-shirt. Coco hurls herself into my arms, nearly knocking me off my feet. 'I can't believe it. Marrakesh. I was so sure you were going to cock it up.'

I refrain from taking my usual sarcastic line of defence and turn my attention to the rest of the hens, in particular Michelle, who is hobbling on crutches. 'What happened?'

Coco speaks for her. 'She's torn a bloody ligament in her foot.' Coco makes it sound like Michelle did it on purpose. 'I've told Michelle she doesn't walk properly. You waddle like a duck,' she tells her. 'No wonder your ligaments are protesting.' With friends like Coco, who needs enemies?

'I've got big thighs,' says Michelle, unperturbed. 'I think I might even have one leg shorter than the other.'

'Really?' I stare at her legs. She's wearing a long flowing skirt so it's not noticeable.

'I fell off the treadmill,' Michelle explains. 'I'm trying to lose weight for the wedding.'

'You don't need to lose weight.' Coco rolls her eyes. 'Just learn to walk properly.'

Michelle laughs. 'The foot isn't so bad, but my armpits are killing me.'

'You poor thing.' I like Michelle; she definitely seems the most down-to-earth out of the bunch.

'Poor me, more like,' says Coco. 'I've got to see what Jorge can do with those monstrosities.'

'I really think you should think about replacing Shell,' says Philippa. 'It'll ruin your format. And exactly how does one hop gracefully down the aisle?' She screws up her pretty face. 'Do you think you can hop down the aisle, Shell, without slipping on the scattered rose petals and going arse over tit?'

'Until the reception at least, then it's anyone's arse and tits,' cackles Andrea.

'I'm sure Michelle will practise to make sure she doesn't ruin my day.' Coco's relaxed veneer is cracking.

I hand the hens their itineraries. Coco raises her brow and I can tell she's impressed. 'You did an itinerary?'

'Yes, I did,' I say in my best teacher's voice. 'I've highlighted the times, places and events—oh, and how to get there too, just in case one of the brood flies the nest.'

They all look up with glazed expressions.

'Okay, girls, follow me.'

It's quite nice to be the one giving the orders for a change. I lead the gaggle, who I notice are ever so slightly inebriated, across the airport terminal out to my pre-haggled taxi. They all stand there looking a little shell-shocked at the hen coop on the roof rack.

Coco crosses her arms and glares at me. 'I'm not getting in that.'

'It's that or walk to the hotel,' I retort.

'Hens on top of hens,' trills Philippa. 'How clever.' She stands by the truck and pulls out her phone, takes a selfie, then hops inside. The rest of the coop follows.

'You better not have booked us into some dive of a hotel,' Coco says, climbing into the back.

'Ye of little faith, Coconut,' I reply.

Coco scowls at her childhood nickname and begrudgingly gets inside. 'If I get *E. coli* you're dead!' she retorts.

'Well, that was hideous,' says Coco, getting out of the truck with a shudder. I watch and wait. Finally Coco stops fussing and turns. The look on her face is priceless. Her mouth gapes open like a codfish.

I smile broadly. 'What did you say about a dive of a hotel?'

'Is this a wind-up?' Coco whispers.

I have an urge to laugh out loud. Coco is never impressed with anything I do—until now, that is. It's enough to make me giddy. 'Nope. Now follow me.' I lead the gaggle of hens across the moat and through to the main lobby. The Carlitz Hotel is just as majestic and exciting the second time round, but it's made even more special by the collective coos and gasps from the hens.

I'm further impressed by the attentive staff. The concierge swoops over to us and in no time the baggage is stacked high on a gold-painted luggage trolley, the front desk get them checked in and we're piling into Coco's room. The entire process is such a doddle that I'm feeling I may well pull this off.

'Wow,' Coco breathes.

‘This place is stunning,’ says Andrea, sweeping back the white flowing curtains from the grand balcony doors. ‘What a sanctuary.’

‘I know! Anything for my sister.’

Coco’s eyes narrow suspiciously. I grin.

‘The view!’ Michelle squeals. ‘I can smell the spices from here.’

‘This bed is to die for,’ Andrea squeals, flopping backwards onto the silk cushions.

‘I have died and gone to heaven,’ says Sarah, flinging open the bathroom and marvelling at the bathtub.

‘I like your hair, by the way,’ I say. ‘Très chic.’ Sarah clearly paid a visit to the salon after her botched home dye job. It’s now a pretty coppery-red colour and has been styled into a pixie haircut.

Sarah looks across at Coco. Coco nods approvingly and Sarah visibly sighs.

The one dark cloud on the horizon is Bernie. She’s the only hen who hasn’t said a word since she got here. Her gloomy aura, a foreboding presence in a horror film. She walks over to the minibar and pulls out all the miniature bottles.

‘Right then,’ I say. ‘I’ll leave you ladies to unpack and refresh.’

Andrea grabs a miniature from Bernie and snaps the lid open, taking a swig. Bernie grunts, gets another and does the same.

As I leave the room, I hear my sister holler, ‘Philippa, no shouting from the balcony or you’ll get us chucked out.’

‘I’ll be back to pick you up later,’ I say to the group.

‘Where are you going?’ Coco snoops.

‘Never you mind. Actually, I have a job interview.’

‘Oh, Dusty, not again.’

‘No, I’m still in the same job, we’re just pitching for a cleaning contract.’

'Oh, I see. Well, good luck.'

'Er, thanks.'

Coco has already turned away and is addressing Philippa. 'No nudity either.'

'What, not even a cheeky …'

'No!' the hens shout in unison.

CHAPTER TWENTY

The interview is going well. Really well. There was an awkward moment at the start when the speaker from the conference, Ikram Hassi, asked us why we left the conference early until I explained that one of our clients had an allergic reaction to a cleaning product and we were just checking on how they were. I quickly moved on to how amazing their heated seats and the automatic flush toilet system in their loos are. Much more hygienical. Is that even a word?

'We have adapted our toilets to accommodate our Western visitors,' says head housekeeper Alif Bassam.

'That is very considerate,' I say. 'Sitting on a toilet can be a right pain in the'—I nearly say 'arse'—'bum.'

Alif stares at me blankly.

'Arthritis sufferers,' I explain. 'A warm seat can help relax muscles.'

'I did not think of that.' Alif smiles. 'This is good. We get a lot of elderly visitors.'

I smile brightly. My time at Port-A-Privy didn't go to waste. 'The bottom line'—the pun gets a smile from Alif—'hotels rely on great toilets, and we ensure that our toilets are sparkling. We want people to sit, not squat.'

'I beg your pardon?'

I get up and demonstrate the squat. 'Some people prefer having less bum-to-seat intimacy, whereas we want people to sit at their leisure.'

Alif and Ikram exchange glances.

'I wouldn't say hotels *rely* on great toilets,' says Ikram. 'But they do play an important part.'

'Yes, they do. And we believe in playing our part too. We believe in establishing and maintaining an excellent interpersonal relationship with all our clients, suppliers, employers and outside agencies. We are Hygenic. Reliable. Tenacious.' I'm pretty impressed with myself. I came up with that on the spot.

Alif is nodding enthusiastically.

'We manage and monitor operation planning and performance, ensuring all operational requirements of the contract are met,' interjects Yaz. 'All our cleaners are recruited and trained by us.' Yaz gives some impressive statistics, losing me at trajectory percentiles.

Alif clasps his hands together and gives me a wide grin. 'This sounds wonderful.'

Yaz's face drops. Whoops! Time to rein it in—God forbid they offer us the contract.

'This is the renowned floor cleaner from Germany that we tweaked,' I say. 'We made some alterations.'

'Can you do that?' interrupts Ikram. 'Adapt another cleaner.'

'Oh, yes, absolutely. We believe in staying one step ahead of the game. We even have a research and development team. Well, it's our friend Genie, he's great at tinkering around and improving on stuff. We've called it … Terminator, 1.1. Our prototype was a bit … the previous model was, um … faulty and we had to recall all the products after the fire. But the point is we … learn from our mistakes, and Terminator 1.1 is it. All the way.'

'Fire?' Alif and Ikram exchange a glance.

'Just a small one. Itsy-bitsy.' I don't know what I'm saying, I'm just making it up on the spot. 'Yes, but that's all water under the bridge. If only we had the right ratio of water in the first place. Those pesky chemical reactions! The hotel didn't press charges and all's well that ends well.'

There's a shocked silence. Alif and Ikram stare at us in disbelief.

'It operates by remote control.' I toggle the on switch and it revs like a car motor. The noise makes me jump.

I was not expecting that. Yaz muffles a giggle. I have no idea what Jacob and Morley did to the floor cleaner. They only said that it would ensure we didn't win the contract, but I hope it doesn't kill us in the process.

'It's a little noisy!' I say over the sound of the engine. I daren't look at Yaz, because I can see she's trying very hard not to laugh, if the little snorts are anything to go by. Suddenly the floor cleaner starts to smoke.

'What's happening?' says Ikram, his eyes widening in fear.

But now the floor cleaner is spinning so fast that it looks as if it might spin out of control.

Ikram and Alif jump to their feet. 'Make it stop!' yells Alif.

I press the remote, but nothing happens and the noise is deafening.

'It's going to explode!' gasps Ikram.

'It's not going to explode,' I say firmly. Although I'm not so sure. I desperately toggle the off switch but nothing happens. Suddenly, a lick of flame jumps out.

Alif runs to the wall and grabs a fire extinguisher, drenching the device in foam. The machine splutters and coughs to an abrupt stop. The silence is deafening.

'Shall I get a cloth?' I offer.

'No!' yells Ikram. 'We take care of it.'

'Okay,' I say.

'Please remove the devil cleaner item,' says Ikram.

'Are you sure?'

'Yes. Enough,' says Alif.

Yaz pulls the floor cleaner across the room, its tracks highlighted by dripping liquefied foam.

'Client who had an allergic reaction to a product. This was the product?' asks Ikram.

'Yes.' I beam. 'How did you guess?'

'That will be all.'

Yaz and I walk to our room, towing the broken floor cleaner behind us, which is still smoking.

'That was brilliant,' chuckles Yaz.

I laugh too. 'I've always loved a bit of improvisation.'

'How do I look?' I say, posing in front of the mirror.

'Beautiful.'

'Why do I feel sick to my stomach?'

'Because you're lying to the British government and jeopardising the entire operation.'

I whip my head around and Yaz looks up from her laptop. She grins.

'Are you sure Adelstein said we don't have to report until tomorrow?'

She nods. 'He was very happy with our performance at the interview.'

'He said that?'

Yaz nods. 'Have you ever thought of acting?'

I swallow the lump in my throat. 'Actually, I did train as an actress but that's all behind me now.'

'Really? Wow.' But her eyes have returned to her laptop.

'Did he say anything else?'

But she's not listening, her eyes glued to the screen. Picture a shark's focus on a blood particle, that's how concentrated she is.

'He's probably going to have an early night,' I answer for her.

But somehow, I doubt it. I can't quite imagine him sleeping, let alone getting an early night. I start pacing, my palpitations getting stronger. It's going to take a miracle to pull this off.

I stub my toe on the rug and tumble forwards, colliding with the oversized bronze urn by the balcony doors. Yaz looks up at the noise. 'Adelstein has a conference call this evening with Ottoman and the Hurst.'

And she only thinks about telling me now!

'He has to wait until the Hurst gets back to his house in Surrey.'

'Oh, right.' I pause for a second as I digest the good news. 'So, it's probably going to be a long call?'

Yaz smiles. 'Yeah, probably.'

'Who is the Hurst?'

Yaz stares at me. 'The Foreign Secretary!'

'Oh, yes, yes, I knew that.' I should have known that.

My heart rate resumes its normal rhythm. Adelstein will have more important things to think about than my whereabouts. Suddenly, I feel a lot better and actually I quite fancy a night out to see more of Marrakesh.

An hour later I am wearing a yellow halter-neck minidress (Miu Miu) and a pair of beautiful bow-embellished sandals (Aquazzura). Yaz is still glued to her laptop, although I notice her occasionally glance up. I suppose the unexpected fashion show of indecisiveness has caught her curiosity. I'm not normally so unsure. Guess I'm still a little freaked out about, well, you know, the whole balancing the mission and hen party without getting caught.

I look at my watch. It's almost eight o'clock. 'Are you

sure you don't want to join us?'

Yaz visibly shudders.

'Okay, well, showtime!' I say.

'Have fun.'

'I will.'

To my surprise, the hens are dressed and ready to go. I clock the discarded bottles of Bollinger scattered around the room. 'It looks like the party started without me.'

'They insisted,' says Coco, smoothing down the 'Hen Party' sash over her little black dress. She also has on a 'Bride to Be' tiara and pink fluffy handcuffs attached to her tote bag.

'Shall we go?'

Andrea's and Philippa's dresses leave little to the imagination. They may well be from the Parisian catwalks, but from the alleyways, not the runways. But I need to keep to the schedule, so I usher them all out of the door.

I rush ahead of the twittering gang and peer over the glossy white marble balustrade. I know Yaz said Adelstein would be on a conference call, but no harm in being cautious.

Happy that the coast is clear, I rally the group down the stairs.

What happens next will go down in memory.

'Coco, how do they get all the plants to go up the walls?' asks Sarah, stopping midway on the stairs. She's referring to a tropical plant climbing up the wall. 'Do they have to stick them on each day?'

This causes a hen-rific domino effect.

Bernie treads on Philippa's satin shoelaces. Philippa loses her balance and falls onto Andrea's back, catching the tasselled diamante strand holding up her halter-neck dress, which subsequently slips down, revealing a ridiculous pumped-up strapless bra. Her left hand punches Michelle in the stomach, which in turn makes

Michelle's corset pop open, along with a few rolls of belly fat, as if someone pulled the emergency cord on an inflatable. Michelle tries to protect her modesty but loses her grip on the crutches. The clatter is deafening, just in case anyone enjoying their quiet pre-dinner cocktail in the foyer hadn't already clocked the circus that has just rolled into town. The only ones to make it down the stairs in one piece are me, Bernie, and Coco.

As I look around, the entire foyer is staring straight at us. I glance over at my sister. Her head is lowered, her shoulders hunched, and she's making a strange whimpering sound. At first I think she's crying, but then I notice they are tears of laughter. Bernie, who was all doom and gloom earlier, is clutching her sides and her shoulders are shaking and she's making this strange wheezing noise. I can't help it, I burst into laughter.

'Honestly, I can't take you lot anywhere,' giggles Coco. The hens pick themselves up off the stairs, checking for injuries, but pride is the only injury here.

I usher the giggling hens out of the hotel and we head into Djemma El-Fna Square, where the atmosphere is even noisier than in the daytime. Loud music fills the air along with clouds of shisha smoke. People are dancing, music is playing. I turn to find Coco shaking her hips to the beat and she has a massive smile plastered across her face. She seems so happy. I haven't seen this side to my sister in a long time.

The colourful stalls are illuminated by lanterns, glowing like giant winged fireflies, their rectangular openings shining brightly underneath. From one step to the next, fragrances change and sounds are anew.

This is a bonkers, crazy place, so we will fit in perfectly.

The hens stop every five seconds, but at least they do it without maiming each other. Michelle stops to look at every food store. Andrea and Philippa are enjoying all the wrong kind of attention with their blonde extensions and barely-there dresses. Bernie walks around like a serial killer—the next person to look at her might meet a premature end. Sarah and Coco keep skipping from one stall to the next. We automatically stop at an opening where a crowd gathers around a couple of fire-eaters.

Coco is giddy with excitement. 'OMG. I am definitely having a fire-eater at the wedding.'

'Don't point,' I say, slapping her arm down. Andrea makes her way over to the fire-eaters before Coco grabs her arm and pulls her back.

'I should have a Moroccan-themed wedding. Wouldn't that be so much fun?' Coco's face takes on a faraway look and I realise she is seriously considering the idea. 'I could have golden everything; the entertainers could be golden; the serving staff could dress like fire-eaters.'

Andrea and I exchange looks.

'I could have a banquet of Moroccan morsels at midnight. M&M's,' Coco continues with her train of thought.

'No one serves food out of a packet at a wedding,' is all I can think of to say.

Michelle's ears prick up. 'Packets of food can be good.'

'You don't seriously want to change the theme of your wedding?' I ask.

Coco claps her hands and laughs. 'Oh, Dusty, you should see the look on your face.'

'You jest, but I wouldn't put it past you to throw everything to the wind and make some "vital,"' I say in inverted quotes, '"last-minute adjustments". As in changing the whole damn theme of the wedding.'

Coco throws back her head in laughter. 'Dusty, lighten up!'

'You're always telling me I don't take things

seriously enough.'

'Talking about packages,' interrupts Andrea.

'No, we're not,' says Bernie crossly.

Andrea ignores her. 'Those fire-eaters are packing …'

Bernie tuts. 'You're so common, Andrea.'

'Common is the new word du jour, my frigid friend,' says Andrea.

'Just because I don't sleep with everyone who gives me eye contact doesn't make me …' Bernie doesn't get to finish as the fire-eaters backflip and land, one in front of her, the other in front of Sarah. Bernie's face flames hot as hers makes eye contact.

Andrea barks a laugh.

'Ooh, um …' Sarah shoos him away with the coyness of a girl being asked to dance for the first time.

'How about we get something to eat?' I suggest.

I grab Sarah and herd the hens to the nearest eatery, push my way to the front of the rambling group and follow the waiter to a long cushioned low table, which is streetside under a pretty pagoda hung with little coloured lanterns.

Bernie plonks herself down right in the middle with the grace of a rhinoceros, then snatches a new mouthpiece out of the waiter's hand and immediately starts toking on the water pipes, making faces at the others.

Finally, we're all seated and looking at a menu I don't think any of us really understand. A fresh pot of green tea arrives on the table with seven little green glass cups with silver rims.

The girls talk at each other in excitement, not listening, just talking, apart from Bernie, who sits in a cloud of smoke.

I lean back and attempt to listen, but that's like trying to decipher Urdu from Yiddish. The noise level is high-pitched, and the pitch is set to nonsense. Coco has now gone into detail about changing her whole wedding theme, with an eager audience coming up with equally loony ideas. When you have a relatively cap-less budget, I suppose nonsense can be acquired. I pick up my little cup and jump as my hand gets covered in a cold liquid. Andrea (not even looking at what she's doing) is spiking the drinks with vodka from a hip flask, Bernie's smoke clouds serving as the perfect cover. Then a plain hairy hand appears *Gorillas in the Mist*-style doing exactly the same thing, but Bernie does it with the speed of a poisoner, each totally unaware of the other. I keep my cup safe in hand.

'Who wants soup?' asks Philippa.

'Me. I'm starving,' cries Michelle.

'What a surprise,' mutters Philippa.

'Just as a little starter, though. We will order more, won't we?' asks Michelle anxiously.

Andrea coos at the young waiter and points at the menu in several places. He comes back with a big tureen and hand-sized soup bowls; another waiter comes with three closed pots and some bits and bobs.

Michelle's eyes don't move off the ladle. As soon as he leaves she piles it in to the brim, takes one sip and pulls a face. 'It tastes a bit weird. What is it?'

'Goat's head soup,' says Philippa.

Michelle spits out a mouthful.

Philippa sniggers. 'It's a local delicacy. Oh, all right, try this instead.'

Michelle eyes the meat suspiciously.

'It's okay, it's not goat. Dip it in this,' Philippa eggs on. A look of panic briefly crosses Michelle's face, then disappears when I also pick up a piece of meat.

Michelle dips it in the cumin and salt mix. I do the same.

'Together?' I suggest.

Michelle smiles and we both take a big bite.

'That one is sheep's testicles,' cackles Philippa.

My reflex is to spit it out, but as I chew, it's not nearly so bad. Actually, it tastes pretty good, and surely they wouldn't serve it if it wasn't meant to be eaten.

'You're eating a sheep's testicle,' snorts Philippa.

'How would you describe it, Michelle?' I ask, ignoring Philippa.

'Tender, and sweet.' Michelle chews thoughtfully.

'I suppose we'll all have to try now,' says Coco, picking one up and popping it in her mouth; the others tentatively reach towards the bowl.

'Okay, here it goes! Down the hatch.'

'I'm not putting my mouth around any testicles,' says Philippa.

'Why change a habit of a lifetime,' retorts Andrea and everyone laughs.

Bernie promptly spits hers out, propelling the round missile into the street and hitting a passer-by on the cheek. He looks around, puzzled.

With everyone getting sloppier by the minute, I wonder if I should talk to Coco about Roger before she becomes completely inebriated. Obviously, I need to be subtle about it. 'You know, you don't have to get married.'

Coco looks at me as if I've grown two heads, and those heads have grown two beards. 'What are you talking about?'

'It's just happening so quickly,' I say carefully.

'Not really, we've been planning it for two years.'

'I just want you to be one hundred percent sure before you walk down the aisle, that's all.'

'Is this because I'm getting married and you're not?'

'Coco, this is not the early nineteenth century and we're not part of the Bennet family. I'm happy for you. I just want you to be certain, that's all.'

'I love Roger,' says Coco.

'Well, that's great.' I cough nervously. 'That's what's important.'

'We have the same goals.' Her eyes glaze over wistfully.

But somehow I can't quite visualise her love for Roger stretching to prison visits or the 'for richer, for poorer' marriage clause.

'We're good together. It works, we work.'

'Coco, you can find a business partner anywhere. That doesn't mean you have to marry them. Go to Switzerland, it's bankers galore.'

Coco frowns. 'Roger already has an account there.'

Does he now!

Still, plenty of people have foreign accounts. Transparency is all the rage these days. Perfectly legitimate. Long gone are the days where having a Swiss bank account meant tax evasion with pools of money. The entire world is a global bank, and of course he has a Swiss bank account with his background—he travels quite a bit. Coco would think this quite normal, not criminal.

'I love him. It's difficult to explain why.' Coco giggles and the tiara slips into the tureen. 'We just fit, and he's such fun and so funny.'

'Funny?' I lapse into silence.

'And he has a big—'

'Right,' I say, standing up brusquely and clapping my hands to get everyone's attention. 'Hens, we need to get back to the hotel now.'

'I wouldn't have room for one more ball anyway,' slurs Andrea, draining her drink and standing up with a sway.

'You've got more capacity than most. Isn't that what the Navy boys said?' screeches Philippa.

'You always were sour at me for that night.'

'Not as sour as your knickers in the morning.' The hens laugh.

I'll be honest, I was not expecting to like Coco's friends, but their lewdness and silliness is surprisingly entertaining. I would have much more fun if I were drinking too, if it weren't for the fear of being caught.

We leave the noisy square and head back to the tranquillity of the hotel. Although tranquillity is the last thing on these hens' minds. The hens link arms in a 'show of love and unity', and I have no choice but to join in. At least this helps to prop the wobbly bunch up—that and Michelle at the other end using her crutch as an extra stabiliser. One massive haphazard walking paper chain, arms intertwined, strutting ahead oblivious to onlookers' gawping curiosity.

As we walk through the courtyard, I intend to take them straight to their rooms, but Andrea takes her shoes off and paddles in the pool.

'Andrea, I don't think you're supposed to do that.'

'There's fish in there,' Michelle says, pointing with her crutches.

'Watch where you're poking that thing!' cries Philippa, as she gets a whack on the bum.

'Sorry, Philippa,' says Michelle.

Finally we reach the open air lobby, herding hens is more strenuous than any army obstacle course.

'Can we have an itty-bitty drink?' Coco asks, sliding down my arm.

'I think you've had quite enough for one night,' I say, hoisting her upright.

'No, I haven't!' says Coco, her eyes rolling backwards. She then plonks herself down on a chair resolutely. Everyone else decides this is a good time to stop too.

'No, no, don't sit down. We have to keep moving.' I

try to pull my sister up.

'Hey!' she protests.

'Come on. Everyone up. Up,' I bark, desperate to get them to their rooms. 'You've got a busy day ahead of you tomorrow.'

'I want to go to the bar,' announces Philippa.

'Me too,' cries Coco, jumping up.

'But you have the camel excursion tomorrow.' But no one is listening.

'It is my hen weekend,' pouts Coco.

'I know, but you'll thank me in the morning.'

That's when I hear footsteps behind me. That must be the staff coming to tell us to keep the noise down. When I turn, my stomach plummets and I dart behind Coco. What's Adelstein doing up so late? Shouldn't he be in bed? Doesn't he know what time it is? Christ, he looks like he's been running.

I peek out from behind Coco, but Coco thinks it's an opportunity to waltz-si-do. Coco spins me around, loses her balance and falls back into Sarah, and as perfect examples of Newton's law of motion my squiffy sister propels the group back and forth, inertia moving them like a pendulum. I clasp my sister's arm and she stops swaying.

'Dusty, is that you?'

My stomach lurches. There is going to be big trouble. Huge.

I turn around and smile. The grave expression on Adelstein's face makes me feel quite ill. The hens, I notice, have gone completely silent.

'You've been jogging,' I say.

I've never seen Adelstein in anything but a suit. Now he is all sweaty and masculine, with pumped-up muscles. His biceps look as hard as rocks and his quads are more solid than … than … What am I doing? I'm going to lose my job and all I can focus on are his biceps. What's wrong with me? Don't answer that!

'I see you have made some new … friends?'

'Yes, totally. I just met them today. I don't know them at all.'

My sister scowls at me. 'We've been to Djemma El-Fna Square. It's an amazing place,' says Coco.

'It's really hot, isn't it? I must get out of these clothes,' says Andrea, nudging me out of the way. 'I'm Andrea, and you are?'

'Dusty's boss.'

Andrea's jaw drops to the floor, as does my sister's and the rest of the hens'. Andrea and Philippa eye him up like he's the next plated delicacy.

'Fitzwilliam,' he says. 'And you must be the blushing bride-to-be?'

'How did you guess?' giggles Coco. The fact she is wearing a 'Hen Party' sash, a lopsided 'Bride to Be' tiara and pink fluffy handcuffs seems to have escaped her memory.

'Lucky guess,' he says, giving her a lopsided grin. 'Are you still planning on having the gazelle as ringbearer?'

My sister's face glows in response. 'Has Dusty told you about my wedding?'

'We have all heard a great deal about your wedding,' he replies, shooting me a sideways glance.

'I've decided against the gazelle. It's so passé, and anyway, what if it pooped on its way down the aisle or nibbled a guest's dress?'

'Good point,' he says, pulling a mock-grave face.

'Would you like to join us in the bar, Fitzwilliam?' ask Andrea.

'Yeah … party!' shouts Sarah.

'You can be our honorary hen,' says Philippa, eyeballing him outrageously.

'Wouldn't that make him our honorary cock?' replies

Andrea, brushing up against him.

Adelstein removes Andrea's hands from his chest. 'I'm afraid I will have to decline the offer, but you ladies enjoy the rest of your night.' Adelstein turns to me and I can feel my face growing hot. 'We will talk about this tomorrow.'

'Yes. Of course,' I reply, swallowing nervously, looking away from his eyes, trying not to cry. He turns swiftly and walks away.

That's it. I'll be jobless tomorrow or, worse … dead. Why did I ever think I could pull this off? It's the MI6, for fuck's sake. They are all-seeing, all-knowing.

'Check out his bum, those hips don't lie,' says Philippa. The hens cackle.

'I'm curious, did you get the job on your academic merits? Was the job advert just "see me"? "See me for all positions"?' Philippa cackles.

'Funny, when's your stand-up gig?' I say as she loops her arm through mine.

The bar is empty as I usher the giggling gaggle towards a corner table. The lush tropical garden setting of the bar is très atmospheric. Moorish wooden screens and plants divide off little sections, each secret corner having its own mix of tables, sofas and chairs, some of which look like thrones.

I ask vaguely what they want, then order a pitcher of cosmos without the alcohol. They'll never know at this point. I order myself a large whiskey. I don't even like whisky, but it seems like the right thing to drink under the circumstances. Pretty unforgivable arranging a hen party the same weekend as a top-secret mission. Pretty much the stupidest thing I've ever done, and that's saying something. Will I be hanged, drawn and quartered, or will it be a bullet to the head? If Adelstein only knew how unhinged my sister is at the moment, he would understand why I did it. He would see I had no choice.

It also proves that I can find a solution to a problem. Killing two birds with one stone, that's using my initiative, isn't it? If he really thinks about it, surely this proves that I can … think outside the box? I'm grasping at straws.

I force a haven't-a-care-in-the-world smile onto my face and return to the table of chaos. If I am going to lose my job, I may as well enjoy my last night in Marrakesh, and quite possibly my last night ever.

CHAPTER TWENTY-ONE

'I can't believe you don't have a boyfriend,' my sister slurs, stroking my hair. 'You've got such pretty hair.'

I have never seen my sister this drunk before.

'Your boss is rather cute. You should totally have sex with him.'

'Cute is not the word I'd associate with my boss,' I say with a kind of shrill hilarity, flapping her hand away. 'And I will not be having sex with him. He doesn't even like me.'

Coco looks at me curiously. 'Your eyes are a crazy green-blue colour, did you know that? They're so green, but blue, but green. Like the greenest fly and the bluest of bottles, butterflies, bluebottles and greenfly.'

'I don't think Hallmark will be calling you up anytime soon.'

'As sisters go, you're pretty cool.' Coco leans over, reaching in for another hug.

My sister is definitely drunk because she would never say this to me sober. I remove her strangling arms from around my neck.

'Isn't my sister the best?' she slurs to the rest of the

group whilst balancing herself on my shoulder. The hens throw a general 'cheers' in my direction, spilling half the contents out of their glasses.

'Let's keep the noise down, okay?'

The suggestion backfires and they all start eagerly shushing each other, taking it in turns to fall under the table to surprise-shush the other.

'I think the bartender is waiting to lock up,' I say desperately.

'Oh, no, he isn't!' the hens retort in the manner of a pantomime.

I roll my eyes. 'Oh, yes, he is,' I say darkly.

Just then a figure sweeps into the bar and I immediately recognise him as the mystery man from the ceramic shop. He looks in our direction and then looks away, seemingly unimpressed by a group of drunken women. He sweeps towards a back wall and disappears behind a large tapestry.

The bartender comes over with a jug of drinks, which I told him to keep non-alcoholic. I look up hopefully and he winks in return.

Michelle grabs his hand in desperation. 'Is the kitchen still open?'

'No, madam.'

'Have you any nibbles at all?' This unfortunately sets off the hens into random innuendo mode. 'You know, food?' She mimes eating out of her own hand.

'Ah, food.' He grins and I really can't help noticing how amazingly white his teeth are. 'Let me see what I can find.' The bartender's face softens as Michelle squeezes his hand in gratitude; he seems to enjoy it and stops to notice her properly.

Just as I get up to see where the mystery man went, Hakim walks into the bar and I quickly sit back down, but he has already seen me. I pretend to sway drunkenly in my chair as he looks over. 'Hi, Hakim.' I wave.

He looks appalled and heads over to the bar. Whatever he says to the bartender, it can't be flattering because the bartender looks in our general direction and seems embarrassed.

Hakim sits behind a wooden screen at the front of the bar; I watch the back of his head through the carvings. After a few minutes, the mystery Arab comes back out from behind the tapestry and joins Hakim. I really need to know what they are saying.

The bartender arrives with bowlfuls of nuts, dried breads and dips. 'Happy lady. Food is good. Lady is good,' he says with a heavy accent. He only has eyes for Michelle.

Michelle beams at him.

Our tipsy table is flaking and the only ones really awake and upright are Bernie, Michelle, and myself. I stand up and pull out my mobile. 'Think this one's for the photo album.' I jump up and switch all the settings to silent, then quickly take a photo of my sister, who is dribbling on Philippa's shoulder.

'I quite agree,' says Bernie, picking up her own mobile and angling a close-up of Sarah, who is curled up in a haphazard foetal position. Andrea has spicy Jackson Pollock'd one side of her face, the harissa sauce acting as a pillow, modern art of the cheek.

'What's your name?' I hear Michelle ask the bartender.

'Akila,' he says, looking over his shoulder towards the screen. He then sits next to Michelle.

I move further back, pretending to get a wider angle, press video and crouch behind a palm tree, pushing the phone between the slats of the screen. Hakim and the mystery man are talking within hearing distance, but I don't know what they are saying. Yaz will know. I'm hoping the recording is good enough for her to translate. It might be useful, but then again, they could be talking about the finer works of how to plumb in the desert for all I know—but somehow, I doubt it.

I stand there until I hear the chairs scrape the floor. They're on the move. Quickly, I unravel myself from between the screen and the palm tree and hurry back to my table, my heart hammering in my chest. Bernie gives me an odd look. Sensing Hakim looking over at our table, I throw myself into Bernie's lap.

'What the—' she says in shock.

'Sorry, tripped over that rug.'

'What rug?' she asks as I gracelessly clamber out of her lap, pretending to be drunk, all the while keeping one beady eye on Hakim. He stares over but then diverts his attention back to the ceramics guy. They disappear behind the tapestry again.

I wait for a minute, then get up and walk over to the tapestry. I look behind me and Akila and Michelle are still engrossed with trying his delicacies (the food ones). Bernie is watching me and gives me a smile. It's the first proper smile I've seen from her since she got here. She then nibbles away at what's left on the table.

I move towards the tapestry and have a peek behind. It's a tunnel. I race back to the table. 'Right, shall we get this lot to bed?'

Michelle looks up, her cheeks flushed with happiness. I look at my watch. It's now two in the morning.

'I'll help,' says Bernie.

Michelle grabs her crutches. 'Pass me the bags, I'll hold them.'

'I can help,' says Akila kindly.

'Are you able to leave the bar unattended?'

'You are my last customers.'

'Then yes, please, that would be wonderful.'

It isn't easy, but between Bernie, Akila and Michelle we have the combined strength of a wrestling team and get the sleeping beauties tucked up in their beds.

'Off you go, Dusty. I'll make sure there's water at hand,' says Bernie.

'You're an angel, thanks.' I stifle a yawn.

I don't know why I thought Bernie was so miserable. She's really rather sweet, plus freakishly strong.

I return to my room and close the door firmly behind me, resting my forehead against it, glad the night is finally over. Can't undo what's been done. Learn from it and move on… tomorrow is a new day. I have just finished my pet talk when I feel a gentle cold breeze on the back of my neck. My body stiffens. I turn and see a figure move in through the white curtains. 'Is somebody there?'

'Yes, me you idiot,' says Yaz.

I laugh in relief. 'What are you doing up?'

'I was just getting some fresh air.'

'It's three o'clock in the morning.'

'I couldn't sleep.'

'Is it my fault?'

'No. Why would it be your fault?'

'Because Adelstein knows about my sister. He bumped into us in the foyer,' I say despairingly.

There's silence as Yaz takes this in. 'You could try to spin it. Tell him you thought it would help your cover.'

'You think?' I say, with a glimmer of hope.

'Perhaps not. What was tonight like?' she asks, climbing into bed.

'Like herding vodka-soaked catfishes in an overcrowded paddling pool.'

Yaz giggles. I trot off to the bathroom to wash the night away from my face and change into my chemise. I return to the bedroom, turn off the lights and get into bed. I'm just sinking my head into the finest Egyptian cotton that's lulling me into slumber when I remember the recording. I jolt awake. 'I saw Hakim in the bar, talking to a mystery man from the ceramic shop.'

Yaz switches the lamp on. 'Did you get a good look at him?'

'Not really, but I recorded their conversation. Not sure if I got close enough. Oh, and there's a secret passageway behind the hanging rug in the bar.'

'Let me listen.' Her tone is urgent.

'What, now?'

'Yes. Now.'

'Okay.' I open the recording app on my phone and hand it over.

We both listen to a snippet of muffled conversation. The colour of Yaz's face turns ashen.

'Is it bad?'

'We need to give this to Adelstein right away.' She jumps out of bed and flings on a tracksuit. She chucks a hotel bathrobe at me. 'Come on, then!'

I pull on the bathrobe, tightening the belt around my waist. I don't want to face Adelstein so soon, but Yaz's vice-like grip means she's not taking no for an answer. 'Yaz, you don't really need me there. Why don't you give the recording to Adelstein yourself?'

Yaz stops and faces me. 'I wouldn't worry about Adelstein. Not when he hears what's on this recording.'

'What did it say?' I ask, twisting the belt tighter round my waist.

Yaz nods. 'All in good time.' Her face is focused and unemotional as she hurries across to the partitioning doors.

This time, it's our turn to barge through the adjoining doors. A sleepy Morley and bedraggled Jacob bolt upright in their beds. Yaz heads straight over to the next connecting door, but before she has time to knock, Adelstein flings open the door. 'This better be good.'

'It is,' replies Yaz, handing him the phone. Yaz appears completely oblivious to the fact that he is bare-chested, with a pair of silk bottoms hanging off his toned hips. He turns, and I gasp in shock. Across his back is a deep, long scar that looks like a hideous knife wound.

'Hakim asks if the swap was made and then'—she pauses for a second—'the other man said yes. He says the stones have been carefully arranged and the USB stick is in place.'

Adelstein's eyes fire up. He pulls on a shirt and marches over to the other connecting door. Morley and a bedraggled Jacob are already at the desk. Morley has the most ridiculous pyjamas on, white with small black and white emperor penguins assembling red and black penguin robots on a production line. Jacob stands straight in a silken robe, a geek Hugh Hefner. Adelstein signals for us to join him at the writing desk. 'Outstanding work, Yaz.'

'Actually, sir, this is Dusty's doing. She got the recording when she was out tonight.'

Adelstein stares at me for a while.

'So, lucky for us that Dusty was there, to get a recording, wasn't it?' Yaz throws me a sly wink. I give Adelstein an awkward smile.

Adelstein hands the phone to Morley. 'Import the video and get the best still you can of the other man. Clean up the image for an identity scan.'

Jacob runs into the other room and fires up his superpowered laptop. Morley plugs in the mobile and Jacob extracts all the photos. My face becomes hotter as photos of the hens pop up one by one, a speedy insight into the stages of their inebriation, even more embarrassing when interspersed with the fire-eater's torso. All eyes are now on me; I cough and look down at my feet.

They return their attentions to watch the computer screen. One face morphs into another. 'I couldn't catch the entire conversation, but they definitely mentioned the swap,' says Yaz, her mouth tightening as she stares at the image on the screen.

'Who is he?' I ask.

'Nothing is coming up. We vill need to release the image,' says the monotonal Jacob.

'Oh, no. Not CIA, you might as well put it on YouTube. They've got more leaks than the LHC tunnel,' says Morley, whatever that means.

'Morley, get it back to headquarters. There's no time to waste. Khan, you come with me. Bring your gun,' says Adelstein.

My heart is shuddering. What the hell has Roger got himself involved in?

Yaz leans over and squeezes my arm in reassurance.

'Sir,' I blurt. 'I just want to apologise for my … um, for bringing my sister's hen party to Marrakesh.'

Adelstein glances at me, his eyes flashing, looking more terrifying than usual. 'And for compromising an operation that's taken a year to set up? That's very decent of you.'

My cheeks flush. 'I promise it will never happen again. I am fully committed to Duty Calls and I want to continue serving the company … country … to the best of my ability, giving one hundred percent every day, now and in the future.' I almost want to add 'amen', an Oscar speech in the making.

For a long moment Adelstein just stares at me and I feel my cheeks getting hotter and hotter under the scrutiny. He finally says, 'Just keep your sister and the hens away from Roger.'

'Yes, sir, I will. I can do that. I will do that. You won't even notice them.'

'You know the family resemblance is uncanny,' he dryly adds.

'Oh,' I say, feeling a little insulted. A belly full of vodka and he thinks our whole DNA pool is set on stupid. ‘She’s not normally like that,’ I say, coming to my sister’s defence. ‘What do you expect? Exemplary decorum? It is her hen weekend. Er …’

‘Wait there,’ instructs Adelstein. Oh, God, I should have kept my mouth shut. He’s gone to get my P45 or equivalent. Do the Secret Service even have normal forms of admin?

Adelstein says something to Jacob and Morley, who return to their software. I don’t move a muscle. I stand there like some spare wheel, square in shape, with no use. I open my mouth a couple of times to apologise, but think I’ve said enough.

Then he’s back. ‘Come with me.’

‘Where to?’ I yelp. ‘What are you going to do to me?’

He shoots me a bewildered look. ‘You? Nothing, but it’s time we had a little chat with Roger.’

‘Can I change first?’

He shoots me another look. This one is a little different and my stomach does a flip. ‘I think that’s a good idea.’

I make a dash to our room, pulling on the first item of clothing that comes to hand when I catch sight of myself in the mirror and do a double-take: I’ve put on flip-flops with the silk colourful kaftan I bought from the market. I look like I’m heading to the beach, not about to interrogate a prisoner. Is that what Roger is, a prisoner?

Adelstein makes no comment on my attire. Talk about a fish out of water then add skydiving towards the rocks. That’s how nervy I am.

We reach Roger’s room. Yaz moves to one side of the door, pressing her back to the wall, gun lowered in two hands. Adelstein does the same on the other side.

I step forward and tap on the door. ‘Roger! Cooey!’ I tap again, louder. ‘Roger, are you awake?’

I put my ear flat to the door. I can hear snoring. ‘Roger!’ I bang on the door. ‘Open up.’

The snoring stops. I hear the plod of sleepy steps getting closer to the door.

'Bloody hell, Dusty. Have you any idea of the hour?' says Roger, glaring at me. His face turns to shock and confusion when Adelstein and Yaz rush at him.

Everything happens so fast. Adelstein grabs Roger's arm and bends it behind his back, pressing the gun to his cheek. Yaz signals him to move back inside with hers, putting a finger to her mouth, signalling to him to keep quiet. Roger is totally petrified.

'Move quietly and you won't die.' Adelstein's voice is low and chilling.

Roger whimpers, staggering backwards. Yaz jabs a needle into his arm, and thirty seconds later he melts to the floor.

Adelstein goes down the small corridor outside looking for I really don't know what, all the while I'm frozen to the spot—the fish has crashed onto the rocks. Adelstein is back seconds later with a laundry trolley and throws Roger into it.

'Don't just stand there, Hall. Get the vase. I've only given him a mild sedative; it won't last long.'

I scour the room and find the vase tucked inside his suitcase.

CHAPTER TWENTY-TWO

By the time we've wheeled Roger back, Morley and Jacob have transformed the room, a makeover orchestrated by Darth Vader himself—dark, menacing and eerie. All the walls have been draped with some dark material, the air is still and black. A single chair stands underneath a bright light. Morley and Jacob have been busy bees. It looks like an interrogation scene out of a movie.

Adelstein places a black hood over Roger's head. Next, he ties his wrists with plastic cords to the back of a heavy wooden chair.

We wait in silence for signs of consciousness. Yaz doesn't look at me. Her focus doesn't flinch from the slumped figure in front of her.

Roger groans and tries to move his feet. Adelstein whips the hood off and Roger blinks in the bright light. He looks utterly bewildered. Yaz pulls a chair up to the left side of him and aims a gun at him. Roger shuts his eyes in terror, then opens them again when he realises he hasn't been shot. *Yet!*

'How long have you been smuggling for Ahmed Al

Sahid?' asks Adelstein.

Roger blinks at him. 'I don't know what you're talking about.'

Adelstein shoves a photo of Roger and Ahmed shaking hands in front of Roger's face. 'Stop the act. You're up to your neck in it, Mr Clinch.'

'I am … a curator,' Roger stumbles out a reply. 'Mr Sahid is a collector.'

'How long have you been smuggling for Ahmed Al Sahid?' repeats Adelstein.

'There's no harm in sourcing ceramics for him. Free trade is not a crime. As a matter of fact, the British museums benefit from his generosity.' His pompous, indignant tone re-emerges.

'Really? No harm in illegal smuggling?'

'Smuggling?'

'The naive damsel act doesn't really suit you. Cut the bullshit.' Adelstein's voice rises a fraction.

I step forward out of the shadows. 'Just tell him the truth, Roger.' I am genuinely worried about Roger's safety.

'Dusty! Is that you? What are you doing here? Is this some kind of practical joke?'

'This is no joking matter. You are up for some serious prison time, or I believe they cut off your hands here,' says Adelstein dryly.

Roger's eyes flick between me and Adelstein. 'I know nothing about smuggling …'

I pick up the vase and start throwing it from one hand to the other. Roger doesn't even wince at the careless handling of his precious vase. 'Roger, aren't you afraid I might drop this? Isn't it supposed to be very rare?'

Roger stares at me, a look of surprise on his face. 'It is. Dusty, be careful.'

'We know it's fake, Roger.'

'I don't know what you're talking about and I demand

to see my lawyer.'

'The only lawyer you'll be seeing is through TV re-runs for years on end if you don't cooperate,' I snap, which gets a chuckle from my teammates. 'Is there a secret compartment? Is that how you smuggle the diamonds?'

Roger continues to stare at me as if he's unable to compute who I am or why I am with these people. 'What? Diamonds? What a preposterous … There's no secret compartment, what a lot of tosh. Now listen here, you peo—' Roger pulls at the plastic ties.

Adelstein gets right up close to Roger's face and places both hands on the chair arms, his muscles visibly pumped, veins protruding through his skin. Roger flinches.

'The museum keeps you very busy, Mr Clinch, but all those pots and vases never go on display. Hiding all the cargo in a vault in case the Nazis come back, are we?'

It stuns Roger into silence.

'After all, no one would suspect a museum curator. The perfect cover for a smuggler. You walk through with the fake and have the original go through with someone else. Someone who just looks like a tourist, or maybe even Ahmed occasionally?'

'Who are you people?' Roger's eyes flit from one person to the next, then he stares at me, still unable to compute.

I feel desperate for Roger but remind myself that he brought this on himself. I shake the vase. Nothing rattles. I poke at it roughly, twisting it in my fingers, first one way then the other, when suddenly there's a click. A wooden rose carving springs open from the base and a USB stick hangs out. Stunned, I peel it off its compartment.

Roger stares at it, all the cockiness gone. 'What's that?' he says unconvincingly.

'You tell me.'

'Where are the diamonds? Shake it again.' Roger breaks off when he realises he's made a gargantuan blunder.

'Roger!' I say, throwing him a disappointed look. 'How could you do this? How could you do this to Coco?'

'I was just helping a friend out.'

'By smuggling diamonds into the country?' I say.

'The import duty is ridiculously high. It's only a few diamonds to sell on the open market. Your old boss, Garibaldy Giraffay, is a keen buyer.'

'So what's this, then?' I ask. We all stare at the small USB stick.

'I actually don't know,' Roger shakily replies. Adelstein gets into Roger's face again, and Roger starts visibly sweating. 'I don't know. Honestly. I swear.'

'Mr Clinch. We have a job for you,' says Adelstein, his voice low and menacing.

'Anything. I swear—'

Adelstein stands up abruptly. 'Hood and gag him.'

Roger whimpers. 'But I said I would help.'

Yaz stuffs gagging material into his mouth and pulls the hood over his head.

Adelstein nods for me to follow him. 'Run it, Morley.' Morley puts a pair of earphones over Roger's head. 'Run it for ten minutes.'

'What are you going to do to him?' I'm slightly concerned with the way Morley is twiddling the knobs. 'You heard Roger, he said he'll cooperate.'

'I know. This is just an extra … guarantee,' replies Adelstein.

'Are you blasting him with the national anthem?'

Adelstein looks at me, half-irritated, half-amused. 'Something like that.' Which tells me nothing.

Adelstein types into an encrypted message service,

cleverly disguised under a wooden shaving soap pot.

'But you will let him go?' I ask.

'For now.' Adelstein holds my gaze; his expression is fierce. I gulp. I wouldn't want to be at the mercy of Adelstein. Being on the same side is terrifying enough.

When I walk back to the room, Yaz is waiting for me. 'You okay?'

'Coco is going to lose her mind completely and forever when she finds out.'

'She better not find out and telling her was taken away from you as an option when you signed the Official Secrets Act.'

'Oh, yes, I keep forgetting.'

Yaz's eyebrows nearly disappear into her hairline.

He's going to end up breaking my sister's heart, and I hate him for it. My parents will be devastated too. They like him. Sometimes I think they might like him better than me. And he did all this because of money.'

'You can take Roger back to his room now,' Adelstein says from behind me.

I jump. 'In the laundry trolley, or can he walk back to his room?'

Adelstein gives me a small smile. 'He can walk. If he gets a little panicky just say, "We are the champions."'

I shoot him a surprised, curious look. 'A Queen song?'

'I think it's quite fitting, don't you?'

'We are the champions.' I smile. 'Got it, sir.'

I have no idea what they did to Roger, but Roger has stopped sweating and is looking quite cheery.

'Hey there, Rodgepodge, you ready to go?'

'Oh, hi there, Dusty,' replies Roger brightly.

'You coming?'

'What? Oh, yes.' Roger gets up from the chair and looks around, then at me, as if he's not quite sure why he's here, then seems to accept it, accept it all.

Walking Roger back to his room takes no time at all. Roger doesn't speak; he seems to glide. I wait until he climbs into bed, pausing in the doorway. 'Good night, Roger.'

'Yes. Good night, Dusty, sleep well.' His voice is polite and untroubled. Bizarre.

I finally get back to my room and to bed. The lights are already out and Yaz is gently snoring.

I roll over and clutch the pillow to my chest. Maybe working as a receptionist for a Portaloo company wasn't such a bad career choice. Life was simpler—dull as dishwater, but simpler.

I fall asleep. Mental and emotional exhaustion at its maximum.

CHAPTER TWENTY-THREE

The alarm on my watch bleeps and I drag myself out of bed, shower, and dress. Two hours is not sleep, it's a snooze at best, but according to my stupid itinerary, I'm supposed to be having breakfast with my sister and the hens this morning.

Yaz expels a loud yawn and sits up. She looks at me quizzically.

'I'm meeting the hens for breakfast.'

She nods. 'Just remember to act normal. Give nothing away. Say nothing, okay? Absolutely nothing, Dusty.'

'Yes, yes, got it.'

She smiles, which turns into a yawn, and then promptly flops backwards, which is exactly what I want to do.

As I approach my sister's room, I notice the door is ajar and my heart gives a jump. Something doesn't feel right. I stare at the door and listen, trying not to panic. Has Hakim found out? Has Roger sacrificed his love for my sister for his own life? I approach the door cautiously, bracing myself for whatever carnage I might find. My heart is beating really fast. If anyone has hurt my sister, they're going to pay.

The scene before me is carnage, but it is not the work of criminals but the devilish work of alcohol. My sister has never looked so ill. It's as though she has been dug up and dragged through brambles. Her hair is sticking up all over the place and her usually glowing skin is grey and sallow.

'Morning,' says Bernie brightly, pushing past with a jug of water.

'Good morning,' I say.

'I don't feel well,' groans Coco. She pushes herself into a sitting position and Bernie plumps up her pillow. She hands Coco the water. Coco takes a tentative sip.

Then Michelle comes barging out of the bathroom. 'I wouldn't go in there just yet. Sarah's still throwing up.'

'What about the others?' I ask.

'Like death warmed up. I don't think anyone will be making it for breakfast.'

'That's a shame. Guess it's just us then.'

'I'll get my bag,' says Bernie, plonking the jug of water by my sister and practically skipping to the door.

'Do you think it's wise to leave them alone?' Michelle hesitates.

'I'm sure they'll be fine,' I say.

'They just need to sleep it off,' says Bernie.

Michelle grins. 'I am rather peckish.'

'This is the best eggs Benedict I've ever tasted,' I sigh, patting my stomach.

'It is,' says Bernie with a mouth stuffed with muffin soaked with sauce.

'How did you find this hotel?' says Michelle. 'It is the most exotic place I've ever stayed in. How clever of you to think of it.'

'And the staff are rather lovely too.' I give her a wink.

'One in particular.'

Michelle's cheeks turn pink. 'Akila is very sweet.'

'You were talking for quite a bit.'

'He was just being friendly.' She shrugs. 'Men are always *just* being friendly to me.'

'I don't think he was just being friendly.'

Michelle blushes some more.

'Shell, he only helped us because of you,' Bernie adds.

Michelle goes quiet. Bernie and I exchange grins, which is precisely the moment I clock Hakim. What is he doing here? Is he following me? Has he found out about Roger? About Duty Calls? About … well … everything!

Don't panic, I tell myself.

Hakim looks over at our table and holds my gaze. Chills shoot right through my body. I lift my hand and give him a wave. He doesn't wave back.

Bernie turns around. 'Who's that?'

'He works at the hotel.'

'Do you like him?'

'Good God, no. He gives me the creeps. Besides, I'm sworn off men. They are a waste of time.'

'Aren't they just,' says Bernie.

'So,' I say, pouring myself another coffee, watching Hakim carefully. 'How long have you two known my sister?'

'We've known Coco since university,' says Bernie.

'She's always been the practical joker,' says Michelle.

My eyes widen in shock. 'We are talking about Coco, my sister?'

Bernie and Michelle laugh. 'Shell and Coco pulled the ultimate classic,' says Bernie. 'We were all in the Cotswolds for Philippa's birthday and, well, Coco and Michelle offered to do a drinks run. They took bloody ages and everyone began to worry, mostly about the lack of wine.' Bernie gives me a wink. While Bernie retells the story, I keep one eye on Hakim. I'm relieved when he sweeps out of the room.

'To fully appreciate the story you need to understand we were out in the middle of nowhere. Pitch black, no orange glow, just darkness all around. Finally, there's a knock at the door, and we thought, *At long bloody last*. I unlocked the door and screamed. Coco and Michelle were standing there covered in blood.'

I turn my gaze to Michelle. 'What … why?'

Michelle grins.

'We rushed them inside, but we couldn't make out what they were saying. Then Michelle blurted out …'

'"They're coming from the woods. It's evil, they won't stop now,"' Michelle says in the creepiest voice I've ever heard. 'Sarah started hugging her teddy under the table.'

'Coco kept repeating, "We are all going to die." I was truly cacking myself,' says Bernie. 'And then Philippa grabbed a knife as if she was Rambo's incarnation, telling them to stand back. The blood started pouring out of their mouths.'

'Joke blood capsules,' says Michelle.

I stare at them open-mouthed, amazed at the story. I have never known my sister to orchestrate a practical joke in my life. She rarely exhibits a sense of humour. 'I can't believe we're talking about the same person.'

'Believe it.'

I wonder why she never shows that side of herself to me.

After a fantastic breakfast, Michelle and Bernie return to their rooms with their bags stuffed with croissants to check the general health of the rest of the rabble and if they are in any kind of state for the camel excursion.

I return to my room, feeling pleasantly full, having

consumed a gallon of coffee, alert and awake. I don't think I could go back to sleep even if I tried.

I step into the lift with a man carrying the biggest bouquet of flowers.

'Oh, those are beautiful,' I say.

He gives me a small smile but doesn't speak.

They really are beautiful. The white and red roses are arranged in a tight spiral pattern. There must be over two hundred perfectly formed blooms. The pattern is only broken with one huge golden bird of paradise flower at the centre of the spiral. (Yes, you might have guessed. I did a stint in the local florist's until they fired me for turning the heating on and destroying the stock in one short afternoon.) Heaps of symbolism are in this magnificent bouquet. Whoever ordered them knows about flowers, or certainly knows someone who knows about flowers.

I step out of the lift, and the man follows me. I find myself feeling a little uneasy. I walk down the corridor, but when the man continues to follow, I discreetly rummage in my bag. I pull out the lipstick pistol and clutch it to my chest. I stop outside my door and when he stops too, I pivot and point the lipstick at him.

The man looks confused. 'I have flowers for Miss Hall.'

I stare at him, shocked. 'That's me.' I drop the lipstick into my bag.

'Most humbly yours, madam.' He passes them over and my arms drop, not expecting the heaviness. He smiles and walks away backwards, bowing as he goes. I give him a little curtsey in return.

Unable to get my key in the door, I balance the flowers on my hip and give the door a sharp tap. Yaz answers and gawps at the flowers.

'I've been given flowers.' I beam.

'I can see that. From whom?'

'I don't know,' I say, feeling excited.

'We better check they're not bugged,' whispers Yaz.

'No, they're pristine, no bugs on these treasures, not one petal,' I say, following Yaz into the room. Yaz brings her fingers to her lips.

Oh, I get it, 'bugged' not 'bugs'.

She takes out a comb and presses the last tooth. When did she get that? I didn't get one of those. When there are no beeps, she grins at me. 'They're all yours.'

'I've never been given flowers before.'

'I've never been given flowers either,' says Yaz.

'I saw Hakim downstairs. I think he might be following me. Do you think he knows something?'

'What can he possibly know?'

I shrug. 'I don't know, I just got a funny feeling about him.'

Yaz smiles reassuringly. 'Our cover is solid. Don't worry.'

'I'm probably just being paranoid. Lack of sleep.' I pick out the card between the masses of petals and look at it. 'They're from Ahmed.'

To one of precious beauty. May your mysteries unfold to me. I feel a huge dart of excitement.

Just then there's a knock from the partition door and in walk Jacob, Morley and Adelstein.

'Really, what is the point of knocking if you're just not going to wait?' says Yaz. 'Ahmed sent Dusty flowers.'

'Did you check it for bugs?' asks Adelstein.

'Yes, they're clean,' replies Yaz.

'Did he send a card?'

I hand the card over.

'"To one of precious beauty. May your mysteries unfold to me."' Adelstein raises a brow. 'Seems like you made quite an impression.'

My face flushes. 'I'm quite an impressive person.'

'That I don't doubt.'

Was that a compliment?

Adelstein inspects the bouquet until he's quite satisfied that the roses can't infiltrate the British government with the malice of their thorns, then turns to me. 'Do you want to explain this?' He pulls out a piece of paper from his inside pocket and it's a copy of Coco's hen weekend itinerary. My heart sinks. 'Did you do this?'

'The itinerary? Yes, sir.'

'I was just wondering if you were planning on reporting for duty at any point today.'

My face prickles. 'Oh, I wasn't planning to go with them. I was just going to wave them off.'

'Where is your sister?'

'Recovering.'

'I want you and Yaz to spend the day with the hen party.'

My jaw flops open in surprise. I glance sideways at Yaz. She looks appalled at the idea.

'Why?' asks Yaz.

'Because … I said so.'

'Yes, sir.' Yaz glares at me. I shrug my shoulders helplessly. It wasn't my idea.

'And we don't want to risk any of the hen party bumping into Roger.'

'Sir, Ottoman is on the phone,' Jacob informs the room hastily.

'Um, sir,' I mumble. 'Does Ottoman know about the hen party?'

Adelstein looks at me for a few moments. 'Yes, he knows.' Then he turns on his heels and follows Jacob into the other room.

Yaz drops to the floor and straps on her sandals. I feel really bad for her. I know she's going to hate every minute of this.

'You look nice,' I say encouragingly. She does too. She's wearing a lovely pair of wide-leg silk trousers, printed with flowers and butterflies, and a white cropped T-shirt. I feel like a proud mummy. Yaz has really come on in leaps and bounds since our first days of training.

The courtyard is already bustling with activity when we get downstairs. Businesspeople nestle into the lobby's furnishings, conducting meetings over coffee and laptops, various parties leaving for day trips. Yaz tuts. 'Where are they then?'

I gnaw at my lip, watching Yaz as she scans each party like the Terminator. 'I'm not sure they're going to make it. They were pretty hungover this morning.'

Yaz puts a hand on her hip and glares at me.

'We could go upstairs and check on them?'

Yaz nods. We turn to leave when suddenly Ahmed appears, sees me and beams. I elicit a gasp of surprise. He looks like he's stepped off the set of *Lawrence of Arabia* fused with 1920s colonial India. Dressed in a white safari suit, he looks mighty fine.

He dips his head to bow. 'Dusty, what a delight.'

'Thank you for the flowers.' I smile. 'They are beautiful.'

'As are you,' he says. My, he's smooth. He takes my hand and kisses it, politely, not like London city leeches. He then bows courteously to Yaz, takes both her hands and nods his head to the side humbly. Yaz's face is barely dusted with a friendly smile. Not that he notices—he only has eyes for me.

If I didn't know he was a criminal, I would willingly go to dinner with him.

'The big orange flower was unusual,' I say.

'Ah, the bird of paradise, most fitting for one who shines as you do.'

I give him a coy giggle.

Just then Hakim slithers out of nowhere, and that chill runs down my spine. I don't care what Yaz says, he is definitely following me. Ahmed doesn't seem too pleased to see him either and holds his hand up to silence him. Hakim closes his mouth. I can feel the hatred in his eyes burning a hole in my forehead.

'And what delights are in hold for the delightful ones today?'

'After the flowers, it might be all downhill, or should I say down dunes?'

He raises a brow.

'We're off for a camel-riding excursion.'

Ahmed smiles. 'The perfect way to explore the Saharan dunes. I have many times watched the sun slip behind the sand and slept beneath the stars.'

I bat my eyelashes up at him. 'Sounds heavenly.'

He nods. 'It is a pity you are not staying longer. I would love to escort you. I would be your personal guide.'

'It is a shame.' I gaze up at him adoringly.

'Will I get to see you later?'

'For dinner?' I nod. Although I'm not sure I will. I guess it depends on what Adelstein thinks. 'I will do my best, but you know it is my sister's last night tonight.'

'However fleeting your presence will be, I hope to see you.'

'Well, when you put it like that, how can I not? It's a date.'

Ahmed bows once more, kisses my hand, and glides away. He moves majestically across the courtyard, greeting his guests while Hakim bends his ear.

'Isn't Ahmed charming?' I sigh.

Yaz gives me a withering glance. 'He certainly lives a charmed life.'

'Hakim though …' I shudder.

'Yeah, I get that vibe too,' Yaz replies.

Yaz and I head upstairs, and I'm relieved to see everyone dressed and ready to go. 'This is my colleague, Penny,' I say brightly, using her codename. 'She really wants to go camel riding, so I said she could come along.'

Yaz smiles politely.

'More the merrier,' says Coco. 'Nice to meet you, Penny.'

Coco is looking much better than she did first thing this morning. In fact, everyone seems to have got their bounce back. It's only Sarah who's still looking a bit peaky and is picking at a croissant in the manner of a small bird. Andrea and Philippa are dressed more appropriately, although the slip-on shoes are a big mistake, but if I tell them now, it'll be ages before we leave. Bernie is reading a paper and Michelle has her feet propped up on the pouf and is digging into her massive tote bag. She pulls out another croissant.

'What about inviting your boss, Fizzy William?' says Philippa, her chest perking up.

'No. This is supposed to be girls only,' says Bernie. 'Right, Dusty?'

'Spoilsport,' says Philippa.

'We should get going, to keep on schedule.'

'You and your schedules,' says Coco. 'You really have excelled yourself.'

This trip, if nothing else, has given Coco and me a chance to bond, which is something I never imagined possible. Out of the corner of my eye, I see Philippa and Andrea making a beeline for the dishy chauffeur. The hungover party bundle into the sleek people carrier while the chauffeur stands diligently at the door. Coco sits straight in the first row; Andrea and Philippa clamber towards the back, disgruntled they can't sit in the front, or on his lap. Sarah, Michelle and Bernie sit together, which leaves Yaz and me to squeeze on the end of

Coco's pew.

'Where are you originally from?' Coco asks Yaz, studying her like it's the first time she's set eyes on her.

'England,' says Yaz.

'I mean your parents?'

I shudder at Coco's heavy-handed, bordering on racist remark.

'My mum is English. My father was originally from Pakistan.' If Yaz has taken offence, she doesn't show it.

'You look a lot like our aunt Agnes, doesn't she, Dusty? Doesn't Penny look like Agnes?'

'You actually do.'

'Aunt Agnes is my mum's sister,' says Coco. 'She ran away with some bohemian French count. She was only sixteen. It was such a scandal.'

'You tell the story as if you remember it. Don't forget these are our mother's words, which I'm sure are exaggerated, and we were only toddlers. I remember thinking it was totally romantic.'

I hear a grunt from Bernie.

'Agnes was a beauty. A real stunner.'

Yaz blushes, surprised to hear beauty and her name in the same sentence. 'You two are very alike,' announces Yaz.

Coco and I stare at each other, open-mouthed. 'We are nothing alike,' we say at the same time, appalled at the very idea.

Yaz chuckles.

The rest of the car journey is surprisingly muted for a group of women. There's the occasional rustle from Michelle's tote bag and Bernie's newspaper. The lack of sleep last night is catching up on me too and I take a brief nap.

'Madam Hall.' The driver taps my arm and I flicker

into consciousness. I look behind me and everybody else is still sound asleep. Bernie's paper has doubled as a sleeping mask, Michelle has a breakfast napkin over her eyes, even Yaz is behind sunshades amongst tousles of black hair.

I climb out of the car and the extreme heat hits immediately. It's like walking into a furnace. The camel owner, a friendly beardy chap, throws his arms out in a welcoming gesture. 'Good mornings to you, Mademoiselle Hall.'

'Mr Youssef?'

'At your service,' he says, bowing extravagantly.

'It's really hot out here,' I say, touching my head.

'Do not worry, we have a headdress for you. The sun is most fierce in the desert. Can cook egg on a bald man's head!'

'You sure could. One moment.' I turn and rap on the window. 'Wakey, wakey, rise and shine. We're here!'

The glamour zombies tumble out of the car in one fashion or another. Philippa causes the first incident of the day. She loses a shoe, which gets buried in a sudden gust of wind, starts hopping on the hot white sand and topples into Andrea. Andrea then falls onto her face, snapping the arm of her Chanel sunglasses. One of Mr Youssef's men rushes to her aid, whips the sunglasses off her head and dips the sunglasses straight into a bubbling pot of gloopy fat, runs his knife along a camel's eye, cuts off some of its eyelashes and binds the dripping fat with the hair, runs back to the horizontal sand queen and pokes them straight back on Andrea's face, immeasurably pleased with his fast-thinking service. A solitary drop of fat lands on her top lip.

We all stand back, half-impressed and half-appalled. Sarah scrambles to help Andrea, but loses her espadrille in the process and topples face down into the sand.

'Oh, for goodness' sake! Hands up, who has two shoes left?' says Coco, stifling a giggle.

'Rather have one than Bernie's chastity boots,' says Philippa.

'If one had half the capacity for thinking that they did for drinking, one would realise sand is granular. You know, a movable terrain,' retorts Bernie.

'Bite me!' pouts Philippa.

Bernie does an exaggerated shudder. 'No, thanks. You're far too soured by men.'

'You two pack it in,' Coco half-jests.

Andrea picks herself up and removes her remaining high heel and shoves it in Michelle's tote bag, spearing Michelle's remaining croissant. Michelle looks so outraged she removes the shoe and tosses it away. It lands next to a camel, who takes one look at the large handmade silk flower attachment and promptly chomps down on it.

The whole group gasp in dismay, but to my utter amazement Andrea laughs and one by one they all topple over in laughter.

Bernie is clutching her stomach, she's laughing so hard. Michelle has collapsed in a knot of giggles. My sister is making little hiccupping sounds and Philippa has tears rolling down her face. Even Yaz is laughing in tiny snorts. Mr Youssef and his helpers look on with bemusement, which only makes us laugh even harder.

After the jovialities have passed, Mr Youssef herds us to the shelter of his Bedouin tent porch and we plonk ourselves on a glorious Persian rug. The helpers bring mint tea and sweet cakes to the vibrantly coloured low table.

Mr Youssef claps and a boy empties bags onto the floor. Out of the bags fall pairs of shoes resembling Ali Baba's moccasin slippers, and out of the other traditional kufiyah headdresses.

'Please help yourself, ladies. A memento of your desert day,' says Youssef. 'My gift to you.'

This piques the attention of the shoppers amongst us and I dive in first, picking a white pair of slippers with a delicate black swirly pattern.

When we're all suitably fed, watered and dressed for the desert sun, the helpers get us to greet our camels by name. We are introduced most respectfully, each of us given a treat to offer our new modes of transport, who bend down (Koosh!) and let us clamber rather awkwardly all over them while they chew on what looks like the camel equivalent of a margarita, an alfalfa cube dipped in salt. With a signal, the camels' back legs rise and some of us hold on, whilst others nearly topple over the camels' heads.

Coco has a particular affinity with her camel. She smiles, posing majestically. I swear the camel flutters its long eyelashes, as enamoured with her as she is with it. Coco grins at me and I find myself grinning back, feeling a dart of emotion for my sister. Coco is blissfully unaware of what an utter shitbag Roger is. My smile fades underneath my kufiyah.

Slowly we set off. I ask Mr Youssef if his team can take the photo, as I think 'two hands when we're going down the dunes' is a necessary rule after Bernie hung sideways for some minutes trying to snap the happy hens. Yaz is a natural, of course; with those core muscles, I reckon she could stay on top of a belligerent brontosaurus.

'This is fun,' says Yaz, as she steers her camel to the back.

'Yeah, lots of fun,' I say. 'Although I can't shake the feeling that we're being watched.'

'Perhaps we are,' says Yaz with a shrug. 'Just stay focused on the activity at hand and try to enjoy yourself.'

'I'll try.'

We trek onwards to an oasis where a table has been set for lunch.

Bernie jumps off, getting her helper to lead her camel whilst she takes pictures for the hen diary. She starts with Bridezilla, naturally.

Then a honk of a noise echoes from behind. Philippa's camel bolts, not enamoured with the click of the camera.

'Yee-haaa! Ride 'em, cowgirl,' Coco cries whilst she carries on posing using her kufiyah as an exotic prop.

Yaz and I look at each other and immediately come to the same realisation. Philippa is in trouble. I don't know how I intend to help, but I jump onto my camel and get it to stand. Meanwhile, Yaz grabs a rope from Mr Youssef and jumps onto her camel.

We both take off after Philippa, leaving gobsmacked faces behind us.

'So, what's the plan?' I yell across to Yaz.

'I'm going to lasso this rope,' she shouts. 'Then when I get control of the camel, I want you to grab hold of the camel's reins.'

'Okay.'

As we give chase we can see Philippa, her body pressed up close to the animal, gripping it for dear life.

'It's okay, Philippa, we're here,' I holler.

Yaz makes a lasso with the rope and swings it wide above her head, and with the skill and finesse of a rodeo rider (for all I know she could be, she displayed those skills during the obstacle course!) Yaz lassos the rope over the camel's neck first throw and gives the rope a sharp tug. The camel tries to resist, but Yaz has a firm grip and tugs again; she continues tugging, forcing it to circle. The camel slows down to a trot.

'Now!' she shouts at me.

I lean over and grab the reins out of Philippa's terrified hands. 'There, there,' I say, leaning towards the camel's ear. The camel grinds to a stop and I kick off the stirrups and dismount. Holding both reins, I continue to walk them in the circle. 'You're positively more skittish than a horse. That won't do, will it?' I purr at the wayward beast.

Yaz slides off the back of her camel and Philippa falls into her arms. 'You saved my life!'

'It was nothing,' replies Yaz.

Philippa hugs Yaz fiercely. 'How can I ever thank you? Both of you?'

'Don't mention it,' I say. But it does feels rather good, being the hero. Yaz and I smile at each other. We do make an awesome team.

When we get back to the group, my sister's jaw is still on the sandy floor. 'Dusty, if Mother saw you now, she'd be so impressed.'

Mr Youssef beams at us. 'You are born riders.'

If the life of a spy comes to an end, I could always become a camel rustler.

We return to the hotel smelling of camels but in high spirits and bursting with stories. Yaz has become everyone's new best friend. I am amazed at how Yaz has fitted into the group, joking with my sister and her friends. She is like a totally different person.

We leave the hens with instructions to shower and rest up before tonight's entertainment, then Yaz and I return to our room, only to discover a huge magnum of champagne and a box of Turkish Delights guarding the door. I open the card and read the message.

It would be most pleasing if you would join us for pre-dinner drinks tonight, my bird of paradise.

Yaz gets her comb and scans them for bugs. When she gives the thumbs-up, I pop a Turkish Delight into my mouth and reread the message again. 'I know he's a criminal and all that, but it's rather nice being the centre of someone's affections, and he's not unlike a greedy banker really … or some dodgy CEO retailer who whittles company off from company until the bare bones crumble. In some ways that makes him more honest.'

'Just different forums?' says Yaz, quirking a brow.

'Exactly. Killing people mentally by awful business practices where they lose everything they've worked for their entire lives. Half the people are in someone's pocket, anyway. What comeuppance is there? A public slap on the wrist and they carry on their merry rich lifestyles, just far away from the country giving the comeuppances.'

'That's deep, Dusty. Greed is one thing, evil and greed are worse,' she says.

'I don't think you can have one without the other.'

The partition door suddenly flies open and Morley stands there in a pair of penguin robot pyjama bottoms and a black short-sleeved shirt. Has he been in his pyjamas all day?

'We've got him,' says Morley. 'The ceramics pickup man is Rashid Zaloum, also known as the Butcher'

Yaz and I rush into the next room.

'Wanted by the Israeli government for the murders of several prominent Israelis and by Interpol for European radicalisations of children as young as ten,' adds Jacob. I glance over at Yaz. Her steely focus has rebooted, and she stares at the screen.

Adelstein steps out from the shadows. He looks like he's been running again or patrolling or worse. He looks clammy and stubbly. Morley scrolls down the screen. 'The Palestinian police arrested and detained Rashid for his part in a bombing of a school for girls, but then released him two days later. Height one hundred and eighty-six centimetres. Eyes brown. He has one scar running from his stomach right round to the coccyx.'

'Looks like he's been sawn in half by a bad

magician,' I blurt out. Adelstein's annoyance is plain to see, I step backwards, coughing awkwardly.

Morley continues, 'apparently the scar is of his own making. It looks like a shark bite but we know this not to be true. It's one of the things he brags about and dazzles his recruits with, belief in your strength and all that bollocks about dying for the cause.' This is the first time I have heard Morley swear or show emotion for the people we're here to uncover. 'Languages: Arabic, Hebrew and English.'

'Excellent work, Hall,' says Adelstein. I almost faint with surprise. He's in a good mood. What a difference an identification of a wanted terrorist can make to someone's day. 'How was the camel expedition?'

I look over at Yaz, but she says nothing. She is staring at the screen with a faraway look on her face. So I recap today's adventures, chuckling a little, but realise Adelstein isn't really following. 'I suppose you had to be there …' I trail off.

Adelstein turns his attention to Yaz. 'Khan, there's some intel we need you to translate.'

'Yes, sir,' she says, still scowling at the monitor.

'What about me? Do you need me for anything?' I ask Adelstein.

'No. You can go.'

'Oh, Hall, can you give me your amulet? I need to update the frequency.' Jacob says.

'Sure.' I slip my amulet from around my neck and hand it over to Jacob.

CHAPTER TWENTY-FOUR

Seeing as I am not needed, I get ready for tonight's party. I have a leisurely shower and wash my hair thoroughly, squeezing the rest of the complimentary humid heat control conditioner out of the bottle. I take even longer with my makeup while enjoying a glass of wine just to take the edge off. I'm definitely feeling a lot calmer about tonight.

I choose a fuchsia-coloured minidress. It's very *Great Gatsby* 1920s. It has layers of swishy sequined beads, sparkles in the light and clings to every curve. It's beautiful. I've strapped on a pair of Manolo Blahnik knee-high gladiator sandals with multicolour Swarovski crystal embellishments. They're a work of art.

Adelstein bursts through the adjoining door.

I turn to him. 'I would explain the etiquette of knocking but what would be the point?' If he burst in just a few seconds ago, he would have got an eyeful of my derrière!

'We kind of expect people to be ready at all times, you know, being MI6 and all that.' As he says it his eyes flicker to my bare legs, making my skin all prickly.

'Roger is in the next room.'

'I'll be there in a sec. I just need to zip up my dress.'

I expect him to leave, but in two strides Adelstein is behind me, his hand on the base of my back. A tiny electric dart shoots up my spine as he touches me.

I push my hair up, and Adelstein slowly zips up my dress. The gesture is intimate, and my skin feels hot as well as tingling and my stomach does this weird flip and I feel sort of breathless. Could be the tightness of the dress though.

I wonder what it would it be like if he took me to bed. What would his hands feel like on my skin? Would he be slow and tender or intense and determined, like he is at work? My cheeks flush with heat. Where the hell did this come from? Oh, my God, I'm turned on! The realisation shocks me, and in a sudden panic, I swivel out of his embrace, only my ankle buckles and get entangled in the fluffy rug. Adelstein grabs my arm to stop me from falling flat on my face.

'Thanks,' I say, in a strange sort of squeak. I cannot meet his eyes. I walk over to the bed, picking up my bag. When I meet his gaze, he has the strangest look on his face, as if something important has just dawned on him. I'm tempted to ask but assume it's not in my pay grade.

Adelstein clears his throat. 'Roger has agreed to be wired. I want you to make your excuses and leave the party. You can use your sister's last night as an excuse.'

'Wouldn't you prefer me to stay with Roger?'

'No. We want them to talk business, which they won't do with you there.'

'Of course.'

His eyes flick to my legs. 'We monitored the rug, I mean tapestry today and it's been a hive of activity.'

It's been ages since I had sex, and it's not just the sex but the intimacy I miss. Did he just say something? I groan. What is wrong with me?

'Are you listening?'

'Yes, yes, secret door behind the tapestry. Hive of activity.'

'We haven't been able to work out where they are exiting. Ahmed's lair in Turkey has also been a hive of activity today, according to HQ.'

My throat runs dry and my stomach churns as I digest this piece of information and the growing enormity of what is happening. The last thing I should be thinking about is sex. I feel flushed with heat.

'Hall, are you all right?' Adelstein steps towards me. 'Hall, you have held yourself together thus so far. You have one last task. All you have to do is sit and be charming and pretty. Then leave. Do you think you can manage that?'

I stand motionless; it takes all my concentration just to breathe. He smells really good.

'Hall?'

'Yes, yes.' I nod, taking a step backwards when there's a sudden knock on the door. Adelstein indicates for me to open it and positions himself behind the door.

I unlock the door and I notice my hands are slightly shaking. 'Coco!' I say, surprised and relieved. 'What are you doing here?'

'Wow, you look gorgeous,' she says.

'Thanks, as do you.'

Coco is wearing a pretty silver minidress and strappy heels, topped off with the hen party tiara on top of her head and pink fluffy handcuffs. She steps inside. 'I just wanted to ask you—' She stops when she sees Adelstein move out from behind the door.

My cheeks flush. 'You've met my boss, Mr—'

'Yes, I remember.' She gives me a sly look, then turns her attention to Adelstein. 'Very sorry about last night. I was suffering from food poisoning and, err … cheap market food.'

Then the adjoining door suddenly bursts open. Yaz, Jacob, and Morley tumble in. They halt when they see Coco.

'It is like Piccadilly Circus around here.' I give an unnatural laugh.

Coco puts her hands on her hips and wiggles provocatively. Jacob's and Morley's jaws drop to the floor.

'Oh, hi, Pen,' Coco says.

Yaz gives her an awkward wave. In fact, everyone stands there looking rather awkward, not knowing what to say.

'Did you want to see me about something?' I ask Coco. 'It's just we have … a meeting to, err, discuss …'

'Cleaning software applications,' says Adelstein.

'Oh, right.' She winks. 'I just wanted to have a word with my sister.'

'Okay,' I say, leading her to one side. 'What is it?'

She bites her lip and suddenly I wonder—'You're not having second thoughts, are you?'

Coco frowns. 'No! I just want to say it's been the best hen weekend.'

'Oh,' I say, taken aback. 'I'm glad.'

'Far better than Angelique's south of France farcical affair,' says Coco in one-upmanship. She opens her arms for a hug, and I step into her embrace. 'Oh, and I was wondering,' she says, her face tightening a little. 'You haven't heard from Roger, have you?'

'Roger?' I squeak. 'No. Why would I?'

'It's just I've sent him a couple of texts but he hasn't responded, it's so unlike him.' She suddenly gives the air a sniff and frowns. I freeze. Coco can smell Roger's aftershave.

I need to get her out of here fast. I grab my Chanel No.5 from the table and start spraying it in front of me, then walk into it. 'He probably doesn't want to disturb you. You are on your hen weekend. Tradition is to leave the bride-to-be to her hens.'

'It is?' Coco coughs and waves her hand in the air. 'Mind where you're spraying that. My eyes can't afford to be bloodshot this early in the evening.' Coco leaves with little persuasion, something about going to check if Sarah's untangled herself from Philippa's mohair handbag.

The others stare at me. 'Roger's aftershave, it's unmissable, unmistakable and unpalatable. Lingers like a Victorian smog.' I wave the Chanel bottle at them.

Determined to be the height of professionalism and maturity for King and country, I follow the others into the adjoining room. Roger is standing in his underpants with a wire hanging from his slight podge of a stomach.

'Was that Coco?' he asks, his face pallid. 'Is she okay?'

'Yes,' I say. 'No thanks to you.'

'What did she want?'

'She wants to know why you haven't responded to her texts.'

'I can't face lying to her.'

I turn to look at him. 'You've done a pretty good job up till now.'

'I swear, Dusty, I thought it was diamonds.'

'And that makes it okay?'

'You won't tell Coco, will you?'

I remain tight-lipped. 'Of course I will not tell Coco. I'll be done for treason,' I mumble.

'You have to help me, Dusty.'

'Just do as you're told and everything will be all right.' Although I don't know that for sure.

'Will you leave us for five minutes?' Adelstein asks.

I step away and Adelstein places a chair right in front of Roger and starts making a clicking sound with his mouth. Roger's face instantly changes.

Morley hands me the amulet and goes with Jacob to their room. I follow Yaz back into our room. Yaz pulls out a dress and takes it into the bathroom. 'I am not having anyone walking in on *me* while I'm getting dressed.'

'Did Adelstein say you could go?'

'Yes.'

This makes me feel a little better knowing that Yaz will be with me.

While Yaz gets ready, I pace the floor. I tell myself it's going to be fine, but I am so confused as well as totally furious with Roger. In fact, I could kill him myself. Did he know the sort of people he was mixing with?

Yaz appears from the bathroom, looking stunning in a beautiful blue satin gown. 'Can you zip me up at the back?' Yaz steps in front of the mirror and gives her reflection a frown.

'You look beautiful,' I say, stepping behind her. I get a brief flashback to when Adelstein zipped me up and my cheeks flush. 'There you go.'

'It is a pretty dress.' She shrugs.

'It's stunning, as are you,' I say, imitating Ahmed. Her face creases into a smile. 'What happened to the woman in the hobnail boots and khaki boiler suit?'

'Oh, she's still there.'

The adjoining door flies open, and Yaz and I share a smile.

'Ready?' Yaz asks.

'As I'll ever be.'

Yaz and I walk into the room.

'Hey, Dusty!' Roger looks uncharacteristically mellow, smiling warmly without a hint of worry on his face.

Morley hands Roger a device—it's a perfect replica of his aristocratic crest ring. How on earth did they put that together in such a short space of time?

Morley pushes it on his little finger. 'This is a transponder.'

Jacob puts some co-ordinates in the computer, and they get a visual of Roger standing in the room.

'If you are in serious trouble, push this three times,' Adelstein instructs. He indicates to the crest on the ring and Roger nods.

'It's a secure line, only we have the frequency and there's a scramble code even a supercomputer couldn't decipher,' Jacob says proudly.

'What lovely craftsmanship.' Roger takes the ring. 'I know that crest from somewhere.' We all exchanged darting looks of concern. He's talking as if they've given him a nice gift.

Adelstein does some weird clicking of his fingers and Roger jolts alert. His hand shakes. Adelstein makes two more clicks, and this seems to get him at the right level of awareness and calm.

'Ready?' Adelstein asks.

'I leave them—no, they leave me—and I ask them—no, they tell me to tell me?' Roger is in a muddle.

'Remember, just natural conversation, Roger, the same as it's been for all these years. Like before. As always.' Adelstein guides him back gently.

'Right. Natural. Just like before. Normal business. As always.' Roger looks at Adelstein with fearful respect. He wants to please him, like an unruly beast being tamed by its master.

'Hall, your ear, please.'

My heart jitters as I walk over to Adelstein. 'If Roger gets anxious, then use these keywords: "Natural, normal, like before. As always." Got that?'

'What about me?'

Adelstein looks bemused for a moment.

'What are my calming words?'

Adelstein leans towards me conspiratorially. ‘Just be yourself.’

‘That’s it? That’s my fighting pep talk?’

His lips twitch into a smile. ‘Do you need a pep talk?’

I blink as he stares into my eyes. ‘Er … no.’ I swallow. ‘I’m good.’ I turn to Roger. ‘C’mon, Rodge, let’s get this show on the road.’

CHAPTER TWENTY-FIVE

We approach the bar and a waiter immediately jumps into action, showing us to a private corner, walled by thick greenery. Ahmed gets to his feet when he sees us. The other men seated at the table follow suit.

'You came.' Ahmed kisses my hand, smiling broadly.

'I'm afraid I can't stay long, but I wanted to see you again.' My voice is soft and seductive. Ahmed seems pleased with my response and invites me to sit next to him. Hakim scowls at losing his place and moves to another chair.

'And thank you very much for the champagne and Turkish Delight,' I say, 'but you must stop spoiling me.'

'Ah.' Ahmed dismisses the gestures as nothing with his hand. 'It is my honour to spoil you. These are just small tokens. The world holds many more.'

The men exchange handshakes, and Ahmed waves his hand to the waiter who showed us to the table. 'Some champagne for the table. Mademoiselle Hall, may I introduce you to Rashid? He is also an avid art collector.' Ahmed gestures to the fierce-looking man with eyes set so deep they look black. Rashid looks at me, but there is no warmth there, just calculation fired with hatred. I shudder.

'An unexpected visit, isn't it, Hakim?' says Ahmed jovially, but I can detect by the intonation he did not find it a welcome one. 'News travels fast when rarity shows itself. But it is always one's privilege to have visitors.'

Hakim's gaze is penetrating.

'Rashid and I often find the same piece enticing. One would think we had the same dealer.' Ahmed looks at Roger and Roger laughs nervously.

Surely Roger isn't mixed up with Rashid, too?

The waiter places the ice bucket at the side of the table and pours three glasses before Hakim shoos him away rudely. Hakim pours water into his and Rashid's glasses.

'It is all simple in the end, my bird of paradise, isn't it?' says Ahmed, touching my hand.

I don't have a clue what he's talking about, but I nod. Ahmed puts his hand on mine. It feels silky and strong. 'Money. It simply comes down to the highest bidder.' Ahmed is so unbelievably charming, truly statesmanlike.

Rashid bows his head and doesn't utter a word.

'I'm afraid his English is even worse than his negotiation skills.' Ahmed erupts with laughter, hitting Roger on the arm. Roger rockets out a laugh, but Hakim isn't amused and doesn't pretend to be. Rashid smiles. Maybe he doesn't understand much English either?

'L'chaim.' Ahmed raises his glass; Rashid's nostrils flare like a dragon about to blow fire. Even I know that was Hebrew. Hakim does a double-take, then throws a piercing look at Rashid. I'm certain now Ahmed does not want his business and wants his company even less.

Besides, I don't want to get too familiar with killers. I think I'm going to have to dye my hair when I get home, just in case.

We've known Rashid has been here for a couple of days, but it seems Ahmed did not. Why would Hakim keep that quiet? Is Hakim up to something that Ahmed doesn't know about?

Ahmed and Roger twitter on about the splendour of old pots from France to Persia sailing over the seas to China and Japan. By the time they've finished, we've travelled the world in a time forgot. Ahmed fills my empty glass; I didn't notice finishing it. I glance at my watch. The hens will be in the terrace room by now. I really should make my excuses, but I can't go just yet as Ahmed may view this as impolite.

Ahmed and Roger carry on as normal, laughing and telling anecdotes about their school days, and I can see how easy it must have been for Roger to be taken in by Ahmed. The man could charm his way out of nuclear fallout even if he was the cause of World War Three. I notice throughout their exchange Rashid and Hakim remain silent. It's all rather uncomfortable but Ahmed doesn't seem to care.

Rashid suddenly says something in Arabic, and Ahmed shoots him a look that could kill. Ahmed then says something in Arabic.

Roger looks at me nervously. I give him a reassuring smile and he reaches for his glass, gulping down more champagne.

'Roger!' Roger and I jump, the sudden switch to English taking us both off guard. Ahmed flashes a smile. 'There's been a change of plan.'

'How so?' says Roger, trying not to sound nervous.

'Fazil won't be collecting my pieces this month. There will be someone else.'

'Why not Fazil?'

'He's been … unexpectedly indisposed.' Ahmed glances at Rashid.

Rashid and Ahmed have another angry exchange, at

which point I think I hear my name.

Ahmed then laughs and speaks in English. 'The game of chess is certainly unpredictability.'

'I haven't beaten you in chess for years,' says Roger.

'You were always too precious about your pawns; sacrifice is a necessity to win. You are a true friend, Roger.'

I half-rise from my seat, gently patting Ahmed's arm and smiling at the table's occupants. 'Well, gentlemen, I must make haste. Unfortunately, my original appointment is pending.'

'You cannot leave me to look at these brutish faces for an entire evening,' Ahmed says.

There is no reaction from the terrible bearded twins, but Roger snorts. 'Steady on, old chap.'

'I'm so sorry, but my sister is expecting me,' I say.

'Of course, family is the most important part of life. Are you sure you will not sit a little longer, my feathered wonder?' Ahmed asks.

'This bird must fly,' I reply.

'Another time, yes?'

'I would love that. Yes.'

Ahmed stands up politely. 'My precious creature, there will always be another time. Roger will see to it, won't you, Roger?' Ahmed kisses my hand and looks deep into my eyes.

'Gentlemen, enjoy the rest of the night,' I say. 'Thank you again, Ahmed, for your hospitality.'

Roger waves a cheerio and I slip away, half-relieved and half-concerned for Roger. A change of collector—is that usual? What does it mean? Ahmed didn't seem too happy about it, and there's some kind of disagreement going on between Rashid and Ahmed. What does 'unexpectedly indisposed' mean? Does it mean what I think it means?

I shake off the uneasiness in the pit of my stomach

and go in search of my brood.

'What kept you?' asks Coco.

Our seats are set away from the centre and to the left of a small stage, surrounding a wave-shaped mosaic-tiled table. I sit myself down.

'Don't be so bloody nosy,' I say, mimicking Pinocchio. 'Just sorting something out.'

'Sorting out or being sorted out?' quips Philippa.

'Are you doing him on the sly?' asks Andrea.

Yaz snorts a laugh.

'Good God. No!' My cheeks flame.

'But you want to jump his bones, right?'

'Oh, darling, that one couldn't jump a red light, let alone six feet of raw sex appeal,' Philippa counters.

Akila arrives with a huge carafe of cocktails.

'This is a Long Island tea with a twist,' Michelle announces to the table, smiling sweetly at her favourite waiter. He pours it steadily into the long glasses. 'The twist being it could hold up a fat continent, not just a long island.'

All the hens whoop for joy, grabbing their glasses to toast the beginning of the night. Yaz glugs hers back and slams it on the table.

Crikey, Yaz is game. I take a sip, the smallest amount possible, and feel my eyes water from the tequila fumes.

'Mademoiselle Michelle, how is your foot?' asks Akila.

'It is feeling much better, thank you,' replies Michelle coyly.

'You must keep the weight off it.'

'That's always been Shell's problem,' cackles Philippa unkindly.

Michelle looks crushed. Akila whispers something in her ear, and a bashful smile spreads across her face.

Tonight's in-house entertainment is a belly-dancing

show, but little does Coco know the belly dancers have strict instructions to take her up on the stage and teach her some moves. She's even got a special costume. The other surprise is the belly dancers are a drag act. I was taken back when the receptionist told me it's a regular showpiece, as I thought transvestites would be frowned upon in this part of the world, but I'm glad to say they don't stone people for cross-dressing in Marrakesh. The receptionist told me that Marrakesh transvestites are tough men, really tough, and performing is in their soul. I can't imagine Hakim approves, but he's not the owner and this is not the Stone Age.

Suddenly, the lights go dim and the restaurant falls silent. I can hear little cymbals from afar. Slowly they get louder, then a simple drum punctures the air, quietly at first, then builds to a faster beat. A frilly pipe melody joins the simple beat. The drumming stops and the cymbals fade. A big puff of smoke fills the room. People gasp.

Out from the smoke emerge three belly dancers, clasping their hands on their silk- and sequin-wrapped hips. They start off with some gentle hip-swaying, which causes applause; I scan the room and find the older male clientele looking especially pleased and keen. Then I notice Hakim and Rashid walking through the back of the room towards the tapestry.

I turn my attention back to the dancers and they separate like the Red Arrows of the belly-dancing world, one to each side of the room and the other racing down the centre of the tables, hips nearly taking the starters with them, filling the room with mystic energy and mesmerising the audience. In this light, I can't tell they're men at all. They get the tables involved in the centre and some serious dad-dancing breaks out.

The girls are clapping away. People are floating up from tables joining in, badly, but it is funny. Coco moves to the edge of the table just so Michelle and Sarah don't feel the urge to get up. And then dinner. After a delicious banquet full of tender meat, grilled vegetables and warming spices Sarah stands up and pulls out a bag with little chickens on it.

'Right, everyone has to pick one, don't unfold it until we're all ready.' The bag flies round the table, closely followed by the cocktail carafe. 'There's a word written on each one and you have to guess who it's about. If you get it wrong, then you have to drink what Bernie says.'

At this point, Bernie produces a huge bottle of vodka from underneath the table. She makes us empty the water carafe and fills it up with the clear devil, throwing in some lemon for good measure.

'But who's written them?' says Coco. 'Surely it will be subjective?'

'Sarah wrote them,' says Bernie and everyone smiles and nods knowingly. 'But I helped. The words aren't descriptive of you, they're something associated with you or what we've done over the years.'

'But that's not fair, you two will know the answers,' Coco points out.

'No, we don't. Everyone apart from you and Pen has written some. We'll think up a forfeit round for Pen.'

Yaz looks at me; I look at her and shrug.

'Yeah, but—'

'Hush your noise, woman, and pick one.' Bernie stands up to dominate Coco, but because the table is sunken, she just looks like a hefty midget.

'I remember you being a lot taller, Bernie,' Philippa mocks.

'Right, but if I feel like this game is rigged, I have the right to allocate my drink to who I wish?' says Coco.

'You'll have no such authority,' I say. 'This is Sarah's game.'

'Sarah. Look at me.' Coco tries to control her faithful

lackey.

'No, Bernie is the jew-dee-caterer. What she says goes, Coco.'

'That's judicator, sweety,' Michelle whispers to Sarah.

'But Sarah …'

'Don't look at me, it wasn't …' Sarah cowers behind Bernie.

'Leave Sarah alone, Bride of Fankless-stein.'

Coco keeps her stern face on, then puts her hands on her hips. 'Okay, shoot.'

I really don't recognise my sister on this holiday amongst her friends.

'Right, Andrea, read yours out loud.' Sarah regains her confidence for the game and Coco sits back, hands firmly folded across her lap.

'Dog Bovril.'

'Andrea!' all of them say in unison. I really don't want to know the story behind that.

Bernie gets up again. 'One person, one guess. For the love of … it's not rocket science.'

A few rounds of successful guess-the-person pass. The carafe of vodka is pretty much intact apart from Sarah's failings.

The music starts building again, and the dancers are working the room. *How opportune,* I think to myself. Andrea and Philippa pretend to act a little lusher than they really are, trying to get out and clap. Coco signals to remain seated. She's sobering up way too fast. This isn't good. Sarah, on the other hand, is way over the side of tipsy. She didn't do so well with her own drinking game.

'I think custard should be made a different colour,' says Sarah.

'You can make it whatever colour you like,' says Michelle.

'I don't think the colours are real.'

'It's the ingredients,' Michelle patiently explains.

'It's not!' says Sarah with as much aggression as a marshmallow.

'It is, sweetie. Either the yolks or the additives. But even naturally, custard is a pale yellow.'

'I think all foods should be different colours,' she replies.

'They generally are,' says Andrea.

Sarah waves her hands and shakes her head in disagreement.

I excuse myself and place a drink order at the bar. The bartender sets to work with the flair of a matador taming ice cubes. 'I make special. My own recipe. You see. We will bring it to the table.'

'Thank you.' I slip out onto the terrace, taking in some fresh air, which is full of the scent of tropical flowers and the past heat of the day, when I hear footsteps. One of Hakim's henchmen appears in my line of sight.

The way he looks at me sends a jolt of panic through me. I manage a smile whilst taking a step backwards.

He takes a menacing step towards me. I turn on my heel and dash inside.

He definitely looked as if he was going to grab me. My stomach curdles. *Okay. Breathe. There's no need to panic. They know nothing.*

But still …

I arrive back at the table just as the waiter turns up with a loaded tray full of highball cocktails. Yaz catches my eyes and gives me a curious look. I force a smile to my lips and raise my glass. 'Well, Coco, here's to you and your future. This is called Amour L'Tropical Paradise, your signature hen weekend recipe with a little help from a professional cocktail-maker.'

The waiter hands each of us a long glass and places

two huge pitchers in the middle of the table, which Bernie moves out of Sarah's reach.

The drinks are delicious, but potent. Passionfruit and lychee are the true masked crusaders of spirits. Yaz comes over and sits next to me. 'What's up?'

'Something weird just happened.' I keep my voice low and steady. 'It's probably nothing, but one of Hakim's henchmen looked like he was going to grab me.'

'Are you sure?'

'Well … I'm …' I shrug my shoulders. 'I'm probably being paranoid?'

Yaz gives me a long look, her forehead creasing into a frown. 'Let me check it out.'

'I'll come with you.'

'No. No. You stay here. I need to pee anyway.'

'Okay.'

Yaz gets up and I notice she's a little wobbly on her feet. Just as I'm thinking about following—

Pow! A dazzling spotlight shines on our table, and I let out an involuntary squeal of excitement. I glance over at Coco, and she frowns at me.

The belly dancer on stage shimmies his way over to our table. Everyone is clapping in time with the beat and when he points to Coco, we all squeal.

Coco's mouth flops open, and she stares at him, then looks at me. He beckons her to take his hand, but she shakes her head vigorously. Despite Coco's protests, Bernie pushes Coco off her seat, then Philippa shoves Coco out and Coco has no choice but to follow him.

'You'll be fine.' I smile encouragingly.

But I'm not so sure. She looks petrified—and they've taken her away.

The lights dim and there's a low, steady drumbeat. Everyone hushes and the drumbeat increases in pace and volume and then, with a loud bang and a puff of smoke, the dancer and Coco appear on stage.

I snort a laugh. This is better than I could have imagined. Coco's face is a picture. She is wearing a bright yellow belly-dancing costume, with tassels swinging, sequined bra and a sheer yellow long skirt. The word we need to focus on here is 'sheer', as in you can see *everything*. I look at the other hens and the entire table is giggling uncontrollably. Coco pokes her tongue out at us all, but the Amour L'Tropical Paradise has given her a sense of humour, and she does a little shimmy. My sister is a lot more fun with alcohol.

We all rush to take out our mobiles and Coco poses as we click away.

The drumbeat starts up again, and the dancer signals for Coco to copy his moves. He's very authoritative, with his big red lips, heavy eyebrows, and fake Bambi lashes. He signals Coco to move her hips in a circular motion and spin around. She does with the grace of a rusty robot in need of a bottle of WD40, and even she laughs as he shakes his head. But then she gets into the rhythm of it. Her dance lessons with Lionel are paying off, and her hips shake, and she is really letting go. I'm impressed. Me and the rest of the hens applaud wildly as she takes her bow.

A spotlight flashes on and focuses on her derrière, and the entire audience goes wild.

Coco turns around to the audience and bows. Flowers are thrown and she catches them like a pro. No problem with her eye-hand co-ordination then. The three dancers turn around to tremendous applause, bowing and still more feminine than anyone at this table. Coco returns to the table looking flushed, shiny, and quite happy to stay in her costume.

'You were amazing!' I say.

Coco grins and reaches over for a hug. 'You're pretty amazing yourself,' she says.

I am shell-shocked and stare at my sister.

'I'm being serious. You did this all for me and these two days have been the best. *You're* the best.'

'Thank you,' I say, a little dazedly. For a moment we sit there, smiling at one another, and it's like we've only just realised how much we actually like each other.

My sister stretches out her arms and we hug again, and it's not the least bit awkward. But something is still niggling away in the back of my mind, like when you know you need to remember something, but can't remember what it is.

Then it comes to me. Yaz! She's been gone for a while—and a terrible thought flashes through my mind. They've got her. I get up from the table. 'Just popping to the loo.'

'Can you order some Amour L'Tropicana … thingamajig on your way out?' asks Coco. The entire table claps their hands in agreement.

'Sure.' I order the drinks and then go in search of Yaz.

The thing is, there are actually rather a lot of toilets in this hotel. My old boss would have been in his element. There's the two nearest the restaurant, one off the other terrace, three off the foyer, and I check them all but there's no sign of Yaz. I reach for my amulet and realise I'm not wearing it. My stomach gives a lurch. I can picture exactly where I left it, on the dressing table in the room. I rummage in my bag for my phone but realise I left that on the table.

Okay, this is not ideal.

Come on, Yaz. Where are you?

There was the one toilet I didn't check because it had an out-of-order sign on it; I bypassed it on the way to the conference hall, and it wasn't far from the restaurant.

I'm legging it down the corridor when the contents of my unzipped bag spill onto the floor. I leave the contents where they fall and halt outside the toilet. It seems eerily quiet. I take a few steadying breaths and ready myself for the unexpected. What if they're behind the door, waiting to ambush me? My heart judders. Clenching my fists, I slowly push open the door.

'Hello?' I step into the room and switch on the light.

I hear a groan from the toilet. I open the door wider and find Yaz slumped across the loo. Thank God for that! 'Oh, you poor thing.'

Yaz's head jerks up, and that's when I see blood on her forehead.

'You're bleeding?' I say stupidly.

'Dusty, you need to—'

But I don't get to hear the rest of her sentence because the door crashes into the back of my head and as I turn something hits me on the side of my face. My ears buzz, and I meet darkness.

'Dusty, can you hear me?'

My mind swirls as I try to open my eyes, but only one eye cooperates. All I can see is a dent in the cubicle door. 'Yaz?'

'Thank God! Look, we don't have much time.'

'Are we going to die?'

'No, we're not going to die,' Yaz says firmly. 'Keep calm.'

'Keep calm? We're tied up,' I say, panic rising. 'What do you think they know?'

'Nothing,' says Yaz. 'He knows nothing.'

I try to loosen the rope, pulling at it frantically. 'Yaz, if you shuffle back towards me I can see if I can stamp your rope with my heel.'

'No, Dusty, stay as you are. Hakim and his two cronies are going to be here any second. We need to stay in character.'

'I think I might throw up.'

'Dusty, we're going to get out of this. Trust me.'

'We are?' I say. *Yes, we are,* I say to myself. *Positive thinking, that's what is needed here.*

'Apparently, you gave them the right run-around.' Yaz chuckles. 'They've been on your tail the whole time you've been checking in and out of toilets. They probably think you've got some weird fetish for toilets or are very incontinent.' She giggles, and I chuckle, feeling a bit better.

'I was looking for you,' I say.

'I was following them and they led me down here, and I walked straight into their trap. I am such an idiot.'

Crash! The door flies open.

'Tell me who you work for.'

I nearly wet myself when I see who it is.

CHAPTER TWENTY-SIX

Hakim's eyes narrow as he gets right up close to my face. 'Tell me who you work for,' he repeats.

'Hakim, is that you?' I squint with my good eye. 'Have you come to help me?'

'Help you? Yes. I will help you if you cooperate.'

'Hey, did you tie us up? You kinky devil.' I giggle.

'Why are you in Marrakesh?'

'Is this like some kinky game?'

'What? What is "kinky"? No. You tell me who you work for.'

'A prank then?'

'Prank? No.'

'It's hardly a crime. We only had a few drinkypoos.' Yaz hiccups.

'Shlokeh!' he spits.

'Don't be such a party-pooper, Hakim.' I giggle.

He then goes on what seems like a five-minute rant in Arabic as his henchmen grit their teeth. I know Yaz understands every word, but she doesn't react. I'm dying to know what he's saying.

'Hakim, my head hurts,' I say. 'I think I overdid it

with the cocktails.'

'Why are you in Marrakesh?' He says some other word in Arabic, then gets up close to my face. His voice is low, menacing, and I have to force myself not to flinch. 'You tell me the truth.'

'Did Coco put you up to this? She does love a prank.'

'Your sister and her friends are disgusting whores. Only whores drink like men.'

I giggle. 'They are a bit of a handful.'

'Who do you work for? You tell me now.'

I let out a whimper despite myself. 'Hhhhhh … Rrrrrr … Ttttttt. Duty Calls Cleaners. Hygienic. Reliable. Tenacious,' I say.

Hakim says something else in Arabic, his temper rising with every breath.

'What's this all about? Did Coco put you up to this?' I ask.

'Shut up about your sister.'

'Does Ahmed know you tie up your guests?' asks Yaz.

'Ahmed is a fool.'

'Will you untie us now?' I bat my eyelashes and beam a smile at him. 'My head hurts.'

He just starts ranting again in Arabic and turns to his henchmen. I take a sharp breath and shut my eyes to steady my nerves. When I look up again, Hakim is sharpening what looks suspiciously like a knife.

Oh, dear God. This is getting serious.

I'm petrified. I can feel Yaz tensing, too.

'Very good, Coco,' I say, raising my voice loudly. 'You can come out now.' But my acting skills are deserting me.

'You will tell me the truth,' Hakim spits out.

'Fuck!' I suddenly hear Andrea's voice, followed by a succession of giggles. Then the door crashes open. 'Watch where you're sticking that thing.'

The world seems to stop for a moment as the hens tumble into the room and stare at the scene in front of them. I don't think anyone can really compute. My good eye catches my sister's. She looks shell-shocked, then her eyes narrow into two angry slits. Oh, God. Hakim's knife and goodness knows what the henchmen are carrying but when my sister has that look, no one is safe.

'Hands off my sister,' she yells.

Everything turns to mayhem.

Bernie charges the henchmen and flattens them. Coco throws her stiletto straight at Hakim's face. Michelle knocks his knife away with her crutches and it flies across the room. Philippa and Andrea takes a swing at the henchmen with their makeup bags.

'Shell, sit on him,' Bernie orders. Michelle rugby-tackles Hakim to the floor.

Sarah springs into action and throws a vase to Michelle, which she catches and promptly hits Hakim over the head.

'Say cheese,' says Bernie. Michelle poses for the camera as Bernie takes a photo.

'Um, Bernie, would you?' I ask.

'Of course.' Bernie locates the knife and cuts our ties.

'Thanks!' I flex my fingers and pull myself up.

'We thought you'd been a long time. We're the search party,' giggles Coco.

'We do not do this in the West,' says Michelle.

'Speak for yourself,' cackles Philippa.

'We ask people out, you know, on a date,' says Michelle, wrapping a rope around the henchman's hands as if she were winding wool.

'Then, if you get on well, and only then, do you get to be tied up and gagged,' adds Andrea, spraying hairspray in their eyes. 'Not on first encounters. Really, no manners at all.' Then she teeters, stumbles, teeters, then stumbles again, and lands over at the mirror, checking her hair like nothing at all has happened.

The men lie hapless and unconscious on the floor. Bernie clicks away and Yaz is doubled up in pain but laughing. She is in hysterics. I'm a little worried. 'Are you okay?'

Tears are running down her face and she gives a little snort.

'We should probably get going, ladies.' I give Yaz a nudge, but Yaz can hardly speak.

Bernie slaps me on the arm. 'Bloody brilliant, Dusty.' She gives me a massive grin. 'We told you about Michelle and Coco's Cotswold prank and you thought you'd come up with your own.'

'What—I—'

'Devious! Who helped you? Was it Shell?' Bernie grabs the vodka bottle out of Coco's bag.

'Shell's always so spot-on with special effects,' says Andrea, touching up her lipstick.

'Hey, that's mine,' I say.

'Found it out in the hall. Finders keepers,' Andrea coos.

I snatch it out of her hand and drop it in my bag. Don't want it firing off accidentally.

'Oh, and here's your phone,' says Philippa.

Sarah grabs Michelle's hand and helps her up. 'It wasn't me,' Michelle says looking confused.

'Was it you, Coco?' Andrea asks.

'Nope.'

I glance over at Hakim and I can see him coming round. But Philippa has crouched down beside Hakim's bloodied face. 'I'm sorry about your nose.'

His hands reach up around her neck. Philippa looks up in alarm. I grab another ceramic vase sitting on the basin and smash it over his head. Then, with the ties he used on us, I tie him up good and tight.

'I bet it isn't every day he is outwitted by a bunch of drunk women,' I whisper to Yaz.

'Now you're one of us,' says Coco, putting an arm around me and Yaz as we all tumble out of the toilets. Yaz beams at Coco, colour suffusing her cheeks.

'Not quite as realistic as my and Shell's zombie attack though,' says Coco with her usual one-upmanship, but for once I'm not bothered.

'Clever to leave a trail of your belongings along the way,' says Michelle.

'Yeah, your eye makeup looks pretty realistic too,' says Bernie.

'It does,' says Coco, peering closer at me. 'It rea … really looks like you've been p-p-punched hard in the face.' She hiccups her words out one by one.

'Cheers,' I say, trying to hold in my wince as she prods me in the eye. 'Yeah, totally realistic.'

As we hurry along the corridor, I notice Yaz has sobered up and is looking at the hens with genuine admiration.

'Shall we have a nightcap in the room? That way we won't lose each other,' I suggest, as we reach the foyer. I can't have them wandering around here. I need to get the girls back to their rooms, to safety. Varying degrees of illegible noises make an affirmative sound.

We wait at the lifts, fifty percent upright, mostly thanks to the fixtures and fittings. Trying to tackle the stairs at this point in the evening would be futile.

Yaz spots something and slaps me on the arm. 'Rashid,' she says. 'I'll be back.'

'Yaz, wait! Don't you think we should speak to Adelstein—'

But in true Terminator style, she charges out of the lobby and out into the night's air.

Ping!

With all of us crammed into the lift, there's no room

to fall down, but when we reach the hens' floor, we all tumble out of the lift in a pile. Then, as we each clamber off one another, there's too much giggling, banging into walls and each other to walk sensibly down the corridor. The hens all collapse in Coco's room. I plonk bottles of water within reaching distance and race back to my room. As soon as I let myself in, the adjoining doors open and Adelstein storms in.

'You didn't wear your amulet.'

'I know.'

'What the hell has happened to your face?' Adelstein's face changes from anger to concern.

'We were kidnapped.'

'You were what? Morley, get some ice,' he orders.

'But we escaped.'

'Where's Yaz?'

'She saw Rashid and took off.'

'She did what? She is not wearing her tracker, no gun, and you let her go?'

'Well, she was quite persistent, sir.'

'Hall. Are you drunk?'

'No, sir.'

'Are you high?'

'No.'

'Worrying,' he says with an arched eyebrow.

'My eye is a bit throbby now,' I say. Adelstein studies my injury. 'He kicked the door pretty damn hard.'

'Who did this to you?'

'Hakim and his henchmen.'

'Jesus, Hall, why didn't you … Morley, Jacob, gather your things. We need to get out of here.'

'No. It's fine. I don't think they were any wiser after we kicked their arses.'

'You did what?'

'Do you think I can sit down?' I swear I can see steam coming out of his eyes, ears, and nostrils. Maybe I *am* high? 'I thought you would be happy we escaped.'

'Hakim attacked you?'

'His henchmen knocked us out cold and then the hens rescued us. Not clucking ones, my sister and her friends.'

Adelstein strides towards me and grabs me by the arms. 'Hall, sit and tell us everything.'

By the time I've finished retelling the night's events, three flabbergasted faces stare at me. My face still hurts and my eye is now swollen shut, but the ice Morley has fetched is helping. That's what Adelstein keeps telling me every time I try to take the cold pack away from my face. What I really need to do now is sleep, but I have to hold it together for a bit longer.

The door flies open and Yaz storms in. She is breathless. 'You'll want to see this. I followed Rashid to the goods yard at the back of the hotel. He was supervising freight boxes having pre-printed flight tags and U.K. customs clearance papers attached. The van being loaded was an airport security vehicle with U.K. plates. They have more people on the inside than we thought.'

Adelstein remains speechless for the next ten minutes. He keeps looking at us. I can barely keep my eyes open, even the good one.

'It's happening, sir,' Yaz says. 'The intel intercepted in Karachi. It reconfirms our intelligence in Istanbul—'Doomsday' is proceeding. They are all prominent public places, twenty attacks to happen one minute after the other in London, maximum confusion, maximum panic. The USB contains a code that will take down the country's broadcasting frequencies and block the Internet. They will broadcast their message to the entire UK. Not only the largest attack on British soil, but a cyber-attack bigger than anything before. They've been communicating offline for months. The pots have been the only messenger. They knew the drones were there; they knew the CIA has been monitoring satellite calls from the hideouts; their CIA informant was killed. They're still after the infiltrator, they know he exists, they're trying to flush him out.'

Adelstein's eyes widen. He definitely wasn't expecting this.

'Sir, they are going to plant bombs everywhere. People will start running from danger only to face more danger.'

My blood turns to ice.

'Morley, get Ottoman now,' Adelstein says.

'Splinter cells are ready; the collector just has to get the final logistics and money to them.'

Oh, God. This is real.

'And, sir, the attack is set for the day after tomorrow.'

I am numb with horror. It doesn't feel like a whoop, whoop moment.

'Another thing, sir,' Yaz says. 'Ahmed and Roger knew nothing. Rashid and Hakim have been working on this together. They are the co-ordinators.'

Adelstein steps over to me. I pull the dripping ice bag away from my black eye. 'Hall, get some sleep and wear shades tomorrow,' he says.

I look at him, trying to process simple instructions, but swooshing round in my head are images of innocent people dying. I take a deep, shaky breath. 'How are we going to stop them? Can we stop them?'

'We will think of something.'

Adelstein seems so sure, but I can't stop the fear and panic running through my body.

'You and Khan are flying out in four hours,' instructs Adelstein. 'Morley, Jacob and I will be on Mr Clinch's flight.'

'What about my sister, sir?'

'We have agents flying in tonight who will monitor

their movements and catch the same flights. Even I know the hen itinerary off by heart now. They won't know a thing. Or suspect. And they'll be safe.'

But somehow, I don't feel reassured. I have put my sister's life in danger, and I have come to like my sister, possibly even love her. I don't want to see her hurt by all this. And what if Hakim moves his suspicions onto them? Surely he has enough brains to work out they're innocent, but would he care? What if he uses them as a bargaining tool?

I pick up my phone and text Coco.

Hi, Coco, it's me. Hope your head isn't too sore today. I've booked a taxi for 3 p.m. to take you to the airport. I'm on an earlier flight than yours. See you back in Blighty. I had a fantastic weekend. Say bye to everyone for me.

From Dusty, with love. x

CHAPTER TWENTY-SEVEN

England

It's good to be home.

The familiarity makes Marrakesh seem like a dream … or nightmare, depending on which way you look at it. I drop my things in the hall of our flat and find Jodie in the kitchen. 'I'm back!'

Jodie's smile drops when she sees my black eye. 'Right. That's it, I'm calling a lawyer. There are laws against this sort of thing. Human rights laws. Physical abuse is not on anyone's contract.'

'Jodie, it's not what you think.'

'It never is.'

'I got into a fight.'

Jodie stops in her tracks. 'With Coco?'

I shake my head. Jodie is waiting for an explanation. I reach over and give her a hug. 'It's so good to see you.'

'What happened?'

'I walked into a toilet door.'

'Oh, for goodness' sake!'

'I was hungover. Those girls have partied me out.'

'A sugary tea, then?'

'We have tea?'

'And in-date milk.'

'Who are you and what have you done with Jodie?'

'I am a proper kitchen goddess now. I even made scones.'

'Are they edible?'

Jodie thumps me on the arm.

'Oh, my gosh!' I shriek. 'You've cut your hair.'

'Oh, that!' Jodie touches her hair self-consciously. 'I took out the extensions.'

'Wow! You look …' Actually, now I'm looking properly, Jodie really looks … different. Still Jodie but … different. Beautiful. Subtle.

'You don't like it,' she says, crestfallen.

'No. I love it!' I say, nodding enthusiastically. Jodie beams. I give her the kaftan, which she adores, and spend the next half-hour regaling Jodie with tales from the hen weekend. It's only when my eyes drop and my face hits the table that Jodie steers me towards my bed.

I don't remember falling asleep but when I wake up I am still dressed, but surprisingly refreshed. I also know my sister got back okay, because Adelstein texted me saying, 'The hens have come home to roost,' which was rather funny for him. I also got a text from Coco, saying what a great time she had and asking if I'd heard from Roger. I'm trying not to think too much about Roger and his whereabouts. I suspect Adelstein has it all under control.

I arrive at Duty Calls on time and ready for duty. If they still want me. I think I now know why I was hired—because of my connection to Roger. It all makes sense now. I'm not sure how I feel about it, but if I can, and they let me, I will help.

I remove my dark glasses just as the lift doors open. And it's the agent who looks like Daniel Craig. The likeness is uncanny.

'Ice bag and an espresso,' the Daniel Craig doppelgänger says, giving me a slow, sexy smile.

'Oh, thanks,' I manage.

He steps out of the lift and I get in.

The room is full of nervous energy as I step into the room. Everyone is huddled around a conference table. I join Yaz's side.

'Good morning,' she says.

'Have I missed anything?' I whisper.

'Not really, we're just studying the museum's floor plan.'

'This is where Roger will enter,' says Adelstein, pointing to the map, which is displayed on a sunken screen in the table. 'He'll make the swap here. Agent Hall and Agent Khan, you will observe from these vantage points. Observe only. We need the collector to do just that, collect. The mission is to track the collector. Morley has embedded a clear microchip inside the vase so we can track where he goes. We want to identify which splinter cell the collector belongs to.'

'The microchip is undetectable,' says Morley. 'We have embedded it into the USB. They will not find it.'

'This is solid intel, thanks to Agent Hall and Agent Khan's work in Marrakesh,' says Ottoman. All eyes turn to me and Yaz, and a flush creeps up my cheeks. 'And is backed up by our man on the inside. But we don't want these groups to know we know. Not yet.'

'Morley and Jacob have deciphered the codes,' continues Adelstein. 'We now know the locations of all the splinter cells and have surveillance all over them. This operation is to identify the collector.'

'Good luck,' says Ottoman.

Everyone files out.

'You okay?' whispers Yaz.

'Just thinking, that's all.'

'You don't want to do that this early in the morning,' she quips.

I give a half-smile.

Yaz stops. 'What is it? Are you sure you're okay?'

'I think they knew about my connection with Roger. I think that's why they hired me. Probably the only reason they hired me.'

'That might be so, but what does it matter now?'

What does it matter? Is she serious? 'They've got what they want. I'm no use to them now.'

'Without you, we wouldn't have even got close to Ahmed or Roger.'

'Maybe, maybe not. It's just … I like this job, I don't want to be fired.' My voice jumps a bit.

'Who says anything about you being fired?'

'Put this on,' says Adelstein, coming up behind us.

Yaz and I jump apart.

'What is it, sir?' asks Yaz, as he hands us both a dress bag.

'Your disguises.'

When he leaves, Yaz gives me a told-you-so face. 'If he was going to fire you, he would have done so already.'

CHAPTER TWENTY-EIGHT

'Roger has entered the building,' I hear through my earpiece.

Roger looks tired, gaunt even. The life of smuggling is finally catching up with him. Adelstein said he was safe and cooperating, but it's good to see him alive with my own eyes.

I watch Roger sign in and pause a moment to exchange pleasantries with the security guard.

My disguise, by the way, is that of a cleaner. I'm wearing a hideous green-and-white-striped tabard and matching trousers. I look like a walking peppermint. I'm halfway between the entrance and the Renaissance section. Yaz is on a different level, but the place has eyes everywhere—tiny cameras you can stick anywhere with live feeds coming in from all directions. I expect the museum's curator had to be brought into the loop, but as he's a distant relative of the King, no doubt they're used to secrecy and discretion.

'Excuse me. Where are the toilets?'

I swivel round and a mum of two is standing in front of me, clutching the hand of a small boy and with another child strapped to her chest.

'Mummy, I need to poo!' says the curly-haired boy in a loud voice.

The mother grimaces. 'We're potty-training.'

I'm not sure where the toilets are and go to make an apologetic face when suddenly the map flashes up in my mind. 'Toilets, down there. Second on the left.'

'Thank you.'

'I did it, Mummy!' the little boy announces and my nose twitches. Oh, dear, so he has.

'Dominic!' the mother scolds. I give the mother a sympathetic smile as she hurries away.

I pass two of the snipers dressed as elderly men. I don't think I will look at an elderly man in a long coat with a walking stick in the same way ever again.

'Roger, try to look normal, would you,' I hear through the earpiece. 'It's not like you haven't done this before.' A pompous, indignant look crosses Roger's face.

Ten minutes elapses and nothing happens. Roger is standing there, clutching the ceramic vase, anxiously looking over his shoulders. He needs to relax if he doesn't want to give the game away.

I stand next to a fierce-looking warrior in bronze behind glass, pretending to dust it, wondering if people are born naturally brave, when out of the corner of my eye I see a man wearing a beanie and glasses approach Roger. Roger turns his head as the man speaks.

'Salam alaikum,' the man says in a thick, heavy accent.

Roger turns and greets the man with a handshake. 'Wa-alaikum salam. Did you have a pleasant journey?' But it's obvious from their body language they have never actually met before.

'Yes. Is this the fritware spouted jug you were telling me about?'

'Yes, it's extremely rare, early twelfth century.' Roger

hands the collector the vase. 'Fritware revolutionised ceramics in the Islamic lands.'

Roger explains the exact history and craftmanship of the vase, but I can see that while the collector is pretending to listen, his sleight of hand has undone the base of the vase and removed the USB.

The collector hands the vase back to Roger, just as another man walks into frame. At first, I think what a nosy idiot. But then something about his gait looks familiar. *Huh?*

Is that Rashid? What is he doing here?

He reaches inside his coat pocket and just as the collector whips his head around I see Rashid has a gun. The collector's head jolts backwards, and there's an ear-splitting crack echoing around the room as a bullet slams into his chest. Roger screams as the collector falls to the ground. Rashid reaches over and snatches the USB from the collector's hand.

'Allahu Akbar,' he says.

I pull my gun from my pocket. 'Don't move!' I yell.

Rashid turns, his eyes widening in recognition.

But the place has erupted into chaos, and people are running for the exit. I get nudged by someone running past me. Rashid uses the opportunity to grab hold of Roger and use him as a human shield. 'Stay back,' he shouts. 'Or I'll shoot.' Rashid holds the gun to Roger's temple and Roger lets out a whimper.

'Let him go!' I yell. 'The game's up.'

Rashid edges towards a staff only door, dragging Roger with him, until he fires some shots in the air, drops Roger's cumbersome frame onto the floor, and escapes through the door.

Out of the corner of my eye, I see Yaz running towards the door. I go to follow when a hand grabs my ankle and pulls me over. I fall to the ground with a thud, my gun skittering across the floor. Before I know it, I'm having a full-on wrestling match with a corpse. Only the collector is not dead and he has his hands around my throat. I slap at his hands, desperately trying to get them off my windpipe. I can feel my eyes bulging. Remembering I put my lipstick pistol in my back pocket (as a precaution), I fumble for my back pocket, using my other hand to push against his chin. I bring the gun up between my stomach and him and squeeze—

BANG!

I recoil at the sight of red spraying from the collector's mouth.

'Hall?'

I heave his body away and stumble to my feet.

'Hall, are you hurt?'

I glance over at Adelstein. His face is twisted in a strange way. 'No, I don't think so. Not much.' My voice sounds croaky.

'Are you sure?'

'Yes, I'm fine.' I look at the body by my feet. 'I think I killed him.'

'No, he's not dead.' The two elderly agents grab the collector by the arms and pull him upright.

'Stay here,' says Adelstein. 'Wait for the medic to check you out.'

'No. I've got to help Yaz. She went after Rashid alone.'

'I'm on it.'

'I'm coming too.'

We sprint to the door. Roger is sitting there, his head in his hands, quietly weeping. 'You did well, Roger,' I say, but I don't think he hears me.

The door leads to a service corridor. 'Which way?' I ask. Adelstein turns left towards a corridor until we hear voices behind us. We double back and see a spiral staircase sloping to the guts of the building. We peer over the railing, and Yaz has a gun pointed at Rashid.

Yes! It's a dead end.

A dead end for Rashid.

We race down the stairs and reach the basement. Yaz doesn't take her eyes off Rashid. She is saying something to Rashid in Arabic. Her voice is strangely flat. Rashid looks into her eyes and laughs. Yaz flinches. A chill runs a course down my back. Something is wrong here. I look at Yaz anxiously.

'Yaz, put down the gun!' orders Adelstein, training his own gun on Rashid. 'Khan!'

Rashid is still talking and I realise that he is revelling in it. Yaz can barely contain her fury.

Adelstein says, 'We need him aliv—'

Yaz aims her gun and fires four shots.

BAM! BAM! BAM! BAM!

His lifeless body crumples to the floor.

Adelstein rushes to check on Rashid. He glares at Yaz. 'What the hell, Khan?'

Yaz just stands there as if she hasn't heard Adelstein. I walk over to Yaz and gently take the gun from her hand.

'Is he dead?' she asks.

'Yes.' Adelstein sounds less than happy.

She nods. 'Good.'

Back at Duty Calls offices Yaz and I have been placed in Room 7. Ottoman is standing at the head of the conference room table. I shift uneasily in my chair because I have a horrible feeling that Yaz and I are both about to be fired.

I hear Ottoman talking, but I'm not really taking it all in. Something about going with a report that a police officer shot and killed an unidentified assailant who was waving a gun, shouting 'Allahu Akbar'. And Roger's story to Ahmed is that Rashid turned up and shot the collector. It's a struggle for power between pure hardliners and a dissident group. Something about it making a merry dance on the circuit via our Islamabad operative. There is a knock on the door, and we turn towards it when Adelstein walks in. He looks tired.

'Khan, come with me.'

Yaz looks up. Her face is pale and agonised, her eyes distant. She gets to her feet and follows him out of the door.

It's just me and Ottoman left. 'Where are they going?' I ask.

He doesn't answer my question. 'Did you know about Khan's brother?'

'I knew her brother was killed.'

'He was killed by Rashid.'

'Rashid!'

'Rashid was known as the Butcher and has killed many, including children.'

'So, it's a good thing Yaz shot him?' I say.

'Yes, but … we do like to interrogate the top ranks. It's MI6 stuff, games we enjoy playing. We love to hold an informative conversation over cups of tea and a few chats.'

'What's going to happen to Yaz?'

'She will need to be debriefed and have a thorough examination with the psychologist. Nothing you should concern yourself with. She will have the best people.'

'And me?'

'You what?'

'What do I need to do?'

Ottoman smiles. 'Well, I think you should go home and take the next few days off. You've earned it. Isn't it your sister's wedding next weekend?'

'Is there still going to be a wedding?'

'We will hold on to Roger Clinch for a few days, but yes, I should think he'll be able to get married.'

I'm just collecting my bag and coat when I see Yaz

standing at my desk. I jump in surprise. 'I didn't see you there!'

'Sorry.'

'That's okay. How are you?'

She shrugs. 'I should have told you.'

'Told me what?'

'About Nabeel.'

'Your brother?'

'Yes. Friends tell each other things.'

Friends. I like that.

'I thought it would make me feel better, you know, killing Rashid. But I don't … I don't feel anything.'

'He killed your brother, and he's killed countless of others. No doubt he would have carried on killing. I, for one, am glad he's no longer a threat.'

'All my brother did is try to save people. He worked for the Red Cross. It's not just. It's not fair. Religion incites hatred. It should just incite peace.'

'Revenge is a bitter mistress. Rashid was deranged and wholly evil. You can't reason with evil.'

'I feel nothing. Empty. Like I'm walking beside myself. A shadow. My brother's face keeps—' Yaz is tearing up. I pull her into my arms and hug her close.

CHAPTER TWENTY-NINE

It's been a strange few days. Coco's been ringing a lot—no change there. Actually, her tone is kinder. She's different with me, she even asked advice about Roger. She's actually worried about him. I had to tell her she's being silly even though she isn't.

I spend the entire journey to the wedding hotel wondering if Roger is really the right man for Coco. Coco deserves to be happy.

I arrive early. Having Jodie's car really is better than five trains and a replacement bus. The hotel is old, a grand Gothic Revival house, and looks more like a mini-castle with its three top floors looming down at you. I'm not surprised at the grandeur. Roger had no budget restrictions then. There's a mini-tower on the right-hand side. I wonder what's up the top of it, perhaps a prison room.

On first impressions, the windows look dark and gloomy. The tall but narrow lancet style reminds me of witchcraft rather than a perfect country wedding. I only know the architectural terms because of the history info pack Coco sent out with the invitations. Bit OTT, but whatever makes Coco happy, including ramming expensive facts in your face. Apparently, some king used it for debauched shooting weekends, stored some of his mistresses in the west wing, and then combined his sports one weekend by shooting one on the grounds. Which king I couldn't tell you—as with science, history wasn't one of my best subjects. It felt like a heavy Tuesday afternoon lesson rather than a happy invite.

The house suffered a fire in the eighteenth century so half the building has a flat roof and only two floors, and the other half of the roof has big stone teeth (i.e. parapets) for battlements. Hopefully that won't be needed today. But at least the building isn't an awful replica, as was in Roger's dodgy world.

I lug my suitcase up the stone steps to an elaborate arched porch. The dark and gloomy wooden doors open slowly, and a member of staff meets me. 'Are you with the Clinch wedding party, madam?' a middle-aged man dressed in an old-fashioned butler's suit asks rather formally.

'Yes, the long-suffering sister of the bride-to-be,' I joke. He bows politely, raises his arm and a bellboy appears out from the shadows, swooping down to take my suitcase.

'Room 101 for Miss Dusty Hall,' he instructs, and a pitter-patter of feet disappear with my belongings into the darkness of the red and black flagstones. 'If you would follow me, please, madam. Would you prefer the lift or the grand stairway entrance to floor two?'

'Stairway.' I need to walk off all the carbs from yesterday.

We amble up the flight of chunky stone steps. I'm not sure if he's being polite and copying my pace or I'm being thoughtful of his age. We move just as slowly down the hall and reach the fifth door to the left, and Jeeves quickly opens the door, bowing for me to go in.

My suitcase has already been placed on a rack by the four-poster bed.

'Please find some complimentary port and fruit by your bureau.'

'Thank you.'

'Our pleasure, madam. We hope you enjoy your stay. If you have any requirement or needs, please do not hesitate to contact the front desk.'

I didn't even see a front desk. Must be behind the masonry somewhere in the grand entrance hall.

It's eerily quiet on the wedding party floor, so I sneak down to the banquet hall to look at the infamous floral arrangements. Jorge's centrepiece is an opulent monstrosity. The plates are gold and the tablecloth is gilded garishness. Even the decorated wedding present table would make Trump blush. This is Coco to a T. It's perfect.

I mosey back up to my room to unpack. Once done I flop backwards into the four-poster bed when I hear an almighty howl.

There's no mistaking who that is. I bolt out of bed, hurrying towards the bridal suite.

'Oh, thank goodness you're here, Dusty. No one has seen or heard from Roger,' Mother bleats while pinning an almost-dead flower to her hat.

'I told you he's been acting strange,' Coco wails. 'He's got cold feet. I know he has. It's because I said he couldn't wear a dickie bow with plus-fours. He was never happy about that. Seethed for weeks.'

'I'm sure there's a perfectly reasonable explanation,' I reply, taking Coco by the hand and leading her to a chair. I glance over at my mother and I can see a look of confusion cross her face. She's not used to Coco and I being civil to one another. 'My guess is that his friends probably took him out for one last drink as a free man.' I wince at my own choice of words. Adelstein told me that

Roger bagged immunity for cooperating and has signed the Official Secrets Act.

'Has anyone spoken to Roger?' Mother asks.

'Eh, yes. I did. This morning,' I lie.

'You did? Did you hear that, Coco? Dusty spoke to Roger this morning.'

My sister stops crying. 'Why isn't he answering the phone then?'

'As Bernie would say, "Hush your noise, woman, and relax."'

She smiles.

'Anyway, it's bad luck to see or speak to the bride on the day,' I say in justification, which may or may not be a thing.

'Oh, yeah, forgot that.' She seems as unsure of the tradition as I am.

'Look, Mother, I've got to go, last-minute bridesmaid duties.'

Mother swipes her hand across the air, then grabs her gin and tonic.

As soon as I've closed the door I pull out my mobile and rush down the corridor, the stairs almost tripping me up with their chunky width as I tap in Yaz's number. It goes straight to answerphone.

I pelt out of reception past a most bemused Jeeves and leg it to the car park. 'Yaz, it's me. Can you call me back?' I hang up while scouring the landscape for signs of Roger. Where on earth could he be?

A flashy car skids in the gravel, nearly running me over. Roger's friends are such knobs. 'Look where you're going,' I rant at the vehicle.

'Hi, Dusty,' says Yaz, poking her head out of the car window.

'Oh, hi, Yaz,' I reply, confused. 'What are you doing here?'

'Your sister invited me.'

'She did?'

'I thought it would be a rather nice to catch up with everyone.' Yaz is positively vibrating with excitement.

'Was Roger released last night?'

'Yes. Why?'

'Err … not sure …' I rub my temples. 'He seems to have gone AWOL.' I look up to the sky. Then I spot something—no, *someone*— dangerously rocking on the roof.

Oh, God, no.

Yaz follows my gaze. 'Is that Roger?'

'I've got to go,' I yelp, leaping into action just as another flashy car pulls up.

I groan. Adelstein! What the hell is he doing here? Don't tell me my sister invited him too. Or has he come to hand me my P45? Well, he'll just have to wait. I turn and dash back inside.

The lift is as slow as Jeeves and takes an age to arrive on the third floor. When I make it to the roof via a rickety staircase, I find Roger standing very close to the edge of the roof. He turns when he hears my footsteps. I feel a momentary sense of panic but force it down with a smile. 'Hey, Roger. Getting a spot of fresh air?'

'My life's a lie,' he says dramatically. 'I can't go on.'

'Inconvenient time to get a sense of morals, Roger.'

He gives me a half-hearted smile. 'Coco deserves better than me.'

'And yet she loves you.'

'I just can't live with all these secrets.'

'I'm sure you'll find a way to forgive yourself. Being a tool is part of your character.'

Roger inches even closer to the edge and I am getting worried. Usually, he can't resist a bit of sparring.

'C'mon, Rodge the Dodge, who will I spar with at dinner?'

Roger turns away from me and looks out.

'It'll be such a shame. Your name really suits you now,' I say lightly, but feeling very nervous.

'It's no use. It's all over.'

'Yes, your little business trips are, and your bank accounts will feel a winter's chill, but that's hardly worth ending your life now, is it?'

'You don't understand.'

'Durr … wrong again. I'm the only one who does. Stop flapping, you big girl's blouse. You've been a prime ham, a greedy bloody kipper, but my sister loves you and I'm quite partial to you. We're going to be family.'

'We are?'

'Yes. As long as you come down off the roof.'

A small smile appears on his face. 'Thanks, Dusty.'

'Just think about all the monumental digs we can muster up in the future. Our sarcasm ping-pong matches will be legendary. It'll be our secret.'

Roger coughs up a reluctant laugh. We walk arm-in-arm to the staircase.

'But if you so much as ever leave my sister broken-hearted, I will hunt you down and I will kill you. You know I can do it.'

Roger's eyes widen in fear.

'It's Liam Neeson, you tool. It's from the film *Taken.* Relax. Or not,' I say, wiggling my eyebrows.

Once I've deposited Roger in his room, I head to Michelle's room, which is acting as the bridesmaids' temporary hairdressers' salon. *Coiffures at noon,* the email said. By the time I get there, Michelle has ordered high teas for at least a dozen. Andrea and Philippa have gone down for a nifty tipple and Bernie has been sent to find Sarah. Apparently, she was last seen in the gardens about an hour ago.

One powerful blow-dry later and more pinned than a

voodoo doll, I decline the offer of two afternoon tea racks and return to my room so I can do my makeup. When I'm done, I head back to my sister's room. 'Knock, knock, anyone getting married?' I walk in and all is calm. Mother, Father and Coco … and Adelstein. What's he doing here?

'Fitzwilliam?' I say, one eyebrow raised.

He smiles. 'Just paying my respects to your parents and the lovely bride-to-be.'

My mother and father seem both delighted and slightly puzzled, whereas Coco is grinning like a giant frog.

'Just a quick update, Roger is at the church,' I say.

'Yes, Mr Fizzywilliam told us,' says Coco.

'Fitzwilliam,' I say, absentmindedly. 'He did? Oh, right.' I turn to Adelstein and give him a questioning look.

'You are staying for the wedding, Mr Fizzywilliam?' asks my mother.

'Yes, do stay. A couple of Roger's friends have cancelled last-minute,' Coco pipes up.

I look at her with a vengeance. She smiles and trills another fake laugh. I wonder who could have cancelled—one's soon-to-be brother-in-law's partners in crime? Ahmed perhaps?

'Silly to let all that scrummy gourmet food go to waste,' says Coco.

Adelstein glances sideways at me. I shake my head slowly. 'I'm sure you've got somewhere else to be.'

'Nope. I've got nothing planned. It is a Saturday.'

'You'll probably be bored.'

'My wedding will not be boring, I can assure you,' says Coco.

'But you won't know anyone.'

'I know you, I know Roger, Penny, Coco and I've met your wonderful parents,' Adelstein says.

My parents glow under his praise. 'It's so nice to see Dusty meet a nice man,' my mother says.

'Mother, he's not my boyfriend.'

My mother winks at me. 'Yet.'

Coco claps in glee. 'That's settled then.'

Coco leaps into action and fusses with my hair. I slap her hand away. 'There's nothing wrong with my hair.'

'I knew you were dating your boss,' she whispers.

'We are not dating. See you in a minute,' I whisper back with gritted teeth.

I stomp out of the room. Adelstein follows. I eye him suspiciously. 'What are you really doing here?'

'Just making sure everything goes off without a hitch.'

'Why wouldn't it?' I ask, suddenly worried. 'Roger isn't in danger, is he?'

'No … but you can never be too careful.'

'You do know my family now thinks you're my boyfriend.'

He nods his head thoughtfully. 'We do seem to play the couple flawlessly.'

'You know you will be expected to show up at every family event.'

'It wasn't me who organised a hen weekend when they were supposed to be undercover on one of the most important missions this decade.'

Hearing it out loud silences me. We continue down the stairs.

'Being a couple might not be so bad, Miss Hall,' he says mildly. He's taking the piss. 'You proved me wrong. Few people can do that.'

'Well, we all know your expectations weren't exactly set to the highest bar.' His expression makes my stomach flutter. 'Is there any other reason you are here?'

He clears his throat and suddenly looks a bit awkward. I realise why.

'Can I just say something first?' I blurt.

Adelstein seems taken aback. 'Sure.'

'I know what I did was wrong. You know, inviting the hen party was an error of judgement—okay, total idiocy on my part'—I can hear my voice rising in emotion—'but in my defence, you haven't been completely honest with me.'

Adelstein frowns. 'How so?'

'You knew about my connection to Roger.'

'We did.'

'Is that why I was hired?'

'Yes.'

'So you used me.'

'I wouldn't put it quite like that, and if you remember, I was against the idea.'

'Yes, you made that very clear.' I swallow back the emotion in my throat. 'But I'm good at it even despite my, erm … error of judgement, which will never happen again.'

'It certainly added an extra dimension to going undercover.'

My eyes are downcast. 'But now I have served my purpose, is that it? Well, it was fun while it lasted.'

'Whatever are you talking about, Agent Hall?'

'Aren't you here to give me my P45 or whatever the equivalent is in the Secret Service?'

'On the contrary, Ottoman and I think the elements you bring to the team are unique and impossible to teach or replicate. Turns out you are a natural.'

I stare at him, confused. 'So, you're not here to fire me then?'

'Goodness, no. We want to offer you a permanent position.'

My jaw flops to the floor, and there's a giddy feeling fizzing in my stomach.

'Courtesy of His Majesty,' he says, a broad smile on

his face.

Not a P45, but a permanent job. I can't quite believe it. 'Do I get a wardrobe allowance?'

Adelstein smiles. 'There are perks, yes. It's all in the letter.' He pulls out a brown envelope from inside his jacket and hands it to me, thinks better of it, then retracts it back into his inside pocket. 'You don't have to give us your answer straight away.'

My mouth feels dry and words have deserted me.

'I would also like the first dance,' he says.

'Sorry, the first dance? You want to dance with me?'

'I hear you're an excellent dancer.'

'Well, I did a stint as a ballroom instructor.'

'Of course you did.' His face is far softer when he laughs. 'First dance?'

'Can you dance?' I ask, doubtful.

'Of course I can.' And I watch as he does a few fancy sets down the stairs like he's a West End star.

While Adelstein heads off to the church I go in search of the bridesmaids. Just as I think that there have been far too many surprises already, and the wedding hasn't even got going yet, my mobile rings. It's a number I don't recognise. I wouldn't normally answer it, but Mr Twinkle Toes has got me all in a dither.

'Is that Dusty Hall?' comes a voice.

'Er … yes.'

'It's Jessica from Chaos Films. We've been trying to reach you.'

'Oh,' I say with a flicker of recognition. 'Er … hi.'

'I hope I haven't caught you at an inconvenient time.'

'Well, actually it's my sister's wedding day but I have a minute.'

'I won't keep you then. We've been desperately trying to get hold of you, Miss Hall. You see, Martin loved your audition tape.'

Is she talking about Martin Spoon, the director?

'Martin wants you to come back and read for Letitia.'

Shock jolts through my body. Hang on … does that mean what I think it means? 'Sorry, can you repeat that?'

Jessica laughs. 'Yes, Martin Spoon wants you to come back and read for the part of Letitia.'

I let out an involuntary squeal of excitement.

'I take it that's a yes,' giggles Jessica.

'Absolutely. I would love to meet Martin Spoon.'

'The thing is your agent said you quit acting.'

'No, no. Just a short sabbatical.'

'Well, we look forward to seeing you soon, Dusty.'

For a few minutes, I stand there. After all those years … all those rejections … I can't believe it. *But you've got a job,* I remind myself. *A very important job relating to national security.* But it's not like I've got the role of Letitia. They only want me to meet Martin Spoon. It might come to nothing. No harm in meeting him.

I find Andrea and Philippa in the grand foyer, concealing something or someone. What are they up to now?

The grave looks on their faces make my own smile drop. 'What is it?'

They step aside to reveal Sarah. Sarah's dress is splattered in algae.

'She fell in the pond,' says Andrea.

'Everyone up to Michelle's room now,' I order. 'Coco is not to see Sarah under any circumstances.'

'I'm so sorry,' says Sarah, close to tears.

'Do not cry!' Philippa snaps. 'You will ruin your makeup.'

'I just wanted to see the grounds,' she sobs. 'I got lost then fell into the pond. I didn't mean to fall in the pond.'

'Happens to the best of us,' I say. But there's nothing

that can be done about the dress. Andrea's got a spare dress, but all eyes have to be on the bride.

Then I have a brainwave and ring Yaz.

'I need your help,' I say desperately. I give Yaz Michelle's room number and within five minutes there's a knock at the door.

After the hugs and cries of 'Penny's here!' Yaz's gaze swivels to Sarah's dress. She gives me a horrified gasp.

'Oh, Ya—um … Penny, you look amazing. That dress is perfect,' I say.

Yaz does a twirl, her cheeks flushing slightly. 'Thank you.'

'Which is why I need you to change into this.' I hold up Andrea's spare dress.

Yaz's eyes flicker with bewilderment as she looks at the dress, then at me. Then her face drains of colour. 'No way!'

'Please,' I beg. 'Coco will have a heart attack if she sees Sarah like that.'

'I am not wearing that.' Yaz's voice rises in repulsion.

'It's Dolce and Gabbana darling not rancid school pudding,' Andrea says sulkily.

'I don't care. I … I will look like a hooker wearing that.' Yaz clasps her hands over her mouth, shocked that she said it out loud.

'A fabulous-looking hooker,' says Andrea, not the least bit offended. 'You've got the legs to carry it off.'

'No!' says Yaz, folding her arms. 'No way. And anyway, isn't the bridesmaids' theme supposed to be blush rose? My dress is yellow.'

'And it looks stunning on you.' Andrea gushes, ignoring the entire point of the conversation.

'Thank you. I chose it myself. It's Carolina Herrera.'

Yaz really has come a long way. The off-the-shoulder dress with a bow-embellished neckline and draped skirt is timeless and elegant. Sarah really needs to wear that dress.

'Please,' I beg.

Yaz stares at me like she wants to kill me. 'Okay,' she says grudgingly.

I reach over and give Yaz an enormous hug. 'You're the best.'

'You owe me,' she says, practically in tears as she takes Andrea's dress from me.

Sarah is thrilled with her new dress. Yaz, on the other hand, looks thoroughly miserable. Personally, I think she looks stunning; her legs run on forever. Bernie wolf-whistles as she eyes up Yaz's legs. Yaz gives her a stony-eyed glare, which seems to encourage Bernie.

'You look great,' I reassure Yaz.

When I glance at my watch, we're running six minutes and thirty seconds behind schedule. 'We need to go. Now. Chop, chop.' I usher the hens and a reluctant Yaz out of the door.

'I'll see you in church,' she mumbles, scurrying over to the lift while I get the hens to the top of the stairs.

'Just keep Sarah at the back,' I hiss to Bernie as we make our descent down the grand staircase.

'Shell, why don't you stand in front of Sarah.' Andrea pushes Michelle in front.

'Happily,' says Michelle as she pops a mini-scone in her mouth. Where the hell did she get that from?

But it appears that we are never to descend stairs as a group in a normal fashion. 'Keep close,' I remind them as we pussyfoot down in a giant ball of bridesmaids.

Mother is waiting at the bottom, looking utterly bemused. 'Do hurry, girls, the photographer is waiting.'

'Shell, look where you're going.'

'Yes, oops,' she says, stuffing her mobile down the front of her dress. 'Akila sent me a text.'

'That's really sweet,' I say. 'But you need to look

where you're going. You've only just stopped using your crutch.'

'Three o'clock,' says Bernie.

My heart gives an almighty thud as Coco turns, mid-laugh at something the photographer has said. She looks amazing. Radiant. Just how a bride should look.

We all freeze.

'Could the maid of honour and the bridesmaids come and crouch on the step before Mademoiselle Coco, please?' Of course Coco has got some French fashion photographer from *Vogue* in.

I hurry over and stand next to Coco. 'You look stunning,' I say, waving at the others behind me to get Sarah to the back.

Coco beams and looks serene.

'This way. Merci,' says the photographer in a comically stereotypical French accent.

Coco is so busy listening to the photographer's instructions that she barely takes any notice of us. It's only outside when Bernie shoves Sarah a little too roughly into the back of the limo that Coco squints at us suspiciously.

I hurry the procession into the church, followed by Andrea and Philippa. Sarah is in the middle and Bernie and Michelle are at the back. Practically everyone I know—all my family, distant cousins, even Alice's parents, Lord and Lady Tambling-Goggin—are here, but Alice isn't, nor Jodie. They're in far flung foreign lands, work commitments,

Yaz, I notice, has cocooned herself in a jacket and sitting next to her is a jacketless Adelstein. My giggles peter out, and my heart gives an apprehensive thud. Adelstein is gazing at me and as our eyes lock there's a weird little beat. I keep walking, glancing over at Roger's side of the congregation, scrutinising each one for traits of criminality.

When I reach the front, I get the bridesmaids to sit down, making sure we shove Sarah to the far end of the pew and out of Coco's eyeline. I give Grandad a quick peck on the cheek, noticing he's wearing all his medals.

As I take my seat, I hear a collective gasp, and the wedding march starts up. I swivel round and there she is. My sister. Looking radiant. And my father, looking so proud as he walks side by side with Coco. I'm almost teary.

I turn to look at Roger and his eyes have filled up with tears. Coco reaches his side, and he bends down and whispers something in her ear and her face melts into a smile.

A big fat tear slowly runs down my cheek. Bernie hands me a tissue. As I take it from her, I notice she is crying too, to my surprise.

The rest of the ceremony passes by in a blur. I notice Roger loosen his tie during the poignant 'for richer, for poorer' vow, but before I know it the vicar is pronouncing them husband and wife and everyone is clapping and cheering.

We follow Roger and Coco back down the aisle. And then it is the usual chaos of getting everyone back to the hotel. Coco only has eyes for Roger and doesn't notice Sarah is wearing a different colour dress from the rest of the bridesmaids, even when the photographer ushers us around, getting more group shots.

When we return to the hotel, the waiters are already waiting for us with large tumblers of pink champagne. After everything that has happened, it's a relief to finally relax and go with the flow. After an hour of mingling, I notice that Yaz has integrated herself into Roger's side of the family. She has shrugged off Adelstein's jacket and no longer seems to worry about looking like a high-fashion hooker. Indeed, she seems to relish the role. My prodigy has bloomed.

When the dinner and speeches are over and our bellies are full of food and laughter, Coco and Roger take to the dance floor, and it's—

Spectacular.

I never thought I'd say that about the newly married couple, but the dancing lessons have paid off. There is no doubt in my mind, they are made for each other.

Yaz comes over and smiles. 'They make a lovely couple.'

'They do, don't they?'

'Do you think they're going to have a happy ever after?'

'As long as he sticks to the straight and narrow and Coco never finds out about his past.'

Yaz laughs. 'Doesn't every family have skeletons?' We share a knowing look.

I sink into a chair, feeling grateful. Grateful that everything worked out in the end. Grateful to see my sister marry Roger, grateful for the new friends I've made. Sarah has been fascinated watching the champagne fountain for at least half an hour. Michelle is glued to her phone. Bernie seems to be mesmerised with Grandad and has been asking about his medals. Every time I look over, their whiskey glasses have been miraculously refilled. She is some 'force de tour', that woman.

My mother is being told off by Great-Aunty Gwendoline for not inviting her beloved bridge group. Mother is trying to explain no one invites other people's clubs along to someone else's wedding and it is Coco who had the last say on the guest list. Father is having a cigar and a cognac with Aunt Agnes.

Then, suddenly and enthusiastically, the hens get up on the dance floor. It's an elaborate display. Oh-my-word. It's a flash mob of hens arising.

'Oh, no!' Yaz says. Yaz and I try to shrink back, but then I notice Coco's face drops as she looks at Sarah.

'Coco, ten to three,' I say as Sarah walks into her periphery. I down my champagne and, dragging Yaz, head onto the dance floor.

'Way-hey, it's Dusty and Penny,' Bernie yells at the top her manly voice.

'Coco knows!' I say.

All the hens except Sarah stop dancing.

'I'd just like to know …' Coco muscles her way into the circle. We all fall silent and still. 'Why is Sarah wearing yellow?'

The group gulps in unison. Bernie and Michelle stand in front of Sarah, either to hide her or shield her, I'm not sure which.

'I don't seem to remember choosing yellow for the bridesmaids.'

'We didn't have a choice,' I begin.

'Sarah fell in the pond,' chimes in Bernie.

'I didn't mean to,' says Sarah.

'And it covered her dress in algae,' adds Andrea.

'I had to swap dresses with Sarah,' huffs Yaz. 'Otherwise your bridesmaid would be dressed like me.'

Coco's face drops.

'It was the best we could do under the circumstances,' says Philippa.

We all glance nervously at one another.

Coco nods, then to our astonishment she starts to laugh.

'You're not angry?'

'Why would I be?' She grins. 'I've just married the man of my dreams and I am surrounded by my friends and the best sister in the world. This is the best day of my life.'

For the second time today, my eyes fill up with tears and I reach over and give my sister a big hug. 'I love you,' I say.

'Yeah, group hug,' says Philippa, and soon we are all hugging and swaying to the music.

I pull away from the group hug when I feel a tap on my shoulder.

'Would you care to dance?' Adelstein asks.

I whirl around. 'Adel—uh—Fizzywilliam,' I breathlessly say, correcting myself.

Then I feel a push from behind. 'She would,' says Coco.

I stumble into his arms. He smells wonderful. It's a mixture of manly adrenaline and musk. Adelstein gazes at me and I feel my face redden.

'Are you sure you want to dance with me?' I ask.

'I asked, didn't I?'

I feel myself prickling with self-consciousness as he takes a hold of my hand and leads me to the dance floor. I catch a look from my sister; she gives me a thumbs-up, mouthing, *Go get him, tiger!* Yaz on the other hand looks appalled.

For once I am lost for words and that's probably not a bad thing because I'm not sure what to think. Adelstein doesn't like me and yet the way he is looking at me, like he wants to eat me up. I drop my gaze.

I can't remember the last time I danced with a man. Certainly not like this, anyway. This is proper dancing, not a mere shuffle from side to side.

'Stop looking at your feet,' he whispers.

'What if I fall?'

'I'll catch you.' His lips curl into a smile. It is cheesy but the way he is gazing at me, so calm and controlled, I believe he means every word.

My body tingles with desire. 'You're a good dancer.'

'I told you.'

'So did His Majesty's forces teach you how to dance?'

'No. My sisters. They love to dance.'

There is so much I don't know about this man.

I lean against his chest and Adelstein's fingers entwine with mine, holding them close to his chest. I listen to his heart, and it's beating hard and fast. I smile to myself. Maybe he's not totally in control.

THE END

ACKNOWLEDGEMENT

And there we have it, From Dusty with Love, our first book in the Duty Calls Series. Thank you so much for reading it. We do hope you enjoyed it, and if you did, please take a moment to write a review. You'll also be happy to know there's another book following in 2023.

We also wrote a free novella to accompany From Dusty with Love, involving Dusty's best friend and flatmate, Jodie Beale. So head over to our website to see how you can get yours. www.ninawhyle.com

Thank you to our wonderful editor, Eleanor Boyall/RJ Locksley. To James Bowden for creating the brilliant cover. And last but not least, our families, we love you very much.

ABOUT THE AUTHOR

Nina Whyle is a writing duo made up of two best friends, Nina Bowden and Clare Whyle. They have published several books: Moving Up On Manolos, Fighting Love, When Life Goes Pop, and My Disorganised Life.

From Dusty With Love is their first book in the Duty Calls series.

Printed in Great Britain
by Amazon

15972193R00171